ADVANCE PRAISE

"A perfect blend of romance, humor and intrigue! Any reader will fall in love with these characters as they struggle in their quest for freedom. I loved it!"

Linda Miranda, author of *The Perfect Blend* and *The Seasoned Butcher's Wife Cookbook*

PUBLISHER'S INFORMATION

EBookBakery Books

Author contact: bucketbooks@outlook.com

ISBN 978-1-938517-22-8

Iniki's Quest

By Nancy James

ACKNOWLEDGMENTS

How to thank so many people in a few short sentences is a truly difficult task. So many of you have encouraged me on this project and I love you for it!

My one-man cheering squad is my husband, Michael. Thank you, my dear, for being there every step of the way and for calming me down when I was a crazy lady. You believe in me. How can I not believe in myself?

Many thanks to Michael Grossman of ebookbakery.com who made the manuscript come alive with his kind suggestions and hard work. He truly helped with his expertise in every step of the publishing of this book.

Good friends offered to proofread the manuscript, draft after draft. So Anna Principe, Debbie Roberts, Lois Diana and Jane Wilke deserve giant hugs for their patience and perseverance.

As does my next-door neighbor and most excellent friend, author Linda Miranda. She provided so much information on publishing and even came up with the book's title!

Special thanks to romance writer Dee Holmes. The characters and plot were born in one of her writing workshops. Her advice proved invaluable.

To my kids and seven remarkable grandchildren, thanks for all the support and love you shower on Grammy.

DEDICATION

For loved ones who have gone away ~

Mom and Dad

and

My sweet brother Joey ~ time to open that champagne.

TABLE OF CONTENTS

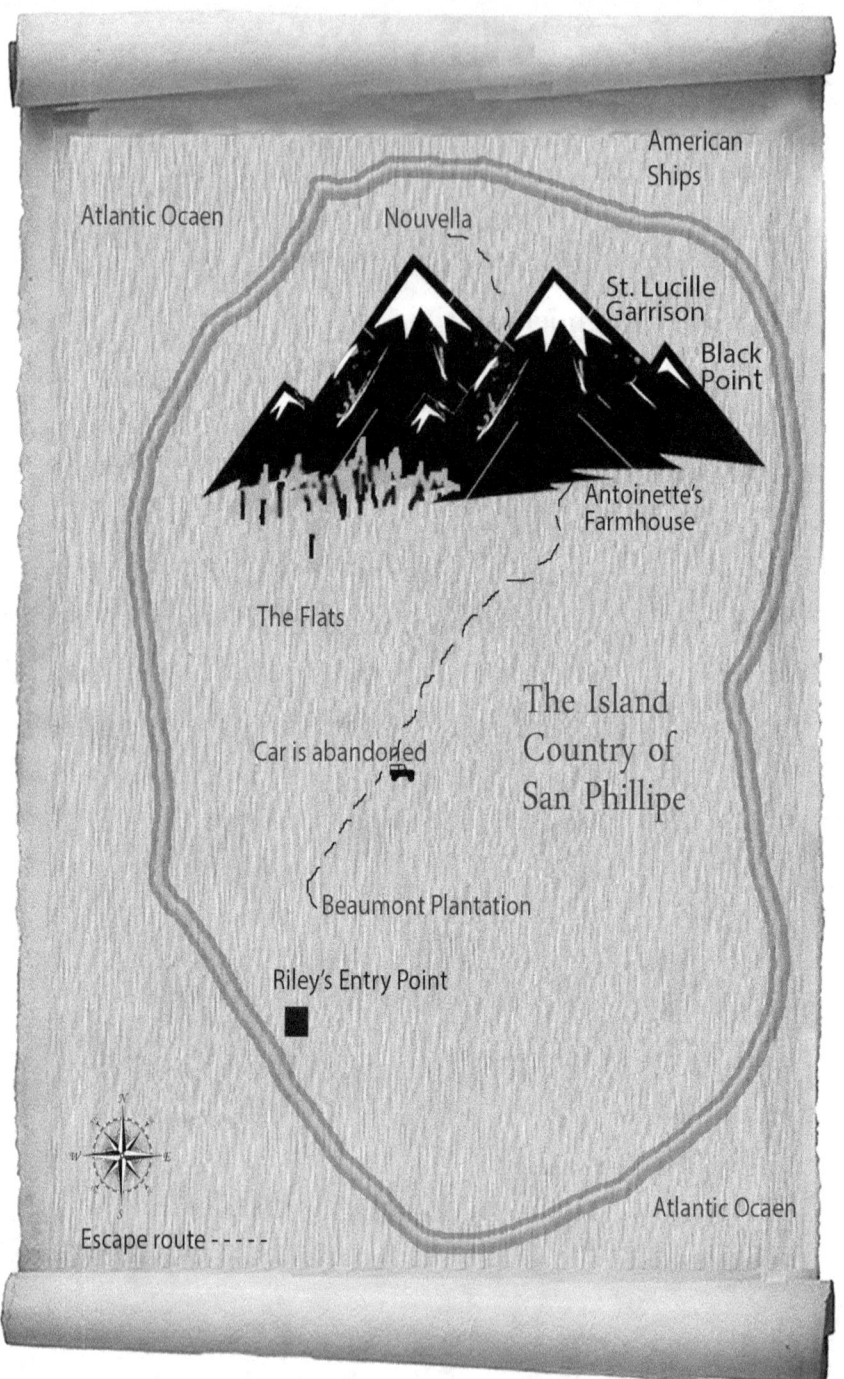

Cast of Characters

Iniki Beaumont ~ The young Frenchwoman who fed the poor of her village when the rebellion began. She started a school for children and was much loved by the peasant population.

President Simone ~ Despotic leader of the independent island country of St. Philippe. He has a strong army which he uses to usurp the property of citizens and kill off rebels who fight against him. The United Nations has warned him of his blatant violation of the human rights of his people and the destruction of independent businesses, farms and sources of income for the working poor.

Spirit Man/Man in Black/ General ~ A mercenary hired by the president of the country to dispose of any landowners who remained on the island. He is determined to find Iniki and kill her.

Riley Taggart ~ Deep Cover American agent sent to rescue Iniki from the island. The UN wants her to testify to the inhumanity of Simone.

Mathieu and Michel ~ Orphaned twelve year old twins who live with Iniki. She treats the boys as if they were her own.

Madeline and Francois ~ Elderly couple who have been with Iniki since childhood. She loves her old servants and vows to protect them.

Antoinette ~ An old woman living alone along the escape route. She bargains with Riley to join the entourage in return for horses and supplies.

Yankee Doodle, Angel and Madonna ~ Very important characters who need rescuing and come along for the ride.

PROLOGUE

Day 1 ~ Beaumont Plantation
"She would not survive the night"

He wore wire-rimmed sunglasses. She could not see his eyes, see what they were searching for, what they could tell her.

He had no name. When he approached, he did not introduce himself. There was no need. She knew the man in black from his reputation.

He was here for her.

"The President, the Honorable Desmond Simone, has commissioned me to deliver a message," he began.

"Ah, I see," she responded, forcing herself to control the trembling in her limbs. She would not let this man see her fear. "So that is your job, is it? Simone's pigeon, his runner? Your president has a way of using people. It surprises me that you allow him this liberty."

"He pays me well, dear lady."

She squared her shoulders. "The words of a true mercenary."

A slight grin flashed across his mouth and was gone the next instant.

"Miss Beaumont, the president doesn't wish to cause undue stress. He strongly suggests, however, that it will benefit you to leave your plantation immediately. You will just have time to pack your valuables, money, jewels, whatever."

"Jewels and money?" she repeated. "You do not appear to be a fool. But perhaps I am wrong. Take a good look." She held out her arms. He could not miss the faded blouse, the worn jeans or the holes in her sneakers.

"Come now, dear lady," he replied, "you don't expect me to believe you have nothing left but the clothes on your back?"

"I don't care what you believe," she fired back. "I have a message you can relay to your president. Tell him my fondest wish is that he burn in hell for what he has done to this country and its people."

"Be careful, Miss Beaumont. Choose your words wisely."

"And what will you do?" She threw the words at him. "You, who have no name and no eyes. Do you think I am afraid? After all this time, do you think I fear you and your ridiculous president? Were that true, I would have left long ago."

She watched as the man reached into his jacket pocket. Defiance froze on her face but her stomach ached. Would he kill her right here? No matter. She would not allow him the satisfaction of seeing her terror.

No weapon appeared. Just a white envelope. "A boarding pass for you, Miss Beaumont. One way. Back to France. For this evening's flight to Mexico City with connections from there. We expect you to be on that plane."

"Do you? And what if I am not?"

"That would be extremely foolish. As I have said, the choice is yours. But I warn you not to underestimate the power of the government."

"So the deal is my life in return for my property. That is generous?"

"Most of the other French landowners believed it was. You are one of the last remaining."

She took the envelope from his hands and staring into the blackness of his glasses, she tore it in half and handed it back. "Tell Simone I refuse his generous offer."

"Think this over carefully, Miss Beaumont. Leave tonight. The consequences of failure to comply will prove unpleasant."

Contempt pulsed through her. "Consequences? Yes, I understand that is your specialty. The villagers call you the spirit of death."

He nodded once but did not respond.

"Well spirit man," she mocked. "Understand this. When you kill me, every peasant in this country will hate Simone more than they do now. Each life he destroys increases their loathing."

He shrugged his shoulders and let the torn envelope fall to the ground. "I'll return by five this afternoon, Miss Beaumont. I expect you to be gone."

She laughed in his face, though her knees barely held her up. "And if I am not? Will you kill me? Will you remove your glasses first, so I may see your eyes? I should wish to look into the eyes of my murderer."

"You're brave, Miss Beaumont. I'll give you that. Your death would be a waste."

"And you are wasting my time. Now leave my land. I will see you at five."

She arched her eyebrows and stared into his glasses. He would come back as promised. There would be no verbal threats the next time. Only pain. Savage, physical pain.

The man turned in the direction of his jeep. He took careful notice of the Beaumont plantation. The estate and surrounding fields would be an impressive prize when restored to its original beauty. Here and there, a piece of grass struggled to survive, a reminder that the earth replenishes itself in time. In this case, it would be a very long time.

He shook his head. His job was not to ponder the future of the island. Nor was it to admire the beautiful woman he just threatened.

She would not survive the night. That was his job.

CHAPTER ONE

Day 1 ~ Afternoon at the Beaumont Plantation
"Cursing will not help us reach a resolution!"

Standing barefoot, ankle deep in mud, she surveyed the barren fields. Fields that were not tilled and planted and coaxed into producing for so long now. In the distance, funnels of black smoke spiraled upward above the trees. Chapelle Plantation was burning. Were there any of them left on the island? Was hers the last? Thanks to her father's intervention with President Simone, she was left alone. Until now. Her reprieve just expired.

Iniki Beaumont had little left. Her land, her beloved home would be lost with the return of the man in black. But that hardly seemed to matter when compared to the people in her service. The old couple could never survive on their own. They were her responsibility, as well as the twelve year old orphaned twin boys she promised to protect.

The reality of her situation was clear. What she needed was a plan; one that would place her and her people out of Simone's reach.

Riley Taggart cursed the dirt roads made rutty by two days of rain. His mission barely began and already it was a disaster. The night before, the Seals delivered him onshore close to the capital. Intelligence provided him with false papers and a car. That was the extent of their help. The papers were up to snuff. The car had seen better days. He needed to complete the mission and exit off the island in five days time. Armed with limited fire power, he carried no cell phone or communication devices. If caught, there was no way to discover his real identity.

But his intel left much unanswered. The man he was assigned to rescue was already shot full of holes by a firing squad. Verification wasn't difficult. The body was splayed out in front of the presidential palace as a challenge to the opposition.

The second name on his list was probably six feet under, too. The young french woman who refused to leave when the going was good. Now, if she was still alive and kicking, he would have to invent some way to spirit her out without either of them getting captured. The way the mission was going, he thought, only divine intervention could save them.

"Bloody woman doesn't know how to keep her ass out of trouble," he complained to no one.

Beaumont Plantation sat some twenty miles out of town. He approached the estate with caution. The last thing he needed was a government patrol right now. He parked the car out of sight and prepared to reconnoiter the area. His first step landed him in three inches of muck covering the top of his boots with mud.

"Damn it all," he muttered.

The aggravation he allowed to fester intensified. After a quick survey of the surroundings, he sloshed up to the front door. Without knocking, he entered. "Isn't a dammed social call," he grumbled.

The house was bare, furniture and paintings gone. Even the draperies were removed, save one solitary drape left on one side of each wide window. Under those lay thick piles of hay, placed carefully.

"Someone's planning a bonfire," he said to himself. "What the hell is going on?"

His tour brought him to the back of the house and onto a large veranda, empty except for two small wooden benches and a stone table. He walked across to a low wall. From that vantage point, he observed fields stretched out at least a half mile in each direction.

A woman stood about two hundred yards away. Although her back was to him, he saw her clearly. He noticed the stance, legs apart, feet planted firmly, hands on hips. She faced the wind, her jeans cut off inches above her knees, her long dark hair streaming back.

"Iniki Beaumont, I presume," he whispered. He was confident he could read character in a person's stature. If he were right, he was dealing with a determined woman. This lady would not be manipulated easily. From where he stood, she was a looker as well.

"Not bad," he remarked.

Then he felt the pressure of a small hard object rammed into his back.

"Not good," he groaned.

"Do not move, Monsieur."

Automatically, Riley's hands went up. Whoever was behind him approached on silent feet while he was focused on the woman. You ass, he chided himself.

"I'm looking for Iniki Beaumont," he explained. "My name is Taggart."

The voice sounded young. A deceiving crack here and there. "You are American?"

"Yes." Riley strained to see who it was.

"Do not attempt to turn around, Monsieur. Your weapons, please. Throw them on the ground."

Bloody hell, Riley thought. How did he miss someone sneaking up behind him? "Look, whoever you are. I'm here to help Miss Beaumont. I'm not her enemy. She's there in the field, right? Just call her over."

"First your weapons. Then I will call Mademoiselle."

Riley didn't appreciate being at the barrel end of a rifle. Normally, he was too careful to make mistakes, too professional to be annoyed when he should be alert. Angry at his stupidity, he toyed with the idea of overpowering whoever was behind him. He had done it before with success. But now he wasn't sure what the game was. He'd play along for a while. He lifted his sweatshirt, revealing a gun and shoulder holster. With careful movements, he pulled the gun out and set it on the ground.

"You may turn around now, Monsieur."

Riley followed directions, facing his captor. Captors, to be accurate. Twin boys not more than four feet high. One held a rifle so old it might once have belonged to a pirate. The other stood beside his brother, armed with a baseball bat. The two were dressed in rags but the determination on their faces left little doubt they were serious.

"Look, boys," he attempted to explain. "I'm not here to hurt anyone. I need to speak to Miss Beaumont. It's extremely important. So you can put the rifle down."

The boys didn't answer. Something behind Riley had their full attention.

"Do not let their size fool you, sir. They are excellent shots. From that distance, they won't miss." The woman in the field joined the party.

"About bloody time," he sputtered.

"Exactly who are you?" the woman asked. "You can explain while you keep your hands up and stand perfectly still."

"Name's Riley Taggart. I'm American, here to escort you off the island."

"Another American? Simone knows where to find his mercenaries. Do not Americans have any sense of fair play? Or is the almighty dollar the only deciding factor?"

"What's that supposed to mean?" Riley fumed. "Am I under house arrest because I'm American? Look, lady, I just drove from the capital to get you off this damned plantation. And I sure as hell didn't come from Simone."

"Then, from where?"

"When I can turn around and face you with my hands down, we can discuss it." How, he wondered, had he managed to get himself into this mess?

"I would not lower your arms just yet, Mr. Whatever."

"Taggart. Riley Taggart. Shall I spell it for you?"

"I believe I am able to figure that out for myself," she responded, still behind him. "Your papers?"

He swore under his breath. Twice, he told himself. Twice he was surprised, once by a child and then by a woman. "In my pants pocket, there are credentials identifying me as a journalist. I carry nothing that shows my true identity, if that's what you're looking for. If your parents weren't so influential, Ma'am," he added, "I wouldn't be here at all."

"And I am not the slightest bit grateful," she countered. "How rude of me."

"Why the hell didn't you leave when you had the chance?" Time for him to ask the questions.

The boy with the gun jabbed it into Riley's stomach. "Do not be disrespectful to Mademoiselle."

"That is enough, Mathieu," she ordered. "Michel, take the papers from his pocket and hand them to me, please."

Riley grunted in disgust. "Can I put my hands down now?"

She ignored his request as the second twin rifled through his pockets, grabbed the papers and gave them to the woman.

She's reading them, Riley thought, and taking her time about it, too.

"Impressive, Mr. Taggart," she acknowledged finally. "With luck you may fool a soldier or two. I doubt these would convince an officer with a brain in his head."

"All the more reason not to delay."

She ignored his comment. "You may put your hands down now."

"Yeah, thanks a lot."

To the boys she said, "Mathieu, the gun is no longer necessary. I think we may have to trust him for the time being. Give Mr. Taggart his weapon and find Madeline. Ask for some tea, please."

The boys nodded, returned Riley's gun, and disappeared into the house.

"May I turn around now? I prefer to face my captor." Riley made no effort to hide his annoyance.

"An admirable trait. I feel the same way. You may turn, Mr. Taggart. But I am amused at the notion that you are my prisoner."

Cautiously he swung round to face her, not knowing whether she, too, held a gun. No weapon was in evidence. Her arms were folded across full breasts, her small bare feet set apart. He scanned her from head to foot. She was young and beautiful but tired lines circled her eyes. No makeup adorned the tanned face and, under her muddy clothes, he imagined her slim body was bronzed. She made no attempt to wipe away the mud caked on her shins. He noticed she stood with shoulders pushed back and hips thrust forward. Under different circumstances, Riley would be attracted to her.

"Do I pass inspection, Monsieur Taggart?"

"The name is Riley."

"Remove your sunglasses, please."

"Excuse me?"

"I said to remove your sunglasses. Is that difficult? I am not asking you to undress."

He shrugged and took off the glasses. When she held out her hand, he gave them to her. Then he watched as she threw them to the ground and stomped on them with bare feet.

"What the hell are you doing?" he sputtered. "You got something against glasses?"

"Yes."

"Anything else I'm wearing that you feel strongly about?"

"No, the rest of you is fine."

"That's a relief."

"Now, Mr. Taggart, exactly how do you propose to rescue me? And from whom?"

The woman was irritating as hell. But he would be honest with her. "Simone's government has declared you an enemy of the state. The rebel Marcel Valois is dead. One by one, the army is wiping out leaders of the opposition. According to American intelligence, you're on that list."

"How do you know this?" No trace of surprise showed in her voice.

"I saw Valois' body myself. Not a pretty sight. As for your fate, that's common sense. How can he leave you alone when the villagers will follow you anywhere?"

"Follow me where? I am not a rebel."

"You bring them food. You nurse the sick. You're responsible for teaching them what little English they know. Simone wants you out of the way."

She shrugged. "I have been told that already. Your news is not startling. An emissary of our wretched president, a countryman of yours by the way, appeared today without warning. His message was to leave immediately. My deadline is five this afternoon."

"In that case, let's get going." Events were escalating faster than he anticipated.

But she didn't move. "I was offered passage on a plane tonight. The deal is my life for my land."

"And?"

"I refused, of course. I will not leave my people to the mercy of his barbaric soldiers."

"Even if you were willing, Ms Beaumont, you won't make it on that plane. Since your murder would incite the villagers, you would simply disappear and they will claim you ran away."

"I am not a leader of any group, Mr. Taggart. Look around you. Do you see any weapons or ammunition? If you search, you will discover that one sorry-looking rifle that Mathieu found in one of the workers' huts. And an even older baseball bat."

She was interrupted by an elderly woman, carrying two steaming cups on a tray.

"You see Madeline here and you are welcome to meet her husband Francois, both of whom have been with my family since I was born. Thank you, Madeline."

The woman bowed and left as quietly as she had come.

"Not very impressive for a terrorist, is she?" The younger woman asked.

"Lady, I'm not the one you have to convince. And if you think you can talk your way out of this with Simone, you're crazier than I thought."

A trace of a smile graced her lips as she invited him to sit at the table. "We have no milk or sugar left. I am afraid you will have to drink it plain." Despite her predicament, she poured the tea as if she were the mistress of a grand salon.

Riley shook his head in disbelief. "You don't seem to understand. We don't have time to waste sipping tea, with or without cream and sugar. It's a necessity that we leave now."

"It is you who does not understand, Mr. Taggart. I cannot go anywhere with you."

"Mind telling me why?"

"If you wish." She shrugged once more. "Simone's men will come soon. They will take over my house and property, including these few workers. Madeline is seventy-two years old. Her husband is seventy-five and in poor health. If they are not immediately executed, they will be forced to work for the soldiers. Or worse still, because they are old, they will be sent to the city where they will starve. The twins face a far more tragic fate. They will run. The only choice they have will be fighting with the resistance groups. So you see, I cannot let you rescue me."

Frustration flooded through him. "No, I don't see. Certainly you must realize what will happen if you stay. You"ll suffer a hell of a lot more than the old couple. And when the soldiers are through, you'll die along with the rest. For an intelligent woman, you're not using your head."

She laughed like he said something amusing. "Did your reports also tell my IQ?"

"Look Lady, I'm not about to argue this. I'm here to get you off the island. And that's what I'm going to do."

With a flip of her black hair, she answered him. There was a smile on her face but fire in her eyes. Eyes he couldn't help but focus on.

"Then I regret you will not be able to complete your mission, Mr. Taggart."

"Riley."

"I am going nowhere. Nowhere. Do you understand?"

"I understand that if you come with me, you have a fighting chance. Staying here only assures your death."

"I am not as foolish as you think, Mr. Taggart . . ."

"Riley."

" . . . . and I do not have a death wish. I would give up everything I own for the lives of these few people."

Again he shook his head. "Ms Beaumont, I've been sent by my government at no minor expense. In the space of five days, I must rendezvous with others to get you off the island safely. If we don't make the meeting spot on time, neither one of us will leave alive. Do you understand?"

"I understand that you do not like being contradicted, Mr. Taggart."

"And I also don't appreciate women who refuse to listen to reason. "

"There is no need to raise your voice!"

"I am not . . ." He stopped, took a breath and started over in a lower tone. "I am not raising my voice. Simply explaining what must be obvious."

"You are raising your voice."

"Damn right I am. I don't particularly enjoy risking my neck to rescue spoiled rich girls who won't use common sense."

Her face flushed, not with embarrassment, but rather with fury. "If anyone is spoiled here, it is certainly not I or my people. You, Mr. Taggart, are a typical man, in love with yourself."

Any advantage he had was lost, he realized. Nothing would be accomplished by infuriating her further. On the other hand, the woman had a sharp tongue and needed a lesson in reality. It went against his grain to apologize. He wanted to cut the crap, throw her in the car and take off. However, he bit his tongue and tried some charm.

"Okay, lady. I'm sorry if I was rude. I'm just concerned for your safety."

She gazed at him with those burning eyes. "I doubt that, Mr. Taggart, but I accept your apology. Now tell me why your government would take the time and expense to rescue one French citizen? There are very few of us left here. But, why me? My parents do not have that much influence."

Smart lady, he decided. "You are part of the resistance."

"At one time, perhaps. Why is that important?"

"The rest of the world is aware of what's happening here in terms of human rights violations. You would be an imposing witness to appeal to the United Nations to intervene on the behalf of the poor on the island."

Disbelief crossed her face. "The United Nations needs me to talk before they will do something? How ridiculous!"

"The world moves in ridiculous ways, Ms Beaumont. You don't have much time. The government forces will return here well before five."

"They are here already," she said cynically. "Do you see the smoke there in the south?"

"What is it?" he asked, aware it wasn't a good sign.

"Chapelle Plantation." Her eyes seemed to water but he couldn't be sure. "The owner is an elderly man who refused to flee when other landowners abandoned the island. He vowed he would not leave anything behind. I believe he is dead now."

14

"He's burned his home? And killed himself?"

"Yes, I think so. And I am next. They will be here soon."

Riley looked at his watch. "That gives us no time. Let's go!"

She didn't jump up from his seat as he did. Instead she folded her arms across her chest and stared at him boldly. "Your mission is to save me from Simone. That is correct?"

"I've said that enough times now."

"Fine. Then that is what you must do. I will go willingly."

The sudden turnabout alerted him. "What's the snag?"

"The snag?" She smiled broadly. "I do not know that term."

"Like hell, you don't. Don't play the dumb broad with me."

"That term I know. Let me assure you, Mr. Taggart, it is not an accurate phrase to describe me."

"As if I didn't know. Look lady, we're wasting precious time here."

"Then I will tell Madeline and Francois to prepare the twins and get set to leave."

"What?" Not what he planned on doing at all.

"Mr. Taggart, I am agreeing to let you rescue me." Her strident manner softened. But her next words were chosen to annoy him further. He was sure of it.

"The problem of my workers is solved. They will accompany us."

He expected something like this and was prepared. "Come with us? I don't think so. My orders specify you only."

"I see. Well, if you want me, you will have to include the twins and Madeline and Francois. Do you wish me to go with you or not?"

"Yes ... no..." He saw no possibility of success with four extra people coming along. "You don't understand the scope of this mission, Ms Beaumont. Our destination is a point some twenty miles from here on the north coast. God knows how many government roadblocks and patrols are between us and there. Not to mention one extremely nasty mountain range. And we have limited time, mind you."

She nodded. "I understand perfectly well. Now you must understand. These people are peasants who have lived here their entire lives. They know the terrain. They will not be a burden."

He knew his temper was showing and didn't care. "Let me assure you I'm not a novice in this business. And I say they are too old for the journey we'll be forced to make. The children will be at greater risk."

"Left here, they will die. You know that. If they come, they will have a ...what is the word?.....a fighting chance."

"Not possible. Sorry." She would not get the better of him, he resolved.

"Then I will stay here and die with them," she pronounced calmly. "I see no other option."

"Don't you see how difficult it will be?" he hammered back. "How can they survive?"

She responded in a voice filled with sorrow. "How can they survive here?"

Taking a few deep breaths, he composed himself. "I have food and rations for only two."

She countered with, "We have some food left. It can be packed into your automobile easily."

He tried it from another angle. "The car can only take us part of the way. We'll have to travel on foot or horse, whatever we come across. Who knows? We'll have to take what we can get."

A flash of deep emotions passed over her face. Anger, sorrow, defiance and fear all mixed together. She rose from her seat and facing him, she placed both palms down on the table. Leaning close to him, she spoke in a hushed tone.

"These people have been taking what they can find for the past two years. Never once have I heard a complaint from either the old ones or the children. When was your last roast beef dinner. Mr Taggart? Last week? A few days ago? These people have not had a piece of meat for a year. Yet they continue on. They continue to fight and hope. They will make the journey even if it becomes their last."

"Bloody hell!" he sputtered out.

"Really, Mr. Taggart. Cursing will not help reach a resolution."

"There is no resolution," he answered. "I can't agree to your plan."

She laughed, shook out her hair and resumed her seat. "I think you should reconsider. Either that or leave here quickly. You are correct to believe the military will be here long before my deadline arrives."

She did have a point, he told himself. "Okay. The way I see it is this. We both have an objective. I need to get you off this island or my superiors will not be pleased."

"I thought you would agree once you calmed down."

Her comment infuriated him but he quashed the feeling. "Taking the same problem from your viewpoint, you have no choice but to convince me to take your people along. So I guess this is a catch 22."

"Yes, neither of us has a choice."

He nodded. "Damned if we do, damned if we don't."

"I get the meaning, Mr. Taggart. You are right, of course. I need you as much as you need me."

"Good," he said with a smile. "So let's stop pussy-footing around and get out of here."

"Not quite yet,"she added. "I have some unfinished business."

"Dammit, we don't have time." He banged his fist on the stone tabletop, pretending he didn't feel the resulting pain.

She rose from her chair. "Do you always lose your temper so quickly?"

"I seldom lose my temper."

"Well you have used enough swear words in our short acquaintance. Or is that an American trait?"

Forcing himself to smile, he admitted to himself that he liked a woman with a sense of humor.

"I'll try to curb that tendency." Like hell, he told himself.

"While you finish your tea, Mr. Taggart, I will start to collect the others."

"Don't suppose you have an extra pair of sunglasses hanging around?"

She didn't answer. Not that he expected she would. His gaze followed her until she disappeared into the house. She didn't glance back.. For some reason that bothered him.

She felt his eyes on her and smiled. She enjoyed sparring with this man, playing with him until his anger raged and waiting for the moment when he agreed to her demands. She understood his assessment of her body. He reacted as a man would, despite her ragged appearance.

"Good God, what am I thinking?" she muttered. This was no time to play the vulnerable female. The lives of her people were at stake. She would not lose those she loved. She knew she had him right where she wanted him. Riley Taggart was caught in the middle, between his duty to his superiors, whoever they were, and his innate caution. Personally she did not care as long as he agreed to her demands. He presented her with a chance of escape. And however doubtful the outcome, it was a better option than waiting for Simone's soldiers. No, she decided, Taggart would not slip through her fingers.

"Good," he said aloud when she was gone. He had her right where he wanted her. She had no choice from the beginning. Where was she going to run? Especially dragging four extra people.

No, he decided. Despite the fact that the woman was far more sharp and intelligent than he expected, he skillfully put her into a no-choice situation.

He did admire her. She was stubborn, no question. That kind of person usually meant trouble on a mission, he reminded himself. On the other hand, his original plan was in shambles anyway. With four more civilians to move, why was he worried about the woman? He would go along with her crazy scheme and hope for the best.

CHAPTER TWO

Day 1 ~ Late afternoon at the Beaumont Plantation
"Are you crazy, lady?"

In the front hallway, Iniki Beaumont issued orders in French to the twins, Madeline and an old man, Riley assumed was Francois. Each held flaming torches. On her command, they each ran to different rooms.

"What the hell...?" he sputtered as he approached.

"Mr. Taggart, do you speak a single sentence without a swear word?"

He ignored her sarcasm. "I've agreed to take everyone. And we leave right now."

"Not quite yet," she objected.

"Why the hell not?"

"I am not finished yet."

"We go now, lady," he insisted.

"Mr. Taggart, you spend too much time arguing and swearing. Stop wasting your energy and make yourself useful." She shoved a lighted torch into his hands.

"What do I do with this?"

"Go set the upstairs on fire. We have little time left, as you say over and over."

"Damn stubborn woman," he said and ran up the circular staircase. "Knows how to send a message though." Takes guts to burn your own house down, he thought.

The second floor offered identical piles of hay at the windows. In less than a minute, he managed to enter all the rooms and light the flammable material. Black smoke choked him as he raced down the stairs. Within seconds, the house would be fully engulfed. Coughing, he ran out the front door and pointed in the direction of his car.

The five refugees, each carrying a stuffed kerchief on a long stick, hurried through the mud. Good Lord, he said to himself, at the sight of them. Tom Sawyer and his band are about to embark on an adventure. He hoped they realized it wasn't to be a lazy journey down a peaceful river.

"Get in the car," he ordered. "The little ones get down on the floor in the back. Ms Beaumont, you sit in front. I hope there's another way out of here besides the main driveway."

"There is," she replied sharply. "Are you aware of the three military jeeps approaching the house?"

"Where? I seem to have lost my sunglasses."

"There. You see the green camouflage."

"I got them. They'll be on top of us in minutes. Start talking. Where to go first?" He shoved the key in the ignition, shifted and headed away from the jeeps.

One of the boys jumped up from his hiding place, pointing the old rifle out the window. "I am ready for them, Monsieur."

Riley caught hold of the boy's arm, pulling his hand away from the trigger. "Dammit, kid! You'll just get us killed quicker." With no time to waste, Riley continued driving. "Tell me where to go, lady. Right now!"

"Continue as you are going," she instructed. Then she leaned over the seat and said, "Michel, you thought you were doing right. But good soldiers know when to retreat. Later, we may need your help."

Riley heard his answer.

"Yes, Mademoiselle. I understand."

"You could have been less offensive, Mr. Taggart," she remarked, turning to Riley. "He is only a child."

The tone of her voice convinced him she was not pleased. Too damn bad, he said but only to himself.

To her, he shouted, "Look, lady, those jeeps are getting closer with every inoffensive word you say. So, are you going to tell me where to go or what?"

She stiffened but conceded the point. "Follow this path around. Shortly, you will see a side road that borders the fields. Take that."

Ignoring her disapproving tone, he increased his speed and peeled through the mud. The car skidded and swerved but went where he aimed it. When he reached the turnoff, he asked, "Where does this take us?"

"Away from the main road. It is an old tract that was used to transport workers back and forth from their living quarters to the fields. It will lead to the workers huts. From there, the path splits in many directions. Most are dead ends to the outer fields. I know of one dirt track that will take us north. We have a good chance of losing them."

"They'll follow us, no matter where we go," he warned.

"Mr. Taggart, you need not instruct me on the dictator's practices. I have lived with them far too long."

Riley raised his eyebrows in frustration but kept his tongue. From what he observed so far, the woman was argumentative and annoying. At the same time, her strength of will and moxie impressed him. Formidable was a good description, he decided. Intriguing might be another.

He stopped himself right there. Rule number two on any mission was to never get involved with a female. He reprimanded himself for almost blowing it.

In the backseat, quiet weeping gradually became louder, blanking out his uncomfortable train of thought. "L"esprit de morte," the old woman cried out.

"No, Madeline," the Beaumont woman comforted. "He is an evil man but that is all. He has no more evil powers than you and I."

"But he comes. I saw him in the jeep. He comes for us."

"Do not fear. Just pray, Madeline."

Riley turned to his passengers. "What the hell is she talking about?"

"Despite your ill-mannered use of vocabulary, I will answer, Mr. Taggart. It is necessary that you know this. The man she speaks of is a representative of Simone. A man dressed entirely in black. The natives call him the spirit of death. It is said that he comes when the government troops are about to take property from the rightful owners. The natives consider him a ghost, a specter, a precursor of death. But he is a man only. I had the pleasure of meeting him this morning."

"Terrific." Riley said in disgust. "Just what we need. A little voodoo to stir up the pot. See if you can keep her quiet."

"There is no voodoo involved here." Again he detected anger in her voice. "My people are too educated for that. But they are afraid, Mr. Taggart, as most would be under these circumstances. However, I will do as you request. And you will kindly eliminate swear words every time you speak. We have young ones with us."

He ignored the criticism, keeping one eye on the rear mirror. Of the three jeeps, only one followed, having a tough time making its way through the black smoke. The other two jeeps stopped at the house, he decided. Unless they had a fire brigade with them, there was little they could do. The structure was engulfed, as Iniki Beaumont planned. And, although the stucco walls and tile roof would not succumb to the flames, the house was a total loss.

"Good job, lady," he found himself saying aloud. "By burning the house, you created just the diversion we needed."

"What is good about that?" He heard the pain in her voice.

"We're still alive, aren't we? The death spirit didn't get us on the first try."

The man in black stopped the jeeps halfway up the drive. One look told him the house was unsalvageable. President Simone would not be pleased. In addition, he held no doubt that the car in the distance contained Iniki Beaumont. The others were unknown. The president would demand an explanation.

"They are escaping, General," his adjutant informed him.

"I can see that. But they can't go far. Radio the last jeep to follow them for the time being. We will stop at the house. I want to search there, regardless. This may be a ploy."

The general laughed to himself though the humor of his thoughts did not show on his face. So the spitfire he met this morning saw through the farce of the boarding pass. She knew the president had no intention of letting her live. Not that it surprised him. She hid her fear well as she spoke her piece. But the general could sniff out fright a mile away. He was a soldier of fortune, a mercenary for too long now, not to realize everyone felt afraid at some time or other. It was how one coped that determined bravery or foolishness. Though the woman was terrified, she didn't let it overwhelm her.

And yet, he did expect her to agree to the bogus flight to Mexico City. His impression of Iniki Beaumont had been slightly in error. He would readjust his thinking. He should have recognized her intelligence. It was right there in her eyes.

She looked back as they drove. Through the rear window, she saw the back of the home in which she spent every summer of her childhood and the last six years of her life. Black smoke poured through the windows, the fire fanned by the island breezes and the open design of the house. Too late, she cried silently, too late to save it now. But if she could not live in her beloved home, no one else would either. She would fulfill her objective no matter what the cost.

"When you reach those huts, you must stop," she directed. "For only a minute."

"Stop? Are you crazy, lady? That jeep isn't far behind. We won't stand a chance."

Another argument, she thought. Did the man ever consider she might know what she was doing? Before this journey was over, he would understand. "I will show you where to turn off and hide the car. They will not see we have stopped."

Riley shook his head but didn't disagree. "Are the outbuildings going up in flames, too?" he asked.

"You bet your life," she answered with no expression in her voice. "Is that not what you say in your country?"

"That's what we say, lady."

He did as he was instructed, making a sharp right turn as they rounded a bend. When she pointed to another right, he followed her lead. The car ended up between the last two of the structures and was well hidden from the road.

She took charge, surprised that the American stayed in the background for once. "Each of you listen carefully. You have your assignments. We have practiced many times. Do your task quickly and return to the car. You have only minutes before those following us realize we have tricked them. As soon as they see the smoke, they will be here."

She watched as the company moved. Piled against one side of the hut were a number of torches soaking in kerosene. She lit a match and touched the flame to each, noticing that Taggart followed her lead and helped. She remained alert, keeping one eye on the surroundings and one ear listening for the sound of the jeep.

"What do you want me to do?" she heard him ask.

"What you do best. Watch for the soldiers and keep my people safe."

"Terrific," he said cynically.

But she ignored him and ran off.

His gun in hand, Riley circled the surrounding huts. Detecting no sign of the enemy, he positioned himself where he could see the car and most of the compound. So far, so good, he told himself.

Two minutes passed. The twins returned first, extinguishing their torches in a barrel of rainwater Riley guessed was prepared for just that purpose. The relief he felt at their safe return surprised him and he patted each on the back. Francois joined them half a minute later. Neither woman appeared.

Herding them into the car, he recognized anxiety on their faces. The old man spoke rapidly in French.

"What's he trying to tell me?" he asked one of the boys.

"Mademoiselle and Madeline should be back by now," he answered quickly.

Riley looked at his watch. Almost four minutes had passed. "How do you know they're late?"

The twin, whichever one he was, gave Riley a knowing look. "We have practiced so many times. We never take more than two minutes to do this job."

"Okay." Riley knew what he had to do. "I'm going to look for them. You guys stay in the car and wait."

"Yes, Monsieur," both responded in unison.

He had not gone far when he heard a faint cry coming from his right. Maneuvering into position took another few moments but once situated he could view the scene without being spotted. Two military men held Madeline by the arms, her burning torch on the ground. One soldier slapped the old woman viciously across the face. Madeline did not cry out.

At the same time, he felt a hand on his shoulder. Reacting as he was trained, he shoved the barrel of his gun into Iniki's stomach.

"Damn, don't sneak up on me like that," he snarled.

"Madeline?" Her voice hid the terror he read on Iniki's face.

He put his fingers to his lips. "I'll get her. Go back to the car so we can make a fast getaway."

"I will help you," she countered.

"No, you won't. Meet me at the car."

"Madeline is my responsibility."

"Look," he ordered, keeping his voice to a low whisper. "I'm in charge. Go back to the car."

Not waiting for a response, he took off, edging his way to the rear of the jeep. The soldiers were busy tormenting Madeline and made no sign that they saw him. He made a split-second evaluation of what he was up against and decided he could overtake both. The gun was useless. His fists and the element of surprise were his best options.

The soldier closest to him was easy. The second one proved to be a different story. Allowing Madeline to drop, the man stood his ground. Maybe this one wasn't so easy, Riley thought, as the man reached for his gun. With a sudden lunge, Riley managed to knock it away. It landed with a thud somewhere in the surrounding brush which was beginning to catch fire. Everything around them was ablaze. Riley's eyes burned, his vision blurred. Not going as planned, he told himself, and threw his best punch, connecting squarely with the guy's jaw. Yet, he didn't drop.

"What the hell....?" Riley muttered, thoroughly annoyed.

Next, he heard what sounded like a cracking tree limb. The soldier collapsed at Riley's feet. Where the guy once stood, the Beaumont woman staggered, then regained her footing. She held a wooden plank, heavy enough to take anyone out. Who was rescuing whom?

"I thought I told you to get in the car?" he shouted.

"And I thought I said I wouldn't," she retorted.

He bent to pick up Madeline. "This damn well isn't going to work, you know, if you don't follow orders."

"Instead of lecturing, Mr. Taggart, you could just say thank you."

"Thank you."

"You are welcome." She ran her hand through her hair. "Tell me, is there any situation in which you do not curse?"

"What the hell does that have to do with this?"

She didn't answer and he understood that somehow she had won their skirmish. He released the shivering Madeline to the pushy broad and watched as they hurried away.

"You could have said thank you, too," he called after her but heard no response.

By the time they gathered together, the wooden huts were a mass of flames. A defiant expression played on the younger woman's face but he noticed her eyes were wet.

"Drive," she said, pointing to a dirt path.

"Right." Despite his annoyance, he had no wish to embarrass her by staring. Once more, he followed her directions. Was she crying? He listened for sniffling. There was none. Maybe the smoke made her eyes water. He was about to dismiss the matter when he noticed her move. A quick glance showed her wiping her cheeks with sooty fingers. Black streaks soiled her nose and under her eyes. Not daring another peek, he fished for his handkerchief and handed it over. "You've got dirt on your face," he said.

"Thank you." She took the cloth and cleaned her cheeks.

He forgot the irritation she caused earlier. He was a sucker when it came to sobbing women. Unnerved him every time, he thought. Still, if anyone deserved a minute of self-indulgence, it was she. He doubted she allowed herself a good cry very often. After all, he was a sensitive male, fully capable of understanding another's pain. Wasn't he?

In the rear seat, Madeline and Francois contributed to the mood, quietly weeping. Only the twins did not share in the sorrow.

"Good, Mademoiselle. Very good." They clapped their hands. "The pig Simone will not get our home," one of them said with surprising vehemence.

Riley listened as their guardian answered. "No, Michel. It is a terrible thing I have done. Do you understand?"

"I do not understand," the boy replied. "The house and the buildings ... They are safe from Simone and his soldiers. No?"

"Yes, Michel, they are safe. But now they are gone. To prevent Simone from using them, it was necessary to destroy everything. But, it is never good to destroy."

"I see," the child said.

How can he see, Riley asked himself. The poor kid is barely a teenager and already he has lost his parents and his home. How the hell can he possibly understand the evil things humans are capable of? Riley found himself wanting to take the kid in his arms, give him some comfort. But the woman beat him to the punch.

"*Je t'aime,*" she whispered to each boy.

Despite their constant disagreement, Riley couldn't deny an odd admiration. She made one hell of a sacrifice back there, one that probably devastated her. Yet, she carried through, thumbing her nose at the president. Riley wondered if either of their noses would get off the island safely.

"We are being followed," she announced calmly.

In the rearview mirror, he saw the remaining two jeeps. In the passenger seat of the lead vehicle, a man with an oversized cowboy hat seemed to be directing the driver.

"The spirit of doom or whatever he's called?" he asked quietly.

She nodded her head.

"Okay. I need a road or path that leads to a dead end," he ordered.

She looked like she questioned his sanity but answered. "Stay on this tract for another minute. You will see a turnoff on the left."

"At the end of it, are there plenty of bushes and trees?"

"Yes. It once headed to the outer fields. The vegetation must be overgrown by now."

"Good." He slowed down considerably, shortening the gap between them and their pursuers.

"What are you doing?" she asked.

"They've got to follow us. I want to be sure they see us turn."

"Why?"

"No time to explain. You'll just have to trust me."

Finally he was in control, formulating a plan and executing it. She would see he was a professional. He was proud of himself until he stopped to wonder why her reaction mattered, why he cared whether she recognized his leadership qualities. Not wishing to answer himself, he pushed it out of his head, took the turnoff and jammed his foot down on the gas. The car took off on the rutted path at top speed, throwing his passengers up, down and everywhere.

Holding on to the doorhandle, the woman spoke. "The car may fall apart."

He agreed with the possibility. How could he not? But he set the strategy in motion and had to see it through. "I've got to get ahead of them. Is there a place where I can hide the car?"

The woman and the old man held a quick conversation, all of it French. Riley understood nothing.

"What did he say?" Riley was barely able to control the car.

"Francois says there is an old path not used in years. Right before we get to the field."

"Just what the doctor ordered. Ask him to tell me as we get close to it."

She did as he requested. Three minutes later, they made the turn. Riley issued orders as he turned off the engine.

"No one leave leaves this car. Not even you." He directed his comment at Iniki as he exited the car. "This is my party."

"It is mine, also," she whispered, seconds after he left. Turning to the ones in back, she explained. "Stay here. You are well hidden. I will be back soon."

"Mademoiselle, where are you to go?"

"To follow Mr. Taggart, Michel. To be sure we can trust him."

"No, Mademoiselle. Do not leave," the other twin said. "We will be lost if you do not return."

"I will return, Mathieu. Do not be afraid."

"*Mon dieu*," Michel said, throwing his brother a dirty look. Mathieu reciprocated with an elbow to his brother's chest. Only a stern warning from Iniki made the two stop.

The car was hidden, embedded in a grove of trees. Iniki removed her shoes and ran almost to the beginning of the turn off. There she dove into the brush when she spotted Riley. He was erasing tire tracks with a handful of rye grass. Then, he squatted down to wait.

It did not take long. Two jeeps flew past within seconds. Moments later, she heard the screech of brakes down the road and orders shouted out.

When Riley skirted through the bushes, she followed. He moved like a panther. Was he as dangerous as one? Iniki realized the man knew how to hunt. Her worry was the identity of his prey.

Just short of the muddy field, he froze. The sudden halt startled her but she managed to do the same. The soldiers were close. She heard hushed conversation only a dozen yards away. For several minutes she watched and waited for Riley to make his next move.

The vehicles stood side by side, flanked by tall trees and prickly underbrush. The soldiers shook their heads, pointing out to the flat fields. The man in black appeared to listen. Tall and broad shouldered, he wore a pistol in an American cowboy-style holster. A thick belt encircled his waist. Atop his head sat a black cowboy hat and his leather jacket sported fringe. The outfit was so bizarre and out of place that, for a second, she was amused. That changed as soon as he spoke.

"They're here somewhere," he uttered to an underling. "They can't be anywhere else. Send two men to search the area."

"Yes, sir."

"And I want the entire perimeter of the field covered. They can't have crossed it that fast. Which means they're hidden in the trees close by. Find them."

Two soldiers were sent off in different directions, leaving the man in black and three officers staring out over the expanse. As soon as the search party disappeared, she saw Riley move. He pulled out his knife and crept closer to the rear of the vehicles.

For a moment, she feared he would attempt to murder each of them in cold blood. If he survived and lived to talk about it, she knew she would not be able to trust him. He would be no better than the men he stalked. She would fear him just as much.

But Riley's plan did not include blood, she soon realized. In no more than thirty seconds, he left his cover, approached the jeeps from behind, gave all eight tires a quick jab and twist with the knife. Then, not even five feet away from his pursuers, he hesitated. Iniki held her breath, afraid to make a sound. The tiniest creak could make them turn around and Riley was still in the open. But, the enemy only looked forward, unaware of what was taking place behind their backs. Get out of there now, she screamed silently. Only when he faded into the woods, did she allow herself a brief smile.

When she lost sight of Riley, she was not alarmed. She memorized a few landmarks on her way from the car. She moved quickly knowing they were still in danger. Her feet ached and bled from the rough terrain. But the trip was worth a little pain. Riley Taggart was exactly who he said he was. And, she would trust him.

Quickening her pace, she made way for the car, expecting to hear plenty from him about disobeying orders. She found herself looking forward to it. The sparring between them would be enjoyable if the situation were different. In fact, it was amusing, listening to him sputter and swear. He would never know that, of course. Let him believe that she answered to no man.

That thought was barely finished when she was grabbed from behind. An arm encircled her breasts, preventing her from moving. Another arm came around and place a knife against her throat. She held her breath, terrified until she recognized the weapon. At once, she relaxed and leaned back against the man who held her.

"It is only me, Mr. Taggart. You do not have to react so dramatically."

"I know I told you to stay in the car," he whispered.

"You did," she replied.

"And you didn't."

"I have a problem taking orders," she explained. "You may let me go now."

"Terrific, lady. Well, you better get used to my orders. I''ve tried to be accommodating as hell but you're damned difficult." He released her but not before he pulled her hard against the full length of his body.

She smiled. "I am difficult at times. That has been said of me. I am sure you have heard the same said of you. However, the trick with the tires was brilliant."

"You followed me the entire way?"

"I had to be sure I could trust you. That you were not giving us away."

"Giving you away? You still think I work for that crackpot Simone?"

"I did question your veracity, I admit. I do not now."

"Well, I hope you are satisfied," he muttered, wiping his hands on his pants. "Because I don't need you on my tail every time I go on a foray."

"On your tail? What does that mean?"

"You know what it means."

When the bullet hit him in the forearm, it knocked Riley to the ground. She gasped, then kneeled down beside him.

"Do not move," the soldier ordered in English. He pointed his weapon to Riley's chest. "Who are you?"

She forced herself to think fast. "We are lovers," she answered. The soldier was no more than eighteen and not a native islander. His English was good. With luck, he would be inexperienced.

"My husband does not know of this. He will kill me if he finds out. Please." She stood up and faced the man, taking a tentative step forward. She forced a vulnerable, wounded look on her face.

"Your name?" he demanded. "Your husband's name?"

"He is of the military as you are. General Fontaine LaForge. Please, I beg of you, do not report me. He will beat me." She was grateful that Riley didn't speak.

"Come with me," the soldier commanded. "I must bring you to my general."

"Please, no." She tucked her arms behind her, her breasts jutting out.

"You are tempting," The soldier said with a smile. "But, I'm not stupid. Come. We must go to the general. You there, " he motioned to Riley, "get up immediately ."

Riley didn't move, a questioning expression on his face.

"He speaks no English, sir," Iniki supplied.

But the man was well briefed. He knew what to do. In an effort to bring help, he attempted to fire a shot into the air. But he didn't squeeze the trigger fast enough. The small figure behind him wound up and swung the bat. The soldier never knew what hit him.

"Pardon, Mademoiselle," the twin said. "You taught us violence is not good. But it seemed necessary at the moment."

"It sure was," Riley confirmed. "Whichever one you are."

"Mathieu," Iniki clarified.

"Well, Mathieu, you just saved our lives. Now, let's get out of here before the rest of them show up."

The boy led the way. Iniki examined Riley's arm as they hurried. "The bullet is still in there," she said. "I am going to have to dig it out."

"Later. Right now we have to vamoose."

"Vamoose?"

"Right. And you should teach those boys the difference between senseless violence and self-preservation."

"I shall." She chose not to argue the point. Instead, she allowed herself to remember how, a few moments before, he grabbed her from behind. She enjoyed the feel of his arm across her breasts. A surge of some emotion ran through her. Not just any emotion, she corrected herself, a sensual thrill. She tried not to smile but it had been so very long since she could feel anything.

The general smiled. They were near, in the vicinity as he suspected. He heard a car engine start up somewhere behind them. It wouldn't be long now, he assured himself.

His adjutant and the two drivers responded by jumping into the jeeps. He took his time swaggering to the vehicle and climbing in. Raising his riding crop in a silent command, his driver shifted in reverse. The jeep went a few yards before it became evident they were going nowhere.

"We have been sabotaged, General," the driver shouted.

"It appears we have," his superior answered. "I have underestimated Miss Beaumont and her party. Obviously we are dealing with someone shrewd and cunning. Get on the radio to headquarters."

His orders were obeyed quickly. As he waited for the connection to be made, the general sized up the situation. Was there someone helping the lovely lady or did she think of this game herself? Whichever the answer, it would prove to be interesting, he decided, as he reported his position to headquarters.

The route took them north, climbing in elevation, leaving behind the fertile lowlands. Since the military patrols would have everything blocked off, they were forced to travel over dirt paths used by farm animals. Iniki knew the area well and directed Riley away from main roads.

The setting sun darkened the interior of the car and the travelers in back fell asleep. The only sound came from the car bumping over the trails. She looked at his face in silhouette. In the shadows, she studied the high forehead with a full head of hair and the squint of his eyes as he navigated the ruts.

She will trust him, she told herself. If they were to survive, she must rely on him. He rescued Madeline and saved them from the military twice within the space of one afternoon. What else did he need to do to prove he was an ally?

Nothing, she decided. If she did not believe in him, they would perish. But she would not relinquish command to him entirely. They will form a partnership, each contributing advice and support to the other. She realized he would not be fond of the idea, not at first. It will take time and effort on both their parts. She started with an announcement he was sure not to like.

"I think we need to speak about the detour," she said.

"What detour?"

"A small detour."

"What small detour?"

"A minor delay," she explained. "But one which is extremely important."

"We can't afford any delay, lady. You do realize that the military is scouring the country looking for you. You're not on the most favored list."

She kept her tone light. "I am aware of that."

"So what exactly is this minor delay?"

Already she was annoyed but would not let him see it. "A small change of plans."

"Like?"

"Madeline and Francois have family in a fishing village on the north coast. They can stay there and be relatively safe. At least, they will not starve. As for the boys..." she hesitated, enduring the pain her words brought. "They will remain with the old couple until I come back to the island to take them with me. I do not suppose you are willing to take the four with us?"

Riley's head whipped around. "Oh no. I understand what they mean to you but taking them would be foolhardy. We'll be lucky to make contact ourselves. Having two kids and an elderly couple with us would be a disaster."

She swallowed hard before she spoke. "Then they will stay in the village. They will be safe, God willing. You are right."

She heard him sigh before he asked, "Where is this village?"

"On the north coast. I assume that is where we are headed."

"I told you it was. But that covers a lot of territory."

She took a map out of her pocket. "Here is the place. Nouvella." She pointed at a spot right by the ocean. "Where is it that we go?"

"There's no need for you to know now. When we stop for food, I'll look at the map."

"Fine." She bristled at his refusal to share information with her but elected not to pursue it. "My people must be delivered to Nouvella. Then we may proceed."

"You've got the whole thing figured out, haven't you?" She detected anger in his words.

"Not at all. I acknowledge you are the expert in this venture."

"But you set down the rules?"

"No," she answered, failing to hide the intensity of her feelings. "Get my people to a safe place and I will go wherever you say."

Riley took a deep breath and continued driving. The detour didn't please him one bit. Yet it did solve a problem. He couldn't drag all of them to the rendezvous point, not with the military on his tail. Too big a risk, he told himself. That she conceded on the point surprised him. Those people, especially the kids, were her life. He had no doubt she would return for them one day, no matter how foolhardy it was. But guilt nagged at him. He was forcing her to leave them behind. Hell, that was his mission, wasn't it?

He peeked at the silent figure beside him. Her head faced forward, eyes wide open. What was it about those eyes, he wondered, that made them so different from others. Sincerity, he concluded. That's what haunted him. Pure honesty shot out at him regardless of what they discussed.

Clearing his throat, he tried to get his mind back to business. But the truth was that he no longer regarded her as an impersonal target. Dirty feet and all, the lady had hooked him.

An hour later, they stopped, hiding the car in a grove of thickets. Iniki insisted on tending to his wound. Opening the first aid kit, she searched for alcohol. He slipped the knife from his shin holster and handed it over.

She smiled as she took it. "You did not surrender this knife to Mathieu when ordered."

"Of course not," he replied, returning the smile. "I told you I was well accomplished at this sort of thing."

"Killing?"

"Nope. Don't do that except in extreme cases."

"Then what else is strapped to your leg?"

He lifted his pant leg and showed her. A small revolver was in the holster.

"I see."

"Good. Now let's get down to business here."

She poured alcohol on the knife tip. "Are you ready?"

"Don't be gentle," he advised. "The faster the better."

"Yes, sir." She went to work. The bullet came out in record time, leaving him gasping.

"Was that fast enough?" she asked.

"Yup. Now bandage it and we're done."

There is anti-bacterial cream here."

"Don't bother." He wanted to get up and shake the pain away. "I've had all my shots."

Despite his protest, she applied ointment to the wound and bandaged it. "You should have it in a sling. It will heal better."

"Forget it. I need two hands to drive." He waited for an argument that didn't come.

"If you say so. You bore the pain well. Does it hurt?"

"Like a bastard."

She raised her eyebrows. "I asked you to refrain from swearing."

"Then don't ask dumb questions. Of course it hurts."

"That would have been sufficient, Mr. Taggart."

"Okay, okay. It hurts quite a bit, Miss Beaumont." Never would she let him have the last word.

"Good," she commented and walked away.

She enjoyed the incident more than she expected. Just as she enjoyed it when he stared into her eyes. At first, she thought it an irritating habit. But now she allowed herself to revel in his gaze. He provided more than an escape from certain death. He made her feel like a woman, something she had not experienced for a long time.

"Their vehicle has not been spotted, sir. The main roads have been thoroughly searched."

"You fool," the general reprimanded. "They won't use the main roads. That would be stupid. And our adversary is far from that."

"Yes, sir," his aide replied. "The helicopter pilots wish to know if you are certain they are headed north. There has been no search of the southern part of the island."

The big man shook his head. "They're going north. I'm certain. The American Navy waits offshore. There must be American intervention. Bring me the soldier who was knocked on the head."

The frightened soldier could barely tell his story, so shaken was he by the summons from the general.

"What exactly did you see?"

"A woman in dirty clothes and a man of about thirty-five. I am certain I wounded him. The woman was French. She told me the man was her lover and that he did not speak English."

"Then what happened?"

"I was attacked from behind, sir."

The general spent the couple of moments rubbing his chin. Then he said. "That means we're dealing with at least three people if not more. This man, did he speak? Have you seen him before?"

The soldier shook his head. "Never, sir. He didn't speak a word. I don't know anything about him."

After the soldier left, the man in black turned to his aide. "Have the helicopter come here to pick me up. I'll organize the search myself."

Riley had a map of his own. Scanning the area, he concluded they would soon leave the protection of the semitropical vegetation to cross the high open plain in the center of the island. The mountains, lined up as far as the eye could see, would have to tackled as well. But they were not the immediate problem. He knew when they traversed the flat land, they would be sitting ducks for any government patrol that came along. The threat would come from helicopters. Whoever was in command didn't have to send out ground troops. The darkness would not protect his group from the searchlights on the aircraft.

"We must cross the flats at night," Iniki instructed as if she was reading his mind. She handed him some dates and a chunk of bread.

"The flats? Is that what the area is called?"

She nodded and went on. "On the other side, at the foot of those mountains, there were once small farms. They may not be inhabited now."

He shook his head, trying to formulate a plan. "Even at night, those patrols can flesh us out."

"It will take two hours, perhaps a little more. If we head in a straight line to the mountains, we may escape unnoticed. If only there was moonlight."

"On the contrary, we don't want moonlight. We want no light." He looked up at the thick clouds closing in. "But your idea about avoiding the paved road is on track. They'll expect us to use it, so they'll search there first."

"And if they don't find us, they won't give up," she reminded him.

"It's possible they'll search the south first."

She shook her head. "Where are the American ships? Off the north coast? They will know we are headed there."

"How the hell do you know about the ships?"

"It is no secret. They have been in the area since the beginning of the revolution. Waiting for God knows what. The people prayed the Americans would act. But they did not. So many lives might have been saved."

He disagreed. "Not quite as easy as you think. But with your help, NATO intervention is a possibility. Your President Simone has managed to piss off the entire world with his human rights violations."

"I pray that will happen. Before it is too late to save anyone, Mr Taggart."

He sat down against a large tree and motioned for her to join him. "Isn't it time we called each other by our first names? Or haven't you decided whether to trust me or not?"

She didn't answer but settled beside him on the ground.

Changing the subject, he asked, "What happened to the furnishings in the house?"

"Piece by piece, I gave everything to the people in the village. Furniture, paintings, clothing, jewels. Everything, so that Simone does not get it. Perhaps if this war ends well, they will be able to sell it to start a new life."

"Why did you burn the house?"

He heard her sigh before she answered. "For some time now, I have known I could not beat him. If anything, I am a realist. Eventually, he would force me into confinement or worse. The property would become his."

"So you planned it all?"

"Down to the last detail." An unmistakable frown covered her forehead and she massaged the area above one eye. "It was only a matter of time. My people would help to carry out the plan and then escape to the village. When the soldiers came, I planned to greet them standing in front of what was once a home. With the buildings destroyed and fields barren, the plantation would be useless to Simone. So you see I was ready to die. My greatest regret was that the boys would be alone with no one to care for them. Your arrival was most fortuitous."

Riley tried to sort out the emotions her story had roiled up inside him. The guilt about the boys came back in full force. Even worse, he believed her when she said she would await her captors with the flames as a backdrop. He could picture the scene. Under the stubborn pride, there was a vulnerability in her that made him want to scoop her up in his arms. Yet he knew she would raise bloody hell if he tried.

"Do you think I am mad?" she asked.

"I think you're something else, lady. But not mad."

"I shall take that as a compliment."

"Do that."

"Then there will be no further discussion about stopping at Nouvella?"

"It takes us miles out of our way." But he knew he would do her bidding.

"No matter," she protested.

He continued to provoke her just to break the mood. If she were angry, she wouldn't be sad. "You don't give a damn if we come out of this alive, do you?"

But she didn't bite. Her voice regained a calm tone as she said, "My people rely on me. There is no one else. Except you, perhaps. They must be my primary concern."

"My orders make you my primary concern."

She stood up and stretched. If she was annoyed, she didn't let it show. "In that case with everyone worrying about each other, we should have no trouble making our destination. Now I will round up everyone and get them ready. It is already late. We need to continue."

He watched her walk away. Who won that round, he wondered? For some reason, he was certain he didn't. His normal reaction should have been frustration. Instead, he caught himself smiling. Despite the danger, the extra passengers he must drag along, the added bother of taking a detour, he admitted Iniki Beaumont was more than he bargained for.

CHAPTER THREE

Day 1 ~ Evening Entering the Flats
"Mon Dieu, a cat!"

Before starting out, Riley took a few precautions. He instructed his passengers to tie the food supply into small bundles and hide it in their clothing. Two water jugs were strung together so that he could carry them over his shoulders, if necessary. The twins were given the chore of collecting a variety of leafy branches and brush that would fit into the trunk of the car.

No one asked questions except for Michel. "Monsieur Taggart, may I shoot at helicopters as they come for us?" He held onto the rifle and aimed it at the sky.

"No, you may not," Riley answered. Then he remembered Iniki's admonition about being too rough with the children. "You must save every bit of ammunition you have for when we most need it," Riley explained. "Do you understand?"

"Yes, Monsieur. You will tell me when it is time?"

"I certainly will. Watch me carefully. That's your official job," he said in a conspiratorial tone.

"Yes, Monsieur. Thank you." The kid ran off in the direction of his brother.

"You have children of your own, Riley." She stood behind him, arms folded across her chest.

Had he heard her right? She addressed him by his first name. Maybe he was making progress.

As he answered, he smiled deeply. He noticed she didn't return the favor. "Nope. Not in my line of work. No time for kids and a wife."

"How did you come to be in your line of work?" she questioned. "Whatever it is."

"I was smart, that's all. Smart enough to get a scholarship to college and then a Ph.D. in political science. The State Department scooped me up."

"I do not understand."

He hoped the damn grin was gone from his face. Why the hell was he beaming at her anyway? Just because she used his given name?

Assuming a serious expression, he explained. "I know a lot about political hot spots around the world. That's my expertise. They trained me to be an expediter."

"In what respect?"

"I'm the guy who gets things done, as quickly as possible."

He searched her face looking for a friendly smirk, anything. He saw only intelligence in her eyes and felt like a jerk.

"Marriage and children?" she continued. "This is not popular where you come from?"

"Texas. I come from Texas." He forced a disinterested pose. If she wasn't friendly, why the hell should he be? "And yeah. It's done, all right. But I've never had time for it. Besides, I don't live in Texas anymore."

"Then where do you live?"

"Virginia. A horse farm."

"And your horses? What do they do when you are away rescuing females who should know better?"

If the comment was meant to be funny, she sure as hell wasn't showing it. "You said that, remember," he pointed out. "Not me."

"I'll remember," she said dryly. "Go on. Tell me about your horses."

"They're Arabians. Two of them. My prize possessions. But I have a stud or two also."

"A stud?"

"Yeah. A horse with a good blood line. Fast racers in their prime. I put them out to stud."

Her expression didn't change so he felt he had to explain. "When a male and a female horse get together..."

"Yes, I do understand. I assume it is similar to the human version, although I have never seen horses procreate. This is what you let them do?"

The laugh escaped before he could stop it. "I don't let them do it. It's a business. The horses don't mind." Was she playing with him, he wondered.

"I see," she went on. "And when you are working, as you are now, who takes care of the animals."

"I have a very capable staff. It's not often I'm away. Lately, I prefer to spend more time at the ranch."

"Then you are thinking of retiring?"

He shrugged. "If I get out of this mission alive, I might just do that. Retirement at thirty-five sounds real good right about now."

"What is Virginia like? A beautiful place?"

He nodded and let her go on.

"It has an ocean border, does it not?"

"Uh-huh."

"I would need to be near enough to the sea."

He smiled again. "Well, there's plenty of that where I come from."

"Good." She turned away, took a few steps, then stopped. "You handled Michel nicely just now. You could learn to be a fine father. It may be your experience with horses." A brief smile danced on her lips before she walked on.

The general spit out orders as soon as he strapped himself into the helicopter seat. "These people are shrewd and cunning.

We'll take this methodically, starting at the western end of the flats and covering every square inch of the area with the lights in overlapping patterns. We won't miss them."

"Yes, sir. The president would like you to phone him, sir. At your earliest convenience."

The sky was black as mud as they made final preparations. The rainy season left the ground saturated. In places where the grass washed away, deep gouges marked the soil. At night, those ruts would be impossible to spot until Riley was on top of them.

It was a close call on the gas, too. The few extra gallons he carried in a tank in the trunk wouldn't go far and the car's tank was nearly empty. As he poured the remaining fuel into the car, he speculated on whether the vehicle would hold up long enough to cross the flats. On a blacktopped road, the few miles they had to cover would be no problem. On uneven ground, however, he couldn't go faster than ten miles an hour. Eventually, the gas would run out.

From that point, they would be on foot. He anticipated that from the beginning. But he expected only the one woman. Now, the burden was increased by four. At best, the detour to Nouvella added an extra day to the journey and required that they cross one of the larger mountains in the range that ran across the northern edge of the island.

Would they make it?

He didn't have a clue.

"We are ready, Riley," she informed him. "I presume these preparations were for a good reason?"

"Damn right. If we have to abandon the car in a hurry, there'll be no time to stop and collect what we need. I don't want necessities left behind."

Iniki took a deep breath. "I gather you have doubts we can make it across undetected."

"It'll be a bloody miracle if this hunk of junk survives. Here's a compass and flashlight. I won't be able to do much except control the car. You're going to be sure we head due north. No wavering. Got it?"

"I was taught as a child to read a compass."

"Good. Tell the others to expect anything and be ready."

"I do appreciate this effort," she said in a low voice.

He stopped what he was doing and looked straight at her. "I would be lying if I said there is no doubt we'll make it."

"I understand. I also realize that taking along my people complicates everything. That is why I thank you for what you are doing."

"It's my job."

"Yes, of course."

When he made no further response, she went on her way.

He watched her go and wondered how he allowed himself to get into this situation. He was breaking every rule basic to survival in the field. He cared for these people, for the woman who barely trusted him, for the old couple and the boys. What the hell was he doing?

Simone asked the same question of his general. The man in black was outraged to be talked to in that manner but did not let his anger show. He had been in the same position many times and his methods were doubted more than once. He would persevere and, in the end, be proven correct.

The idiot president would hand over another medal to be displayed on the general's already overloaded official uniform. A multi-cultural uniform, he called it, as it held medals from many countries, particularly third world. It was surprising what poor countries could afford to pay to get a nasty job done.

"The flats are not appropriately named," Iniki remarked. "Even in the dry season, the natives use only the road that skirts the savannah."

His only comment was abrupt. "I see what you mean."

She did not question whether he chose the best option available. The man was far too skilled to make that mistake. And, she told herself, even if his plan presented obstacles, he would not give up. That was the kind of man he was. Then she wondered why she was so sure of it.

"This reminds me of a mine field," she heard him say. He was forced to drive with his head out the window in order to see a few feet ahead of the car.

She spotted helicopters far to the east. Though they were tiny darts of light, she knew they had a plan as well. Simone and his military attacked their problems with precision. Despite the fact they were miles away, she was sure the aircraft used high-powered spotlights that covered wide swaths of ground with each sweep. She acknowledged her foe and held a certainty that Riley did also. Eventually every square foot of the flats would come within the boundaries of the searchlights. She kept a tight rein on her fear. The fact that she was frightened was revealed only by the slight tremble in her voice.

"You were right, Riley. They are looking for us."

He slowed almost to a standstill while she pointed them out.

"Yup," he confirmed. "But they haven't caught us yet. Hold on everybody." He increased his speed. "No point in creeping along. We'll go for broke. Keep an eye on the helos. Tell me when they get closer."

"Aye, sir," she quipped to overcome her anxiety.

"Hope you still have a sense of humor when this is over."

"I do, as well." She forced a smile. "In the meantime, I will be your co-pilot. Is that acceptable?"

"You bet your life, lady."

The car bumped up and down like an amusement park ride. Michel let out whoops of laughter as they hit a deep hole and the passengers in back got bounced almost to the roof.

"Michel, no more noise," she scolded.

Riley put his hand on her arm. "Leave the boy alone. He has a sense of adventure and no fear. I like that."

"I do too." She kept her voice low as she went on. "He is the brave one. But he is also impetuous. Mathieu is the opposite, quiet and sensitive."

"I noticed," Riley said, matching her quiet tone. "I'm beginning to tell them apart just by their expressions. Michel's eyes are constantly about to pop out of his head."

She nodded. "And Mathieu seldom smiles. Life has become too serious for him since his mother was killed. I worry for him more that I do for his brother. He can not shake off his sorrow as easily."

"A loss like that is difficult for anyone," Riley offered. "I can't imagine how a twelve year old deals with it. What happened to their parents?"

His question reopened a wound in her heart she believed would never heal. She refused to discuss that horrible night with anyone. Not even Madeline. Yet, she was ready to tell the story to a man she hardly knew.

"Blanca and her husband were good, kind people. Both were children of workers on the plantation. She and I were the same age. As children, we played together. We swam in the ocean and shared our childish secrets. We were the best of friends. I was welcome in the workers' huts and she was welcome in our house. At least, Maman allowed that. But my family spent only summers here. In the winter, I was educated in France. Blanca had no education. It was an injustice, Riley, because she was bright and inquisitive. She wanted to learn everything. Always, always asking questions."

"Wait a minute," he interrupted. "If she was your age, she had those kids when she was what?"

"Not quite sixteen. She married Carl when she was fourteen. It is an accepted custom here for the natives. They marry early and have many children, to help with the work. A large family would afford them a larger hut and more food for the family plus more money in payment."

She stopped to relive the excitement she, herself, experienced when Blanca announced her wedding plans. "I was so jealous when she married. I knew about the marital bed. I envied her. I think I was more thrilled with her marrying than she. Of course, I had not figured out what Blanca already knew. Her life was mapped out for her. She would live on the plantation, work in the house, and that was it. No future that promised anything different."

"What about her husband? Did he treat her well?"

"Oh, yes. I believe he tried to make her happy. She never complained about him. But as we grew older, I wondered if she really loved him or whether they were bound together by loyalty. I still don't know. I remember she told me Carl never drank. She explained that some men would have too much to drink and go home and beat their wives in an angry rage. But not Carl."

"I see."

"Yes. So did I, for the first time. Even though she had a handsome husband, Blanca's life ceased to be enviable. When I took over the plantation, I gave her books which she devoured. Eventually, she helped me with the children's school. Her husband was eager to improve his prospects and accepted my suggestion to organize the workers. He became an overseer in the fields. This was before Simone came to power, of course."

"What happened then?"

"They joined the local underground movement as most of the workers did. It was Blanca who got me involved."

"How did she die?"

"It was after I left the rebel cell. I begged her to follow but she could not understand why. She was determined to fight for her country's freedom. Her last words to me were, 'You are rich, Iniki. What care do you have if some wild man comes and rules your life? You have only to return to France and live a life of luxury'." Those words still haunt me. That is why it is so difficult to leave the twins to fend for themselves. They need a mother. And I am the only one they have. That, at least, I can do for Blanca. Maybe she now sees how I love them and she will forgive me."

He took his eyes off the road for a moment. "Lady, from what I've seen, there's nothing to forgive."

She appreciated his remark, the sincerity in his voice. But it did little to ease the pain in her heart. "Later that same night, Blanca asked if I could watch the children. She did not say where she was going but I knew she and Carl were on a mission for Marcel Valois. I waited all night for their return. In the morning, I took the boys to the plantation. Blanca's body was found in the center of a nearby village. Her husband lay next to her. Both had died from a single bullet to the head." Iniki fought to keep back the tears. She never allowed grief to consume her. She would not start now.

"I'm sorry," Riley said and reached over to touch her hand.

At that instant, the car came to an abrupt halt.

"Dammit!" Riley blurted out.

"Please watch your language in front...."

"Yeah, yeah. I know." He opened his door and appeared to survey the left rear quarter. "The tire is buried in muck up to the rim," he announced. "Watch those copters. If you notice them coming closer, let me know."

Despite the problem, she wanted to smile but knew enough not to. Instead, she asked, "What will you do?"

"Try to get this blasted car out of the mud. What else?"

"With the hole in your arm? It will begin to bleed again."

"If you've got a better idea, lady, I'm all ears."

She did not, so she shut her mouth.

"Another first," she heard him say as he slammed the door. She found herself grinning and the pain of Blanca's story lessened.

Riley couldn't afford to abandon the car. They had too far left to go. The older ones wouldn't make it on foot. He had to free the car, provided those copters stayed the hell away. The twins and Francois were called upon to help.

"We need wood pieces behind the tire to give it traction. I think there's some sand in the trunk. Francois, you help me look in there. The twins can position the wood as they find it." Shin deep in mud, they tackled the job.

The old man located the soil while Riley went to lift it. "What the hell is that?" Riley pointed into one dark corner of the trunk.

Next to him, Michel let out a surprised, "*Mon Dieu*, a cat!"

Riley was not pleased. "I know it's a cat."

"Then why did you ask, Monsieur?"

"Excuse me," Riley explained. "Now who put the cat in the trunk? Michel? Speak to me. Why is there a cat in the trunk?"

The accused answered sharply. "I am sure I do not know. It is not my doing. I know nothing of it."

"Michel…" Riley was annoyed at the boy's unwillingness to admit the truth.

"It was I, Monsieur," the other twin confessed softly. "The poor animal would die in the fields alone."

"How long has this thing been in there?"

"Only since the beginning of the flats. I was carrying it in my knapsack until then. It is well fed, I assure you."

"That certainly takes a load off my mind," Riley growled. "One more thing to take along." He picked up the brown and white ball of fur and handed it to Mathieu, taking full notice of the unhappiness on the boy's face. The kid has lost everything, he remembered. Despite the inconvenience, could Riley demand the boy abandon the animal in the middle of nowhere? Riley found himself in another corner. He seemed to be in that position far too often.

"Take it to Madeline," he ordered. "She can hold it while we finish the job."

"Yes, Monsieur," the boy answered joyfully. Riley realized it was the first time he saw Mathieu smile.

The next order of business was to set things straight with the other twin. "Sorry, Michel," Riley apologized. "I shouldn't have accused you."

The kid didn't seem to be bothered. "It is not important, sir. I would have done the same thing if I had found the cat first."

"Don't I know it," Riley agreed.

They worked for ten minutes until the tire was framed in wood. When it was ready, he asked Iniki to gently depress the accelerator while he and the others pushed from behind. The plan worked and the car was freed although he and his helpers were wet and filthy.

When he returned to the driver's seat, he was worn out and his arm ached. He winced as he put his hand on the steering wheel and got the car moving again.

Iniki questioned him immediately. "Is your arm all right?"

"Yeah. Just hurts like a bast...er, it aches."

"Let me drive for a while," she offered. "You can rest."

"No, I'll be fine," he insisted.

"Riley, this no time to be a hero. I need you to stay alive."

"Then I guess I'll just have to stick around."

"Good."

A grin popped onto his face. He knew it and didn't care. "Have you seen our latest addition?"

She nodded. "Mathieu was thrilled that you allowed him to keep it. You handled it well."

"Thanks. Did you really think I was such an ogre?"

She shook her head. Her eyes seemed to light up. At least, he wanted to believe they did. "No," she answered. "But this trip has not gone as you planned."

"No shi.... No, it hasn't." Did he hear her giggle? One look told him he was mistaken. Her expression remained as serious as ever.

"How do you say cat in French?" he queried.

"The word is *chat*."

"Hey, Mathieu," he called. "What are you going to name your *chat*?"

"*Votre chat*," she corrected.

"Whatever."

"I have not decided," the boy answered. "I must think about it."

"You do that."

Iniki enjoyed the conversation and grinned.

"What?" he asked her.

"It is amusing, I think. You came here to rescue a man and a woman. You end up with only the woman plus her servant couple and two orphaned boys."

"And a *chat*," he added. "How is that funny?"

"Fate plays silly games," she explained. "You can not deny that."

"I'll admit it when we're home free." He forced himself to concentrate on the mission. With luck, he would have time to enjoy her smile later. "How close are the copters?"

"Still way off. They must not see us. I was wrong about the moon. If it were a clear night, they would be on top of us."

"Probably. On the other hand, I would be able to see where I'm driving."

"The compass shows you are still on track."

"Good." Damn good, he told himself, considering the distractions. To her he said, "What are you doing alone on this island, anyway? Why didn't you leave when ..."

".....when the sensible ones did?"

"Yeah. Why didn't you go? At one point, Simone was encouraging everyone to leave. You could have taken your people to France."

She shook her head. "Simone wanted the land owners to abandon their property. In return, they were allowed to leave. His peaceful solution, he called it. I refused to give in. As for my people, this is their country. They would not forsake it. I understood their reasons because it was the same for me. You see, when I was a child, this was a beautiful place. However, since it received independence from France, no one government stayed in power for long. There were peaceful takeovers and not so peaceful takeovers. But the French landowners always took care of their workers. The poor depended on the plantations for their livelihood. The landowners knew their responsibility."

"What changed?"

"Simone. Piece by piece, he began to usurp the land. At first, he bought it legally. Then, he intimidated and, finally, he used his particular brand of pressure on some of the largest land owners. Soon, most of them left."

"This started when?"

"Maybe three years ago. My parents urged me to give it up. But, at that time there were many workers on the plantation. I could not abandon them to whatever fate Simone decided on. I could not allow that."

He sympathized with her but didn't quite grasp why her situation became so desperate. "Why didn't your father come and get you?"

"He did come once but I refused to leave," she declared. "I do not do what I choose not to do."

"So I've learned."

"When he was here," she went on, "my father visited Simone and reminded him of the favors he received when he first came to power. Papa thought that would keep me safe."

"Obviously, that didn't work out."

"No, although Simone waited a long time before trying to get at me. If I had not been part of the cell ..... But that made no difference in the end. He needed no excuse."

"I'm impressed, lady," he told her. "You've taken on quite a burden."

She shook her head. "These people have nothing. And the land is rich. This island can feed itself twenty times over. Tourism can be encouraged. There is no reason for the poverty that exists today."

"Isn't that a bit naive? Poverty exists everywhere."

"Perhaps," she conceded. "But someday my land will be given over to the people. Not to some despotic leader who tortures and kills innocent women and children."

She gave him the perfect opportunity to bring up another subject. "If you feel so strongly, why did you leave the rebels?"

A peculiar emotion, one he couldn't decipher, washed over her face. "I was eager to help Marcel Valois and his rebels when they formed a small cell of opposition in the neighborhood. Their mission was to help the poor and sick. I gave Marcel food and money whenever he asked. During that time, I let myself believe that Marcel was the salvation of his people. Together, we accomplished much good. But when he began to accumulate guns and weapons, he lost sight of the people. He became frustrated, as we all were. But he decided to fight back."

"Not an extraordinary turn of events," Riley interjected.

"I suppose not," she agreed. "Marcel and his advisors came up with elaborate plans to use weapons against Simone. I argued against the idea. But they prevailed. On the first mission, several unmanned jeeps and arsenals were blown up. No loss of life for Simone's men. But the civilians, the innocents who happened to be nearby, were killed."

"Is that why you left?"

"I had to," she explained. "Marcel called them martyrs for the cause but, in truth, they were sacrificial lambs. Meeting violence with violence can not win. The price is too high. You are right. Perhaps I am naive. But I refused to continue and, in doing so, I abandoned the group and Marcel, as well."

Riley still had unanswered questions. Her personal relationship with Marcel Valois was a good place to start. "I'm sorry I announced the news of his death in such graphic detail."

"It does not matter," she answered in what Riley took to be a sad tone. "Marcel was not who I thought he was. That man did not exist." She went no further and Riley stopped the questions.

Less than a hour later, the car succumbed to the terrain's abuse. Hitting a deep gully Riley felt a sharp pull to the right. Iniki slammed against the passenger door. Those in the back were tossed around from side to side. Riley fought the steering wheel for control, barely managing to stop the vehicle from flipping over.

"Everyone okay?" he asked first.

Iniki checked on the refugees in the back. "We are fine. What has happened?"

"If I were to guess, I'd say we lost the right front axle. Stay here. I'll go look."

"I will come," Michel offered.

"No, you will not," Riley countered.

"But you said I was to keep my eye on you, Monsieur."

Mumbling under his breath, Riley opened the door. "Not this time. I need you to continue surveillance on those helicopters while I'm gone. Okay?"

"Okay," the boy said happily.

"You will need someone to hold the flashlight," Iniki announced and opened her door, not waiting for approval.

"Of course," Riley muttered.

He did need both hands to dig away the mud. The flashlight she held illuminated the wheel that twisted grotesquely away from the chassis. She was wise to accompany him, she thought, though she did not expect him to admit it.

"Well, so much for driving," he commented. "From here on, we hoof it."

She smiled broadly, resolving not to show the anxiety she felt. "That means we walk? I have not heard that expression before."

"You're going to wish you never heard it. Let's get them out and organize this little band of runaways."

Special agent or not, the man showed his feelings, she decided. Once, she was the same. But civil war wiped away the tiny joys of life. No longer could she allow any deep emotion to surface. If she suppressed it, she did not hurt as much. For so long now, she faced every hurdle with stoic reserve, doing whatever was necessary, not daring to dream of the future for fear she would be disappointed.

This man was different. His sense of humor never failed him, even in the most trying circumstances. Every time he looked at her, he smiled. And the gesture, she understood, was a way to communicate what he felt inside. With him, it was difficult to maintain her guard. He made her want to smile. And against her better judgement, she did succumb several times. Even more disturbing was the realization that she looked forward to the next time.

Following his lead, she motioned to the others. "Come," she said. "We will hoof it, as Riley says. Another adventure for us."

"Hoorah," the twins answered.

"Exactly," she agreed and prayed she was right. She watched as they complied with her wishes. The old couple put on a brave face. She was their only hope. And Riley was hers. The thought encouraged her.

In minutes they were prepared. She watched Riley take rope from the trunk and tie together the branches and brush the twins gathered at the beginning of the journey.

"What are they for?" she asked.

"We're going to try a cowboy trick."

She frowned. "I do not understand."

He kept working as he explained. "When we went goose hunting as kids, we would hide in the bushes as they flew by."

"You would shoot them?"

"Of course."

"The geese? You shot the geese?"

"Look, I was the son of dirt poor farmers. If we were lucky enough to bag a goose, we ate for a week on it. Nothing was wasted."

Embarrassment reddened her face. "I see. And now? Are we looking for geese?"

"Now the goose is searching for us," he answered. "When those helicopters spot the car, they'll know we're on foot. It won't take them long to spot us. We need some kind of cover."

"The branches?"

"Right. If we huddle together and pull them over us, we may appear to be just another sun dried bush when they fly over us."

"You think they will ...pass over us, I mean?"

"I'd bet on it." He tied the brush so that it hung from a single rope. The he circled it around his waist.

She offered to help. "I will pull some along as well."

The twins appeared in front of him, armed with rifle and bat. "We also will carry some," Michel added.

"Thanks, guys, but your job is to keep Madeline and Francois with us. Mathieu, you are totally in charge of that animal. We've got a good distance to cover to get to the woods. The mountains are beyond that. I figure we have another five hours of darkness. If we make it to the trees, we can rest during daylight. Now, let's get going."

"Yes, sir," the twins chimed.

"Good God," Riley said under his breath.

"The captain has a sorry-looking crew," Iniki added.

The general placated the president with news he was hot on the trail of the Beaumont woman.

More intriguing was the suspicion that the Americans were somehow involved in her escape.

"How are you sure of this?" the president demanded, showing his displeasure that the woman was not yet captured.

"We have a witness who places her with a man in his thirties. This man has not been identified. We also know there are others in her party."

"Who are these people? I want them dead."

That was all the man seemed to want these days. At the rate he was going, he would rule a country with corpses as its only citizens. "I have not identified them as yet. I suspect Americans are helping her."

"Why do you think this?"

"The woman could not make it this far on her own. Someone trained in evasion tactics is guiding her. They seem to be heading toward the north coast where the American carrier sits offshore. I'm convinced I'm right."

The president was overjoyed. "Ah," he informed the general. "That would be an ideal chance for us to deflate the United Nations and their complaints about human rights violations. "You must bring the American to me alive. Once he confesses he is a spy, the UN will back off."

The general was not convinced the president's reasoning was sound. Yet, he had every confidence he could do it. The American and the woman would be his.

The enthusiasm with which they started helped a great deal. The twins helped the older couple as ordered. Each boy held on to their respective weapons as if they alone could ward off Simone's entire military. Riley admired them as they marched along, encouraging Madeline and Francois and making sure the cat kept up with the parade.

Iniki kept them on a course due north. Riley watched while she checked the compass, then turned to check on her people behind her. He brought up the rear, keeping a careful eye on the copters in the western sky. In his mind, a plan formulated for when the aircraft came. It would take less than fifteen minutes to put into operation. The copters were taking about twenty-five minutes to complete one sweep of the pattern. That would give Riley enough time to get ready. It wouldn't be long now, he estimated.

His supposition turned out more accurate than he expected. And the helicopters had little to do with it. Five yards in front of him, Francois went down on one knee. The old woman clutched her husband's arm, urging him to rise.

Riley caught up to them. "What's wrong?"

Madeline looked up at him, a mixture of panic and sorrow on her face. "He is sick and weak, Monsieur. I do not know why. It is best if you leave us. Save the children."

Riley put his arm around her. "No deal, Madeline. We are all safe or none of us are. Tell Francois we will stop to rest soon."

The woman spoke so softly to her husband that Riley couldn't make it out. But he knew the woman followed his orders when Francois struggled to a standing position, shaking off his wife's attempt to help. Riley made no move to support the man. Instead, he waited as Francois lifted a trembling hand to his forehead and saluted. Riley returned the gesture, nodded to them both and moved up the line toward Iniki. An unfamiliar ache in his stomach ate at him but he didn't wonder why.

"The old man isn't doing well." Riley explained the problem as they walked side by side. "Give me the compass and go help Madeline."

A flash of panic showed on her face. But determination replaced it immediately. "How much longer will it take us?" she asked.

"At least another two hours. He'll make it if we give him time to rest every half hour."

"Riley, what do we do if he is seriously ill?"

He identified the anxiety in her voice. "Look, let's not worry about that now. The important thing is to take one obstacle at a time and we've got a huge one coming in about thirty minutes. See if they can continue for that long."

"Perhaps I was wrong to insist they come along. If they die on this journey . . ."

"Whoa, lady. Who said they were going to die? He's just feeling punky. Maybe because he's been walking in muddy drenched clothes. And he is not young anymore."

When she didn't respond to his encouragement, he addressed the entire troupe. "Keep walking, my *amies*."

"*Mes Aimes*," she corrected.

"Whatever. We should sing a marching song as we go. That'll keep us moving."

Michel jumped at the idea. "Yes, yes. What song shall we sing? I know many but they are in French."

"Monsieur Taggart's French is a bit rusty," Iniki mentioned.

"More than a bit," Riley added. "How about an American song? It has only a few lines so it won't be difficult."

"No swear words," she whispered.

"My word of honor as a gentleman. It's called *Yankee Doodle Dandy*."

"Sing it for us," Michel begged as he hopped along pulling Francois with him.

"Okay, folks, here goes. And no comments from the peanut gallery."

"What is peanut gallery?" Michel asked, as Riley knew he would.

"Never mind. Listen to the words of the song." In no time he had the group of them singing along.

Michel had a million questions. "What is Yankee Doodle? What is macaroni? What kind of feather is it and why did he do such a thing?"

Riley began to regret he had suggested it. Yet, the activity worked its magic. The group moved quicker.

"An excellent idea. Thank you." Iniki came to walk beside him. "They needed something to boost their morale."

"No thanks necessary. It's an old trick."

"A Texas trick?"

"Nope. Military, I guess. Whatever, it works."

"Yes. There are many sides to you, Riley Taggart."

He laughed. "I don't know about that."

"I do," she assured him.

Fifteen minutes later, they stopped. It was no coincidence that Riley picked that moment. The copters were about to make their first pass directly over them.

"Hold up there, guys," he shouted. "This is a good place to rest."

"I agree, Monsieur," Michel confirmed. "Francois is very tired. He needs to sleep."

"Not yet, I'm afraid. But soon. First, we fool the helicopters."

"And how do we do that?" the boy asked.

"We play Hide in the Bushes."

"Oh yes. This is grand fun." He ran to Iniki with the news.

A second later, Mathieu came to stand next to Riley, the baseball bat under one arm and the cat under the other. He did not speak until Riley acknowledged his presence, a significant way the boy differed from his brother.

"Hey, how's the cat doing?" Riley asked.

"He has a name, I believe." There was no smile on his face but a glimmer of happiness was evident in his dark eyes.

"That's good," Riley encouraged. "Everyone should have a name."

"This is what I think also," the boy responded in a serious tone.

"So? What is it?"

Mathieu smiled for the second time in their acquaintance. "Yankee Doodle," he said proudly. "Do you approve?"

CHAPTER FOUR

Day 2 ~ Midnight on the Flats
"God, you feel good."

Iniki knew it would not be long before the powerful white lights passed over. She whispered soothing words to encourage Madeline and Francois. Even Michel's natural jubilance was tempered as they looked west into the black sky and observed the noisy machines approach.

"They look like extraterrestrial space ships, do they not?" She asked in an attempt to lighten the mood.

As usual, only Michel answered. "No, Mademoiselle. They look like giant bees. Alien spacecraft are silent."

"Are they? And what do you think, Mathieu?" she asked.

"I would rather they be spaceships. I do not think aliens want to kill us."

"That is also what I think, Mathieu." She patted the heads of both boys and moved over to Madeline and Francois.

"*Mon Dieu*," the old woman cried. "We will be killed."

"No," Iniki comforted. "Riley will find a way to keep us safe."

"He is brave, your Monsieur Taggart. When he looks at you, it is as a man should look at a woman."

Iniki felt herself redden. "How is that?"

"With growing affection, great respect and lust."

"Lust?"

"That is not a bad thing, Mademoiselle. It makes marriage so much more . . .magic. Yes. That is the word."

Iniki smiled. "Yes, I understand. Many women would be eager to receive those looks from a man."

"Then, Mademoiselle, you should think about it carefully. If he is worthwhile, you will know. And you may want to share those feelings with him."

She did want that, she confessed only to herself. Riley assumed a place of monumental importance in her life. Not only was he her lifeline, but he made her feel as a woman should feel. Until Madeline mentioned him, Iniki did not want to admit that she basked in his attention. He respected her intelligence, consulting her at every turn. His attraction to her was not difficult to recognize especially when he smiled. Those thoughts made her aware of sensations in her body that she had not felt for so long. Madeline's assessment of the situation was correct. Yet Iniki felt no shame. A woman should enjoy this experience, she told herself, and wondered if she would live long enough to tell him that.

The copters came closer. She looked to Riley with questioning eyes, anxious for him to give orders. Please God, she thought, he had an order to give. If not, they would be like the terrified deer she remembered as a child in the Le Bois Colombe outside Paris. Caught in the headlights of a car, they froze. Standing firm, they would wait until either the car hit them or managed to swerve away. She vowed she would not be the frightened deer. She would not freeze, hoping that death came swiftly and painlessly. If death were her fate, she would fight to the end.

When Riley finally gave the word, it was in short concise sentences. Each person was assigned a position in the small circle they formed on the ground. Each had a job to do. He gave careful instructions on how to place the brush and larger branches. Then he stood outside the structure, observing the finished product until the last possible minute.

"Hold on as tightly as you can," he urged. "When the copter goes over, it will seem like the end of the world. Everything will fly around. Remember, whatever happens, don't let go of the branches you're holding."

"Will they see that we are not a real bush?" Michel asked. "We are made of different kinds of vegetation."

"Good question," Riley answered, though he wished it hadn't been asked. "They'll pass over quickly and we'll resemble other vegetation scattered everywhere. There's no reason to examine this bush any closer than the rest."

"Aye, captain," Michel said bravely. But Riley didn't miss the quiver in the boy's voice.

The twins nestled in the middle of the group. Their job was to hold down the top most part of the brush with both hands. Rifle and bat were tucked safely in between their legs. The cat slept in Madeline's lap unaware of the pending trouble.

"It is not time to shoot, Monsieur," Michel stated. "It is time to hide."

"Right. I'll let you know when you need the rifle."

"Yes, captain."

No questions came from the other twin. Mathieu, his face pale and frightened, looked to Riley, who nodded. Mathieu returned the gesture and assumed his job holding on tightly to the 'roof' of the bush.

Riley, Iniki and the two elders formed the outer ring around the boys. Madeline and Francois held on to each other with one arm and the branches with the other.

"Put your arm around Madeline's waist," Riley whispered to Iniki. "I'll do the same with the old man."

She swallowed hard and followed his instructions. She could not remember ever being so afraid as the giant machines approached, creating powerful noise and vibrations.

"Here they come," Riley shouted. "Close your eyes and don't open them until I say. Whatever happens, don't move an inch."

Iniki expected their leafy protection to go in the first second. Her fear increased when the aircraft's deafening roar was directly overhead. She could feel the group sway with the tremendous force of the wind. Sand and small stones pelted their bodies. But the man-made bush held together. Just as suddenly as it came, the copter passed.

"Hot damn. You did an excellent job, but stay where you are," Riley urged. "Open your eyes but don't move. They'll make another pass that will include us in the light again."

Iniki checked with each of them. They were shaken but kept their silence.

Except for Michel. "Those pilots are stupid," he pronounced. "We can not look like a real bush. Impossible."

"Let's be grateful they thought we did, Michel. And try to keep in mind they're not as stupid as you think," Riley added. "A good soldier never underestimates his enemy."

"Yes, Monsieur," the boy said meekly.

Riley turned to Iniki. "You okay?"

"Yes. That was indeed as dreadful as you predicted."

"You did fine. Everyone did. If they didn't catch us that time, I think we're okay."

"Riley," she whispered. "If they do capture us . . ."

"They won't."

"But if they do . . . I will not let them take me. I would rather die."

"They won't get you. I promise."

He let go of the branches with his left hand and slipped his arm around her waist. She leaned against him and rubbed her face into his shoulder as if his body could blot out reality. It was a long time since she allowed a man to comfort her. For that brief moment, she let her vulnerability show. She felt his lips brush over her hair. In the midst of the danger they faced, she felt strangely at peace.

Then the helicopters came back.

The general rode shotgun at the pilots side. They located the abandoned car less than an hour before and he knew the prey were now on foot. The direction in which they headed puzzled him. However, if their objective was to make contact with the Americans, then they would have to move to the northwest. The ideal spot was the Black Point area.

Still, the general kept to his methodical plan. He would cover the entire area of the land called the flats. If that did not uncover them, then he would move east toward the spot where the mountains were easier to cross. Regardless, if he approached his objective in a logical manner, he would find them. It was only common sense.

The ground flew past in a haze of dust and debris. There was nothing of note. Just a continuation of low vegetation and stretches of mud. Certainly, he thought, a man and a woman would have no way to hide.

Iniki recovered quickly, Riley thought, as he watched her feed something to the cat. For those long minutes while they waited for the second pass of the copters, she allowed him to witness her fear. The same fear he felt. Sharing it together, with her head buried in his shoulder, made the experience easier.

"Ain't that a kick in the head," he said aloud. Her vulnerability and strength mixed together like a potent elixir. Since when had a female ever touched him that way? Something to think about.

After the helos passed, the group rested longer than anticipated. Madeline and Francois needed time to regain some strength. He regretted having to move them, particularly the old guy. But there was little choice. He was running out of darkness and they must reach the tree line below the mountains before first light. Those copters would return once they failed to pick them up on the night search. Sooner or later, they'd be back. Riley wanted to be well into the trees by then.

He studied the bunch of them. Anxiety and weariness strained their faces. They needed sleep. The plan was to rest during the day and travel only at night.

"Let's go, my people." He clapped his hands together to rouse them.

"Your people?" Iniki stood behind him.

He wondered to himself when they had become 'his'. He didn't have time to formulate an answer. "Okay, troops. Up and ready. Only a short distance left to walk. There you go."

The group mustered at his command, stretching sore muscles that screamed for sleep. Yet, no complaint was heard.

"Listen, folks," Riley started. "This is the last track to cover before we can take a long rest. You've been good soldiers up to now. Let's continue that. I estimate we have a little more than a mile to travel. We can do it. We fooled those military aircraft, didn't we? Certainly we can accomplish this little hike. Now, let's start moving."

"May we sing our marching song, Monsieur?"

"Sure."

This decision was regretted sorely as the boys repeated the tune ad nauseam. "Do you not know another song," Iniki asked Riley after an hour. "Any song?"

"They like that song. Besides, look at them. They seem happy enough. Do you notice that Michel doesn't march. He prances."

"Always. And Mathieu, I have observed, is constantly watching you."

"He needs more encouragement than Michel."

"You surprise me at times, Mr. Taggart."

"And why is that, Mademoiselle?"

"You understand the boys well, even though it has been only a short time."

Riley wanted to think of a smart reply but couldn't. The boys were becoming important to him. He wanted to understand them, give them a chance at life.

"They sing that song really well," he commented, hoping to change the subject. His fondness for the boys, for all of them, confused him. He didn't know how to put into words.

She laughed softly. "Yes. Though I do not wish to hear about Yankee Doodle ever again."

"I agree."

They made the tree line just as dawn approached. Riley led them deep into the woods to a sheltered spot. There he found a thick copse of trees and settled them in the center. After eating a bit of the fruit and bread and a sip of water, the elderly couple made their bed in the leaf cover and fell asleep. Iniki instructed the twins to do the same. They huddled close to each other, with the cat between them. Mathieu gently stroked the cat's fur. Michel kept an eagle eye on Riley and Iniki, rested against a tree trunk some yards away.

"Thank you," she whispered.

"For what?"

"For saving us. For saving them." She looked toward the tired band of travelers.

"We're not out of this yet, lady. Somehow, we've got to make it over that mountain and Francois isn't going to do that on foot."

"Yes. He is ill. He never was a healthy man."

"If he gets worse, we'll have to find medication for him. God knows where."

"I would have thought God spoke to you directly," she said with a grin. "You arrive at the solution of each problem so quickly. After all, you have brought us this far."

His eyes lit up when he smiled. She liked the lines streaking out from his eyes like tiny sunbeams. She had not noticed that before.

"I saw smoke coming from a chimney not too far from here," he told her. "Did you see it?" He pointed in a westerly direction.

"Yes. Someone must still live in this area. It surprises me. There is no easy way to get supplies except over these mountains.,"

He nodded. "Maybe a small farm that can support itself? That's what I'm hoping. After I get some rest, I'll investigate."

"I'll go with you."

"No. And before you get on your high horse, that's not an order. Just common sense. If something happens to me, you're going to have to lead these guys over that mountain to the village."

"Then nothing must happen, Riley. Not only do you do a better job as tour guide but I think I might miss you if you are not around."

He raised his eyebrows at that. "You would? A day ago you didn't trust me as far as you could throw me."

She was amused. "Another of your American phrases. It is difficult to learn them. They do not mean what they say."

"Most of the time, they mean exactly what they say."

She smelled the musky odor of his body and realized he was much too close to her. "Riley, I will be truthful. I did not trust you at first. Until you saved us from danger time and time again. I have decided you are an honorable man."

"You have?" he questioned with a grin.

She nodded. She saw the tiredness in his eyes, the worry and the excitement as he looked at her.

"Thank you again," she said and leaned closer to place a light kiss on his cheek.

"Is it customary to reward an honorable man with a kiss?"

She pretended to think it over. Then she shook her head. "An honorable man would say good night and go to sleep."

Riley made a face. "My ma always did say I had a bit of the devil in me."

"I do not see any horns."

"You will." He leaned toward her, pulling her closer with one arm around her shoulders and the other just above her waist.

She did not resist. "Riley," she murmured as his face came so near. She traced the beginning of his two day beard. "I like your name. Is it a family name?"

"My mother's maiden name."

"Ah. I see." Their lips were only inches apart.

"And Iniki?" he asked. "Where did that come from?"

74

She shrugged. "From nowhere. My mother thought it fit me."

"I remember a hurricane of that name."

"Yes. They named it after me."

"I believe it."

Tentatively she rested one hand against his chest and bowed her head, making it difficult for him to seek her lips. Putting his forehead next to hers, they sat frozen for a long moment. She found herself experiencing a myriad of emotions. Anticipation was the strongest.

"Riley . . ." She moved away and studied his eyes as if there were knowledge hidden there that she needed. "An honorable man . . ."

"With a bit of the devil in him . . ."

"Ahem." A voice spoke from above them. "Pardon, Monsieur and Mademoiselle. We will take the first watch." This time Mathieu carried the rifle and his brother held the bat. "You may rest now."

Iniki jumped to a standing position. Riley was not amused.

"No need, boys," he answered with a calmness he did not feel. "It's time for you two to get some sleep. You may have to relieve me later today. Go lay down."

Immediately Mathieu did what he was told. Michel lingered. "I think the captain should rest now," he argued.

"And I think the captain will be displeased if his soldiers don't follow orders," Riley answered.

"Yes, sir," he said with a pout and went away.

Riley sank back against the tree. "What am I going to do with him?"

Iniki moved closer. "You give both boys hope and courage. Those are fine qualities."

"I know. But they have an annoying knack of being under my nose when I least expect it."

She touched his face. "They did us a favor. It may be better to . ."

"Come here," he whispered. "Just let me hold you."

Her decision was made in an instant. She nestled in his arms, her breasts against his ribs.

"God, you feel good, lady."

"Riley . . ."

"I know. You're right," he admitted. "This isn't the time or place for what I have in mind. Since I'll never sleep now with you so near, I think I'll take a look around. Stay here and rest. You'll be safe."

"Where will you go?"

"Just to reconnoiter the area. I'll be back soon. Don't leave this spot. No matter what. Do you hear?"

"Yes, sir," she obeyed, disentangling herself from him. "It is written in the rules that there is to be no fraternization among the crew."

He traced her lips with his finger. "It is also written that the captain makes the rules."

Daybreak forced the helicopters back to base for refueling. The hunt for the refugees was unsuccessful. Yet, the general was not surprised. His theory of American intervention was verified by the inability to locate them easily. He gave orders to return to base. They would resume the search in the eastern quadrant.

In spite of his confidence, a slight uneasiness crept into his brain. He was no longer hunting a woman alone. His prey had become much more dangerous. He enjoyed a game of high stakes. Not often was he involved with formidable opponents. He would find them, he was sure. But the game would be just a bit more challenging than he expected.

"We will not resume the search right away," he instructed the pilots. "They will not take a chance on traveling during the day. I will return to the city to prepare for another night search. There is new equipment that will help."

"Yes, sir. The weather report is not good. Perhaps you should read it?"

"Hey, lady. Wake up." He hated to disturb her. Worry and stress drew deep lines on her forehead and mouth. Even as she slept, she frowned. Her dark hair spread out over the ground like a pillow and he wished like hell he could bury his face in it.

"Riley," she said with a deep sigh. "I don't like to sleep. My dreams terrify me. I can not make them go away."

"You? The woman who managed to get me to do your bidding. Lady, you can be afraid. That's normal. But, as far as courage is concerned, you've got an extra helping."

When she smiled, he knew he was melting. This woman who had the ability to exasperate him, also could reach a part of him he had buried away. The growing attraction, the wanting, the desire he felt for her surprised him. Yet, he knew it was right.

"What did you learn on your foray?" she asked. "Is that the right word?"

"Sure is. I've been gone an hour or so. Wanted to take a look at the source of that chimney smoke. It's a rundown farmhouse but someone is living there. There's no military in the area."

She sat up leaning against the tree. "Does that make sense? They know we crossed the flats. They will guess we are heading for the mountains."

Riley agreed. "There haven't been any helicopters in the region. They may have concluded we're going to try crossing further east of here where the mountain passes are easier to traverse. Our detour to Nouvella may have thrown them off."

"So they will look to the east first?"

"I hope so."

"What do we do now?"

"Get as much rest as possible," he advised. "Later, I'll approach the farmhouse. American dollars may convince the inhabitants to give us food and water. Horses, if we're lucky."

She disagreed. "They will most likely speak only French. Perhaps I should go instead. I will appear less threatening than a strange man. And I am able to communicate with them."

"No way," he pronounced. "I'm trying to save your life, remember?"

"Riley, your French is terrible."

He shrugged as if it didn't matter. "Won't need French. Money is a great communicator."

She said nothing more. He was fighting exhaustion. This latest disagreement could be postponed despite the fact she knew he was wrong. He would be taking a risk approaching civilians in a war-torn country. The island people were not quick to trust. No amount of money was going to change that.

"Will you be able to sleep?" Riley asked.

"Yes. I believe so."

He was tempted to suggest that he sleep close to her. Ridiculous idea, he told himself. Not now.

"No more bad dreams," he instructed. "They aren't allowed on this mission by order of the captain. By the way, where are the two little devils?"

"Over there. In dreamland. And, yes, I will sleep better now that you are back."

He stood up and faced her as she sat against the tree. He wanted to press her body into the tree with his own. He wanted to feel her body facing his. He wanted so much . . . But he stopped the fantasy at once. Not now, he reminded himself.

"Put your foot up here." He patted his right knee.

"What?"

"Your left foot. Put it up here. I thought we were pals now."

She laughed. "You want my foot?"

"Yup. On my knee."

She did as requested. Riley took hold of it and retied the loose shoelaces. That job done, he placed both hands on either side of her foot. "Thank you," she said but did not move it.

"You're welcome." He moved both hands slightly upward, palms flat, across her ankles and then to her calf. Finally, he reached her knees and lower thighs. He could hear his breathing become heavier. He let her leg down.

"I'm going to be over here." He moved about a yard away. "I think that's best." Was she having the same difficulty breathing as he? He couldn't be sure and didn't want to stare at her breasts any more than he already did.

"You are the captain," she responded.

"Right, damn it all."

The thought of her so close was just as distracting whether she was three feet away or leaning against him. Before nodding off, he tried to recall any occurrences of sexual attraction on previous missions. None came to mind. Women were seldom involved and he was too busy trying to stay alive.

Many females danced in and out of his life during his career. Some were more important than others. But none were willing to put up with his disappearing act every few months. More importantly, he could find no one for whom he would give it up.

Iniki was different. He admired her qualities; her bravery, honesty, loyalty. They were missing in other love affairs, mostly through his own doing. He made a habit of avoiding commitment.

He saw those traits in his own parents. They owned little and worked hard but there was a dedication, an owing to each other that made their relationship deepen. He learned about marriage through the example of parents who loved each other well.

Iniki was important to him. He knew the danger of involvement with a mission target; too easy to lose the ability to evaluate the situation with a clear head and too easy to think of someone else when survival was the only concern.

What was it about Iniki that tugged at his heart? Whatever it was, he didn't find it in previous relationships. Together they must survive. He would not take a chance on losing her.

He was a damn fool. He'd be lucky to get out of this alive. On previous assignments, that thought didn't enter his head. Now it did. Iniki and her people, especially those damn twins, must come out of this in one piece. So would he, he vowed. He refused to accept the alternative.

CHAPTER FIVE

Day 2 ~ Daytime Antoinette's Cabin
"No, absolutely not!"

Iniki watched as Riley carried Francois to the trees surrounding the farmhouse. The old man grew weaker by the hour and she was worried. They needed medicine; at the very least, aspirin. Stronger medication would be essential before long.

Riley made the man as comfortable as possible, then issued orders.

"All of you are to remain here in the trees. Under no circumstances are you to follow me. Do you understand?" He focused squarely on Michel who stared innocently at his captain.

"Whoever is in there will think I'm alone. Until we see how many people we're dealing with, I don't want any of you to show your faces. I can take care of myself if the situation turns sour but you could be injured."

Michel and Mathieu took in every word Riley uttered like he was Moses on the mount.

"Yes, yes," they repeated.

Riley raised his eyebrows higher with each response from the pair. Not for a second did he believe their acquiescence. By now, he was well acquainted with their devious ways.

Iniki listened to Riley repeat the usual warnings yet again. You can tell them a million times, she wanted to say to him. The two could twist the facts to suit their choice of action. No matter what orders were given, if there was a loophole in there somewhere, they would find it.

Despite her reservations concerning Riley's scheme, she said nothing more. It will not work, she told herself. A French woman lost in the woods might be somewhat believable. But an American man coming out of nowhere? Insane. However, Riley was the expert. This time she would not interfere.

The group settled down to await the results of Riley's grand plan. Madeline tended to her husband, oblivious of what was going on. The twins positioned themselves in the bushes where they had an excellent view of the house. Michel checked his rifle, making sure it was loaded.

"*Merde*," Iniki muttered as she watched Riley approach the house.

It was nothing more than a broken-down hut with a scrawny patch of garden. A few vegetables prospered here and there and the fruit trees offered limited produce. No one was in evidence. Off to the side, a dilapidated lean-to protected two horses and a wagon. From Iniki's vantage point, neither was in good condition. On the other hand, she reminded herself, beggars could not afford to be choosers. They would take what they could get.

No lights burned in the growing darkness but smoke circled up above the chimney. Someone was in there. Someone who would be asked to accept a lone male stranger, an American at that, into their home. Foolish, she told herself.

She knew Riley would make no effort to explain his presence since nothing but the truth would be believable. They talked the issue round and round before he started out. His plan was to tuck his gun into his belt, take out a wad of bills and knock on the door. She watched as he did just that, keeping an equal eye on the twins. The last thing she wanted was for them to be involved in the impending disaster.

As he waited for a response to his knock, Riley kept one hand on the butt of his gun. Iniki held her breath.

The heavy door opened slowly with a pronounced creak. An elderly lady, not more than three and a half feet high, poked her head around to peer at him.

"*Bon soir*," he said. That was all he managed to utter. Despite her size, she shoved the door open wide, lifted a rifle that was twice as long as she was tall, and took aim.

"*Merde!*" Iniki said again.

Since Riley was so tall and the woman so short, her rifle pointed directly at his genitals.

"Damn. Not again," Iniki heard him shout. He put his hands up immediately. "I come to buy food and clothing and horses." He waved the money in the air.

The woman's response was brief and to the point. She fired one shot. Had she been able to handle the heavy weapon, she would have hit Riley squarely in the groin. But the rifle was far too ungainly to manage. The shot landed in the dirt a few inches from his feet. The recoil threw her against the door and gave Riley a chance to take a giant leap backwards that would make Barishnikov jealous.

"*Amis!*" he yelled. "*Amis*. Money *pour vous*."

He pointed at his shirt and tugged at his collar. "Clothing? Shirt? Food?" He acted out a pantomime of eating soup.

"*Mon Dieu*," Michel muttered.

"Damn. That was close," Riley yelled.

Regaining her balance, the old woman reloaded and fired again, this time hitting the doorstep. Pieces of stone splintered up at them both. But it was impossible for her to pull the trigger and remain upright at the same time. She bounced once more against the door. Then she and the rifle fell to the ground.

"No, no," Riley protested. "I give you money. *L'argent*? For horses?" He giddyupped around in a small circle, arms holding imaginary reins.

Iniki covered her mouth so as not to laugh aloud. She did not notice Michel slip from cover and proceed toward Riley.

Meanwhile, the woman, still sprawled on the doorstep, placed a hand over her heart and began to speak in French. She gave up trying to shoot a hole in Riley. Her only movement was to beat her fist against her chest. Riley was stunned, not quite certain what to do.

But Michel did. "Monsieur" the boy said quietly, standing behind Riley, rifle at hand. "Is it time to shoot now?"

"No, no shooting." Riley turned in a panic and pushed the raised gun barrel down.

"Les amis, good amis," he said in his best French. Pointing first to himself and then to the woman. "Michel, tell her we are her friends. We are her good friends. Tell her that we ask for food and clothing and horses. We will give her American dollars."

Michel sighed in disapproval but followed orders. The woman began to speak profusely, accompanied by the constant shaking of her head.

After a good minute of this, Riley asked, "What did she say?"

"She says no, Monsieur"

"Ask her why."

"I have done so already."

"And . . ."

"She says she will not take the money but she will give us what we want if we take her with us."

"What. . .?"

"She says she . . ."

"Never mind. I've heard this story before."

"Then, sir," Michel asked innocently, "why did you ask?"

Iniki saw enough. She stomped out of the woods, fire in her eyes. "Michel," she said angrily. "Go to your brother and put down that damned gun."

She could see that Riley was relieved to see her, though he would not be eager to admit it.

"You could at least help the poor woman up from the ground."

"What for? So she can shoot off my . . .shoot at me again?"

"For heavens sake . ."

"What," he answered. "I didn't swear this time. Not even once."

She ignored him and turned to the old lady. "Madame." She helped the woman to stand and spoke to her in rapid French. Then she faced Riley.

"She is terrified of you. She thinks you will rape her."

Riley's eyes nearly popped out on that one. "Rape her? Why does she think that?"

"Because you waved money in her face like a lunatic. She thought you mistook her for a prostitute."

"Her? She's got to be eighty years old."

"Regardless, this is what she said. She claims she is suffering heart palpitations because you scared her so."

"Dear God! Is she all right?"

"I suspect she is fine. She has invited me inside. I will speak to her about what we need."

"Good." A grin appeared on his face. "Did I hear you mention something about a 'damned' gun a few minutes ago?"

"That is not important now."

"That, my lady, is cursing. Something I have been lectured on numerous times in our short acquaintance."

"Riley, deal with the woman's request first. We will discuss the other matter later. Michel was correct. She insists on coming with us. Although she does not want you near her. You are *diable*, she says."

"What's that?"

"Demon."

He shrugged. "I've been called worse. Is she done taking pot-shots at my feet?"

"The poor thing could not even hold the gun up."

"From where I was standing, she didn't do too bad a job. Offer her money. Here."

Iniki refused to take it. "I do not think the money will convince her. I should have approached her first, as I suggested." Iniki took a deep breath. "The money is the reason she thinks you want to buy her body."

He sighed and shook his head. "Okay. Okay. Never have I had this kind of trouble before." He hoped she was sympathetic. Instead, a cynical smirk greeted him. "How is this funny? You find it amusing that she wants to assassinate me?"

"Really? She missed you twice and I doubt she could hit anything with that weapon. But, that is what stirred Michel to action. He was protecting his captain."

"This captain bullsh . . ."

"Riley . . ."

"Okay, okay." He threw up his hands. "Why is it I can't curse but you can?"

"We decided to discuss that later. The matter at hand is the woman. I will speak to her. Meanwhile, you should go to Michel. He thinks he did something wrong. He was only trying to defend you."

"Wait a minute," Riley huffed. "Aren't you the one who yelled at him?"

"Riley, there are more vital issues to be settled. Please see to Michel."

"Okay, I'm going. Speak to this woman, please. We can't take on another person."

He found Michel polishing the barrel of his rifle. The boy did not seem unduly upset by whatever it was Riley supposedly said. Riley wondered if Iniki was trying to pawn her own guilt on him. She was the one who swore at the kid, wasn't she?

"Hello, Monsieur. Are you here to lecture me on the use of my weapon?"

"I guess so. What I want to know is why you disobeyed my orders?"

"What orders were those, sir?"

"You heard me clearly, Michel. I said no one was to follow me to the house."

The boy nodded, the picture of innocence. "This is true. But earlier you gave me definite orders to keep an eye on you at all times. Since then, I have done that. Are you telling me to forget one set of orders when you give another?"

"No. I am telling you to follow every order I give you."

"That may sometimes be impossible," the frowning child replied.

Riley had no answer for that one. "Right," he said and moved away as fast as he could. No wonder people who had children wore a pained expression, he realized. Children were enough to undo the sanest of men.

"Don't even suggest it!" He stamped his feet as he paced in a circle around Iniki.

He was being stubborn. But she was not worried. "The woman is a widow, Riley. Her two sons went to fight in the rebellion over two years ago. They have not returned. She assumes they are dead. The poor thing is alone and frightened."

Still orbiting Iniki, he responded with an adamant, "No. Absolutely not!"

"Then we shall have to walk over that mountain." Folding her arms across her chest, she determined that he would capitulate. Why did the male of the species have to be so obstinate, she asked herself. To him, she observed, "Antoinette will not give us what we need unless she accompanies us to Nouvella. And please stop circling!"

He did as she requested. Arms extended, he asked, "What do I look like? The Pied Piper?"

Sometimes, she just wanted to laugh at him. "A pied piper? I do not know this expression."

"Oh, yes you do." He resumed trotting, a frown across his brow. "All I need is a damn flute!"

She tried but failed to suppress a grin.

"This is not funny," he objected. "I was sent here to get you. And I end up collecting half the country as I go along. What are we going to use for food?"

"Antoinette has food and dry clothing and some medicine we need for Francois. Most importantly, she has horses and a wagon. We must have them to travel the distance to the foot of the mountain. Francois can not walk another step."

"Uh-huh. Then we can use the horses as pack animals and Francois can ride."

"And Antoinette as well, " she added.

"No. Not Antoinette as well."

"What do you propose to do? Steal her property? Take her food?"

He stared at her in disbelief. "Of course not!"

"Then what is your plan?" she asked.

"I don't have one," he said in exasperation. "Why should I? Not one of you does what I say. I specifically instructed the lot of you not to move from the trees. Next thing I know, you're following me like I was a . . ."

" . . . a pied piper?" She could not resist.

"That's not funny."

"Riley, we are obeying your orders like a perfect band of soldiers."

"Let me tell you something." He pointed a finger at her. "If this platoon gets any larger, we're going to resemble Hannibal crossing the Alps. All that's missing are the elephants."

She continued to annoy him on purpose. It was an amusing experience. "Riley, I needed to intervene. What were you thinking? Running around in a circle ? Bobbing your hands up and down?"

"You damn well know what I was doing."

"Yes. I do," she confirmed. "Acting like a lunatic. No wonder the woman thought you would attack her."

"Stop saying that!"

"Well, it is true. Is it not?"

"And stop laughing. Getting my body parts shot at is not amusing."

"Very well." She made a sorry attempt to control her reaction. "You have nothing to complain about where these people are concerned. When this is finished, they will surprise you."

He was circling again. "Oh, I don't doubt that. There's a surprise a minute around here. You change the game plan every hour on the hour. First, we must go here. Then, we must go there. Next, we must take this one with us. Then, we must take that one. And we don't dare leave behind any homeless animal within a five mile radius. I don't know why I'm even here. You can do this without me. Then there's Michel just waiting for permission to blast holes in someone. Now some troll of a woman thinks I want her body. This is crazy."

She folded her arms and cocked her head. "You are whining, Riley. And do stop that tramping around."

He froze in position. "I'm not whining. I'm telling it like it is."

"I disagree."

"What else is new?"

"Well . . .?"

"Well, what?"

"What do I tell the old woman?"

"Damn it all," Riley blustered. "Tell her to get ready quickly. We also need blankets and bandages. Francois needs aspirin at the very least and my arm needs to be dealt with. I'd like to make the foot of the mountain before midnight."

"A wise decision, captain," she said.

"Don't call me that again." He pointed his finger at her and then marched off mumbling something about stubborn women.

Forty minutes later they departed the farmhouse in the old wagon with the two still-older horses pulling. Iniki and Riley sat up front, dressed in peasant clothing the woman provided. The five others were tucked under the hay along with a meager but fresh supply of water and food.

"We'll be lucky if we make the foot of the mountain in this thing."

Iniki touched his arm. "It is better than hoofing it."

The wagon did not deserve his derisive abuse. It rolled along smoothly on the route Antoinette suggested to Iniki. The old woman refused to speak to Riley but assured Iniki that she visited Nouvella many times. With a piece of charcoal, she drew a map showing a narrow passage that would take them close to the higher elevations of the mountain but would eliminate many hours of treacherous travel. The wagon could go only so far, she warned. Then, they must unhook the horses and leave the wagon behind.

"Antoinette says to watch the skies," Iniki mentioned.

"What does that mean?" He looked up. "Looks okay to me."

Iniki observed for herself. Streaks of purple and pink shot through the indigo sky as the sun sank to the west.

"The wind is gusting. She thinks a storm is coming. She says the sky turns these colors when a bad storm approaches the island from the east."

"There was a tropical storm headed this way when I came ashore. The weather people said it would turn to the north."

"I hope your weather people are more accurate than your intelligence people."

"Don't count on it. If we can just get to the place where the road ends and the path begins, I think we'll have a shot. Helicopters will have trouble spotting us with all the foliage cover.

"Then, you think they will be back?"

"I'm sure of it. It's been almost twenty hours since they found the car. They've had the entire day to search the eastern perimeter. When they don't find us, they'll move west."

The general returned to the capital after spending almost ten hours in helicopters. Then, he followed the progress of the search from his office in Simone's palace. Frequent reports came in - all negative. The woman and her companion were not found.

"They're somewhere out there," he told his adjutant. "We keep looking."

"There is more uprising in the city, general. Should we waste our resources on one french woman?"

The general disagreed. "She isn't just one woman. She's an intelligent person who will make your president look like the butcher he is if she manages to get off the island. She hasn't gotten as far as she has without help. There's an American with her. I'll bet a week's salary on it."

"And that is important?"

The general shook his head at the man's stupidity. "If we prove American intervention, we have bargaining power. Sooner or later, we'll need it with the president killing off half the population."

"Then, what are your orders, sir?"

"Contact the helicopters and instruct them to retrace the area to the west. Especially near the mountains. If we didn't spot them in the eastern sector, then there's only one other place they can be."

The adjutant cleared his throat. "The latest weather report warns of a severe tropical storm heading for the island from the east. We will have wind and rain in a few hours. The weather men expect it will be a minor hurricane before long."

The general cursed. "That will ground the copters. On the other hand, it may also do in the refugees. Instruct the pilots to search as long as weather permits. They are to report to me if they see anything."

"Yes, sir. And what are they to do when the woman is found?"

"The American must be brought to me alive. Dispose of the woman."

Less than three miles into the short ride, the helicopters came. Darkness gave them some cover. But traveling in the wagon meant sticking to the bumpy dirt road. A road that was easily picked up with the powerful spotlights on the aircraft.

Riley heard them coming. "Everyone under the hay. Don't move," he shouted to his passengers. He turned to Iniki. "Climb in the back with them. Hurry."

"No. It may look to them that we are just a peasant couple. Pull your hat down and slouch your shoulders like you are elderly."

The copters were closing in. "Do we argue about this too?"

"No argument," she conceded. "I think you are wrong."

"What else is new? Okay, lady. You win. Here they come."

The aircraft swept down, illuminating them in the spotlight. The pilot slowed down and followed the wagon for a half mile or so. Then it flew off banking to the right.

"You see?" Iniki exclaimed. "They did as I predicted. They thought we were an innocent old couple."

"They'll be back. Get under the hay."

"I will not. Why is it you hate to admit I may be right?"

"Okay. You're right. They won't be back. Keep still so I can listen."

"For what?"

"For the helicopters," he answered.

"Riley Taggart, you are the most stubborn man I have ever met."

"Quiet."

"Do not tell me to be quiet."

He didn't have time to answer. His ears were trying to hear the thumping of the aircraft.

"Riley, answer me."

"Lady, can you shut that mouth for one second? Please," he added.

"Why?"

"Cause they'll be back."

And out of nowhere, the copter swooped down on them, positioning itself directly over the wagon. The horses spooked and Riley fought hard to control them and stay on the road.

"Get down," he shouted. "And stay there."

This time she followed orders without debate, scrunching down on the floor boards of the wagon's seat.

They had only a short distance to go before they reached the pine tree cover near the foot of the mountain. Riley spurred on the horses, shivers of fear rippling down his back. He waited for the first shot to be fired.

It did not come immediately. Riley had time to see Michel climb over the backboard and onto the seat of the wagon. In his hand was the rifle.

"I shall ride with you," he informed the driver.

"You shall not," Riley yelled. "Get this kid out of here."

At that instant, the helicopter began to fire. Michel was pulled down by his feet into the small space under the seat. The first run of gunfire strafed the right side of the wagon where the boy had sat seconds before. Riley felt the wood splinter next to him.

Michel popped his head up, pointing the rifle upward. "I will get him, captain."

"Get down," Riley demanded. Michel disappeared onto the flooring. Iniki shielded him with her body.

A second round of gunfire erupted. The old women in the back screamed in terror. Riley was helpless to do anything but drive the horses as fast as he could and pray that the antiquated wagon stayed in one piece.

The third round struck him in the left thigh. It startled him and burned but he could tell it was not too serious. They were nearly to the trees. He encouraged the horses on with a last bit of hope. They were so close when the final burst began. The wagon was strafed on both sides and down the middle. The barrage was so extensive Riley expected that his passengers were dead or severely injured.

Bursts of gunfire spooked the horses to the point where Riley couldn't control them. Recklessly, they sprinted for the trees. In a matter of minutes, they would be there. The wagon would crash into the pines, as the horses continued their wild escape.

Riley knew their only hope was to gain control. He tugged on the reins with every bit of strength he could muster, his wounded arm and leg screeching in pain. The horses responded somewhat although Riley was certain they would not stop in time. The wagon would hit the first copse of trees at top speed. His only concern now was the passengers.

"Iniki, jump out," he screamed. "Michel, jump."

The two climbed up onto the seat. Both were horrified at the idea.

"When I tell you, jump. Everyone in the back, jump out now."

But there was no time left. The old wagon surpassed its maximum use. The back right wheel spooled off like a spinning top, causing the vehicle to list to the right. The back corner gouged out a line in the earthen road as it bumped along. The result was a slowing of the wagon as the dead weight forced the horses to hold back. Riley fought to keep the wagon from tumbling over. The best he could do was to pull hard left. The wagon didn't flip. Instead, it rolled gently on its side. Iniki and Michel jumped clear in time. Riley was the only one to ride it to the end which turned out to be anticlimactic. The vehicle slid along for a short distance and stopped. The horses whinnied and snorted but remained upright and unharmed.

With the tree cover around them, the helicopters couldn't get to them easily. They continued firing, but their target could no longer be pinpointed. Bullets hit the tops of trees but the crew could not tell if they reached the refugees. The wind was coming in stronger gusts and the pilot was not going to chance a landing in a forested area. Even if he could make a landing, there was no guarantee he would get off the ground again. The general would not be pleased. Nevertheless, the pilot pulled away from the spot, instructing his co-pilot to note the coordinates where their quarry was last seen.

On the ground, Riley jumped from the mangled wagon and raced back to where his cargo had fallen. He could see bodies lying along side the dirt path under the trees. Fear clutched at his heart and he could feel actual pain in the pit of his stomach.

"Iniki?" he yelled. "Where are you?"

"I am here." She was standing brushing dirt from her clothes. He reached out to draw her into his arms. Then he remembered the boys. "Oh my God, where are Michel and Mathieu?"

"Michel is here." She pointed to the boy who stood behind her.

Riley bent down and picked up the boy. "Are you okay?"

"I am fine, sir. But my brother . . .?"

"We'll find him. Thank God you're not hurt. Iniki, help me check on the others. We have to get out of here fast. Michel, can you start unhitching the horses?"

"Yes, Monsieur."

"Good boy."

Antoinette and Madeline were shaken up but otherwise fine. Mathieu helped them to their feet as Riley approached.

As he did with the other twin, Riley lifted the boy in his arms. "You're not injured?"

"No, sir. And Yankee Doodle is fine, also. But you must see my bat." He held up the long piece of wood, in which was a bullet.

"The bat saved my life. I was holding it against my chest. I believe it made a bruise but no damage." The boy opened his shirt and, in the darkness, Riley felt a long straight welt raised down the center of his chest. The bat saved Mattieu's life and the boy held the object as if it were a first place trophy. Riley closed his eyes in silent prayer that the twins escaped unharmed.

The old man was found last, lying unmoving by the side of the wagon. Hay covered most of his body. Riley cleaned away the hay and examined the frail old man. He was hit in two places; his head and his left side. The head wound was superficial and he was conscious but in pain. The other injury was deep and ugly.

"I'll need something to stop the bleeding. It's bad."

Iniki searched through the supplies and found a cotton compress and tape. "Here, use this."

Riley managed to bandage it tight enough so Francois could be moved. "He's going to need that cleaned out but we can't stop here. The military may arrive any minute."

"Mademoiselle," Antoinette called in French. The two women spoke for a moment. Then, Iniki translated for Riley.

"Antoinette tells me that the pass through the mountains is only a short way from here. Once on the path, we need travel for an hour or so. But it is dangerous as it climbs up. She will show you a cave where we can stop. She is sure the rain will come soon and heavy winds. I believe she is correct."

"Then Antoinette's plan sounds like our only option."

Carefully, he lifted Francois. The old moaned in pain.

"Is he able to ride?" Iniki asked.

Riley doubted it. "Maybe we can put one of the boys on the horse seated in front of Francois. Then he can hold onto the kid."

"I will get Michel."

"While you're at it, confiscate his rifle, will you please."

"We have a report from one of the copters, General."

"Yes. What is it?" It was almost twenty-four hours since they located the abandoned car. He was anxious for the chase to begin in earnest.

"One of the pilots patrolling the central section of the flats near the mountains reports seeing a wagon with a man, a woman and one child in it."

"A child?"

"Yes, sir. Approximate age, about eleven or twelve."

"What action did he take?"

"He strafed the wagon, sir. He reports hitting it several times. The man was injured. He does not know of the woman and child. But he is certain that the wagon crashed into the trees on the side of the path. The pilot could not land because of increasing winds."

The general was irritated. "Isn't there someone in this army who asks questions before they shoot? I gave orders the man was not to be harmed."

"This man did not appear to be our target, sir."

"Why not?"

"He was old, sir."

"And the woman?"

"The pilot said the woman had long dark hair. That is all, sir."

"Long dark hair. Show me on the map where they were spotted."

The soldier did as commanded.

"When the storm passes, I want that area thoroughly searched. If the pilot says the wagon crashed, they may still be there."

"Yes, sir. We will recover the bodies."

As the soldier left the office, the general spoke. "There will be no bodies, fool."

"Monsieur, I apologize for my mistake. Mademoiselle said I must give my rifle to you."

Riley took the weapon and made a mental note to thank Iniki for making him the meanie. "Listen Michel. You've got to learn how to follow my orders if you are to be my . . . corporal."

"Your corporal? I . . we may be your helpers?" Excitement made his eyes widen so much that Riley thought they would pop right out.

"Exactly. You and Mathieu are to be my right hand men. But you must listen to what I say and do only what I say. Do you understand?"

"Yes, sir."

"Good. Now get up on that horse. And remember, I don't want to hear you ask about shooting the rifle again. I'll tell you when I want you to fire. Is that clear?"

"Yes, sir. But will you allow me to hold the rifle?"

Riley tried hard not to laugh. "Okay. If you promise to obey the rules." He handed the weapon over.

"Thank you, sir." Michel gently fingered the beat up object. "You will instruct me when to fire?"

"Yes. Now get up there."

He watched as the boy scrambled onto the horse, then call to his brother. Such good kids. They don't deserve to be orphaned like this, Riley thought. They don't deserve to live in constant danger.

Riley organized the group in less than thirty minutes. With no firm idea of the military's plan, he could only assume they would not abandon the search for Iniki. Allowing her to escape the country would not be in Simone's best interests. He knew she would be a compelling spokesperson once outside the country. To the dictator, she was a liability that must be eliminated.

"Everything is ready. Is your leg painful?" Iniki came up behind him as she frequently did.

"It can wait until we reach this cave Antoinette talked about. I hope she knows what she is doing."

"She said the same about you."

He frowned. "I thought I was doing a pretty good job around here."

"We think you are also. Do not fret. However, Antoinette still believes you will ravish her. She will not listen to me."

Damn women! Would he ever figure them out? "You have got to be kidding."

"Unfortunately, I am not. Nevertheless, we must go. Everyone is ready."

"Then let's get this show on the road. I don't doubt the military has pinpointed where we're headed by now. They're probably waiting for us on the other side of the damn mountain."

"Get the show on the road. It means to move on? I like these colorful phrases. But when you curse, Riley . . ."

"When did I curse?"

"Just now. The damn mountain . . . ?"

"That's cursing?"

"Certainly. There are the boys to consider. They should not learn such words."

"They probably have already."

"Yes. If they have listened to you," she recounted.

"Which reminds me, Mademoiselle. The discussion you insisted we postpone? Is this a good time to resurrect it?"

She put her nose in the air but he detected a hint of a smile on her lips. "Very well," she answered. "What is it we are to discuss?"

"The fact that you cursed this afternoon and that was fine. But if I say the word 'damn' . . ."

"Riley . . ."

". . . I get the evil eye from you. Doesn't sound like equality to me."

"It is not. Has no one explained the war between man and woman and the lack of equality therein?"

No shit, he said silently. "Yeah. Seems I've heard that before. But that's not the issue."

"Put simply, this is the issue, Riley. I was overcome with emotion at the circumstances and used an unfortunate choice of words which in my native country, in fact all of Europe, is not considered swearing."

"Whereas I . . ." Riley waited for her to complete the sentence.

" . . you use these words as part of the vernacular. Not in the heat of the situation."

Riley was offended. "That's how we do it back home." Well, wasn't it?

"Then you will have to change."

"You're one tough cookie, lady." He would never win this point.

"You may explain this 'tough cookie' to me as we start up the path. I believe the rain and wind are worse."

"Goddam it! What else is going to happen?"

"Riley!"

"What?"

"The cursing!"

"Well, excuse me," he mumbled in frustration.

"What?" she asked.

"I said excuse me, dammit."

CHAPTER SIX

Day 2 ~ Late at night in the cave
"This is most educational. Please continue."

Francois sat on the first horse behind Michel. The old man's entire weight pressed against the child's back. Supplies were tied to the second horse. The weather worsened, making a difficult ride more treacherous. Thunder and lighting brightened the sky like fireworks. The wind pounded, pushing them forward, then back, then sideways as it gusted, then ebbed, then gusted again. Drenching rain beat on them sideways, piercing their skin like tiny slivers of steel.

The horses suffered just as cruelly. Riley knew it would not take much for them to spook and take off. On that pathway, the result would be fatal. He took hold of the lead horse, holding on tightly at the muzzle and tugging to force the animal to move forward without taking off at a gallop. Iniki and Mathieu did the same with the second horse while Madeline and Antoinette trudged behind, supporting each other on the slippery path.

Francois clung to Michel atop the horse but the old man's grip gradually weakened. The boy fought to keep the injured man on the saddle but the heavy weight became too difficult to bear. At one point, they both began to slide sideways.

"Monsieur, please help."

Dropping the reins, Riley managed to steady both at the last second, preventing them from falling to the muddy ground. Francois was barely conscious and mumbling incoherently.

"He's too heavy for you, Michel. We can't risk him falling. He'll injure himself further."

The boy nodded solemnly. "You are correct, sir. But who can take my place?"

Riley stopped and waved Iniki forward. "Michel can't bear the weight of the old man," he explained. "Will you get up there? Put Francois in front of you?"

"I will try, of course. Would it be better if you rode? I could pull the horses."

Riley shook his head. "These animals are ready to bolt at the next clap of thunder. I'd rather be down here where I can hold them back."

She agreed, shivering in the rain.

"Are you all right?" he asked, taking her cold hands in his own.

She nodded. "Just tired and freezing. You make my hands warmer with your own."

He smiled. "Underneath this calm facade is a man who is on fire, lady." He said it to be funny but knew it was true.

"Why? I want to know why." She did not smile. She looked into his eyes and shivered once more.

"I want you," he said quietly. "I want to make you warm. I want to hold you and be near you."

"Yes. I believe I want the same."

"Then let's get on with this journey as fast as we can."

"Oh yes. Please."

Despite the miserable conditions, he laughed. "I don't know which one of us is the leader here. I figure you got me hook, line and sinker."

She mounted the horse and positioned herself in back of Francois. "When we reach shelter, I want to know about this hook, line and sinker."

"I think you know already, don't you?"

She nodded and took hold of Francois, who leaned forward, almost doubled over. Since she was behind him, she could keep him steady only by wrapping her two arms around him.

The storm intensified, the wind doing its best to knock the two riders over. Riley knew she was using every bit of strength to steady Francois. The strain on her face was painful to watch.

"Riley," she shouted over the wind. "Francois is very ill. We must find somewhere to stop soon."

Again Riley stopped his marchers and confirmed Iniki's diagnosis. The man burned with a high temperature.

"Where's the fever coming from?" Riley was puzzled.

"Can it be his wounds?"

"Doubt it. It hasn't been long enough for an infection to set in."

"Then what?"

"You got me there. Can you ride further?"

"Yes. Antoinette says there is a cave about less than a kilometer from here."

"We'll make it." He reached up to squeeze her hand. "Just hold on a bit longer. Okay?"

"I will. Check on the others."

The rain and wind were unforgiving. The twins struggled to hold up Madeline and Antoinette while dragging the pack horse behind them.

"Why have we stopped, sir?" Michel was full of questions despite the rough conditions.

"To check on you. Everything all right?"

"All right," he answered and saluted. Mathieu copied his brother's gesture.

"Where's Yankee Doodle?"

"He is safe in my knapsack," Mathieu assured him. "He does not seem to want to leave it."

"Smart cat," Riley said. "You are both good soldiers." He patted each on the shoulder.

Riley wondered if any of them would survive. The rain was so fierce that he could hardly see ahead. The path clung precariously to the mountain side. It narrowed as they climbed higher. Where there once was ten to fifteen feet on either side of the horses, now there was only five. He was concerned about the horse with the twins and the women pulling. If the path were only a few feet across, could the boys steady the animal and help the women as well? He could do nothing to help them. Giving Iniki the responsibility for managing the horse while steadying an unconscious man at the same time was asking too much. Would any of them live out the night?

They continued on, the path tapering more. Riley hoped there was no erosion since Antoinette had last used the path. In the stormy blackness they were moving blind. One misstep would take them into thin air. The thought of Iniki or the boys or any of them tumbling into the blackness sent a shiver through him that no amount of cold and wind could surpass.

"Riley, can you hear that? I think it is Antoinette," Iniki shouted breaking into his dark thoughts. He fought to block the roar of the wind, and in doing so, he heard a woman's scream.

"I hear it. Can you hold the horse still?"

"Yes, go quickly. The twins!" Panic laced her words. The same panic he felt as he ran back to the others.

His fears were nearly realized. Antoinette hung over the side of the path, her feet dangling into empty space. All that saved her from sailing to a horrible death were the twins, lying face down across the trail. Each held one of the woman's arms. They stopped her from falling but could not pull her up. In the background, Riley heard Madeline praying.

"She is stuck, sir." Michel's face was covered in mud as was his brother. Riley lay down across the path between the boys and spoke gently to her. She continued to scream at the top of her voice. After a moment, he gave up trying to calm her. She wasn't going to be any help in her own rescue. He turned to the boys.

"Okay, now listen. I'm going to take over where Michel is and grab onto her right arm. Michel, you help with the other arm. Do it now."

The boy snapped to action.

"Good. Now when I count to three, we pull. Dig your feet into the mud to give yourself some traction. Then inch backward, digging in again. Keep pulling until I say to stop. Got it?"

"May I do the counting, sir?" Michel looked up at Riley with a serious face.

"Go ahead."

"*Une. . . deux . . trois*," he shouted.

The woman came up slowly but made it over the precipice and lay flat on the ground. Madeline continued to pray. Antoinette continued to scream. But the boys smiled through muddy faces.

"Give me five, guys," Riley said.

They looked at him in confusion.

"I do not know that expression, sir," Mathieu explained.

"Then, let me show you." And he did. "Now go to Mademoiselle and tell her Antoinette is fine."

They did as ordered, practicing their new trick as they ran.

Antoinette did not stop bellowing even when Madeline assured her she was safe. She quieted down for a moment then resumed when Riley tried to examine her ankle. One look told him it was swollen.

"Damn," he said, checking first to see if anyone could hear him. Madeline was the only one close enough and she didn't appear to care.

"She'll have to ride." He tried lifting the woman but she fought, punching him with her fists.

"What's her problem, Madeline?"

"She still believes you are evil."

"Not again! Well, she'll just have to scream then. I don't have the time to prove my good intentions right now." With quick effort, he scooped up the woman and sat her on top of the horse. The action startled her so that she stopped her blathering.

"Women," Riley muttered and made his way back to Iniki and the boys.

105

"Boys, go help Madeline with the reins. We don't have too much further to go."

"Why did she scream so?" Michel asked.

"It's a long story," Riley stated. "No time now. Go."

The boys resumed their posts. Riley took the reins from Iniki. "How's he doing?"

"He has been unconscious for a long while."

"Can you still hold him?" Francois was limp in her grasp. His eyes remained closed and his arms dangled beside him.

"Yes. He is so frail. Please get us out of this storm, Riley. That is all I ask."

The general did not appreciate the news he received from his adjutant. "What do the other helicopters report?"

"They found nothing in the western quadrant. The wind and rain are worsening. They were forced to go back to base at St. Lucille."

"Let's revisit the area where the wagon was sighted. There are old farms at the foot of the mountains, aren't there?"

"Yes, sir."

"Then it's possible they found shelter. The whole area will have to be searched when the storm abates."

"Sir, that area is nowhere near the Black Point location."

"Yes." That worried him. It made no sense that the only place where travelers were sighted was so far from the most logical escape route.

"When the storm passes, we investigate this wagon incident. Also, I want a report on any villages near that location. They may be heading in a different direction entirely."

"Yes, sir. But it will be well into tomorrow afternoon before the storm clears enough for us to continue."

"No problem. They can't move any faster than we can."

Ninety minutes later, they made it to the cave entrance. Despite the fact that she was a raving lunatic, Riley was grateful Antoinette came with them. Without shelter, he doubted they would last much longer.

The place was large and deep enough to give both refugees and horses protection from wind and rain. From the remains of campfires and the wood and horse blankets there, he gathered this was a stopping off point between the flats and Nouvella and was used frequently by local people.

The storm raged for hours. Riley estimated the wind gusts were reaching sixty to seventy miles an hour. More than likely, they were caught in a minor hurricane, which would not blow itself out until the morning. He settled the horses near the cave entrance, then turned his attention to the others.

Madeline and Antoinette changed into dry clothing. Iniki covered them with the cleanest of the horse blankets. Madeline was exhausted and worried about her husband. Other than that, she was relatively healthy. Antoinette could not put any pressure on her ankle. She would not be walking for a few days.

"Will you see to Antoinette? Every time I go near her, she thinks I'm about to attack her."

"She is a crazy old lady, left alone for too long. You are perhaps the first male she has seen in a few years."

"Whatever," he shrugged. "Do I look like someone who stalks elderly women?"

"Right now, you look frightening. You are covered in mud."

"That's what I get for saving that crazy lady from certain death?"

Iniki laughed. "Crazy lady," she repeated. "I very much like that."

"Good. And when you talk to her, ask her if there's a pharmacy or apothecary in the village. She's been there before. She should know."

"For Francois?"

Riley nodded. "Without medication, he may not make it."

"But if we have no doctor, how can we get medicine?"

"We'll get it. That's one of the things I'm good at."

"What? Stealing?"

"That, too. I was talking about doing the impossible."

She smiled and went to the woman, elevating the ankle on some leaf-covered rocks next to the fire the boys built with wood pieces.

Francois was the worst off. Riley cleaned out both wounds and applied what salve he carried and an antiseptic from Antoinette"s provisions. The head wound, just a scrape, was not serious. The bullet that passed through the man's side near the waistline was a different story. Riley knew the deep gash should be sutured, but the best he could do was tape it tightly and hope no infection set in. From Antoinette's supply of medicines, he found more aspirin. It was the strongest medication he had and he gave the man three of them with water.

"How is he?" Iniki came up behind him.

Riley just shook his head. "I don't know what else to do for him except keep him warm. He needs antibiotics. Whatever is spiking that temp is not going to disappear without that."

"What of the wounds?"

"Not that bad. Certainly not life threatening if he had a doctor and medication."

"Then we will see that he gets one or the other."

"Just like that?" he asked.

"We accomplished more than I thought possible. We can do more."

"You may be speaking of miracles, lady."

"Miracles do happen. You must believe."

"Okay, Jiminy Cricket. What did Antoinette say about a pharmacy?"

"Not good. It may be necessary to do the impossible yet again."

"Meaning?"

"There is no such store. The people must go to the military garrison on the edge of the village for medication. They may get it only if they are treated by a military doctor."

"So there's an encampment in the village?"

"I believe so. It will be difficult to find Madeline's people with soldiers about."

"But not impossible. I thought you believed in miracles?"

"We seem to need quite a few."

He could think of no suitable reply, so he asked, "Care to do some nursing on my leg?"

"Of course," she said. "Take off your pants."

"What? Like hell I will."

"Riley . . ."

"Swearing? Okay. Sorry about that. But you shocked me."

"Riley, do not be foolish. How else am I to clean out the wound?"

"I don't know but I have no intention of removing my clothing." He took out his knife and slit a section of the pant leg so she could get to it.

"Very good." She instructed him to sit. "If you shed your trousers, Antoinette may start screaming again." She cleaned and bandaged the affected area. Then, she did the same with the arm injury. "You will live," she pronounced.

The twins appeared at his side ready to give their report. "The cave is secured, sir. The horses are tied and everyone is as comfortable as possible. We collected rain water and passed out some food."

"Excellent, Mathieu. Now I want both of you to change into the dry clothes Antoinette gave you. Put the wet things near the fire to dry. When that's done, both of you settle down and sleep."

"But . . ."

"No buts, Michel. Tomorrow we must decide on a new plan. I need you rested and ready to act."

"Yes, I see, sir. But should there be no one to keep watch?"

"Not in this storm, Michel. There's no one out there. We barely made it ourselves. There's no danger, at least for tonight. Now go."

The two went off and accomplished their chores. Despite Michel's concern, he was asleep as soon as his head hit the old blanket near the fire.

"They did well, did they not?" She looked to Riley for confirmation.

"Extremely well," he agreed. "Not only the boys, but all of them. I just hope our luck holds."

"Riley, do you remember when we began the journey, I assured you they would be strong. The best troops you will command."

"Several times, as I recall."

"Then you must admit I was correct."

"Absolutely. Undeniably. One hundred percent correct. And now that I have humbled myself, may I wash some of this mud away?" He stripped off his shirt, laid it beside the fire to dry and headed for the mouth of the cave.

"Certainly," she responded and followed after him, as he hoped she would.

Then wind shrieked across the mountainside but just inside the dark opening, the air was calm. A steady but tranquil rain spilled over the outer walls forming a natural shower. He dove into it, tilting his head back so the water poured over him.

"The bandages, Riley. They are soaked."

"Then you'll have to change them again," he replied and offered his hand to her. "Come on. It feels good. Join me."

She accepted the invitation and was instantly as soaked as he. Her clothing molded to her body, revealing so much Riley wanted to see; strong thighs and rigid nipples. He watched as she caught the droplets with her open mouth. That mouth, he thought, he must possess that mouth. Or was he the one possessed? She was so young and so damn fearless. She chose to trust him. In doing so she entrapped him like no other woman had. Bracing himself against the rock wall, he reached for her and she came willingly.

"Yes," she whispered. "Yes, it is time."

He felt the pressure of her fingers on his chest and asked, "You mean we agree on something?"

"On this matter, we do."

"You're one hell of a lady," he murmured into her hair.

She pushed away from him but he saw a sly smile on her lips. "I thought we had an understanding about cursing?"

"Cursing? What did I say now?"

"Hell," she answered, planting her hands on her hips. "Always, it is hell this and damn that. They must be your favorite words."

"But I intended it as a compliment."

"Ah, I see," she teased. "Then American women appreciate cursing?"

He knew she was enjoying the sparring. "It's just an expression. There are other ways to say it, I suppose."

"Tell me."

He crossed his arms on his chest and realized he was enchanted by her; this woman he wanted so badly it hurt.

Still standing away from him, she asked, "Well? Do Americans know how to flatter a woman without using swear words?"

"Of course they do. Let's see." He pursed his lips and feigned serious deliberation. "Okay. I've got it." He put one hand over his heart. "I could say, 'You're extremely impressive, Mademoiselle'."

She shook her head. "Too formal. We have known each other for two days now."

"Right. How about 'you're something else'?"

"You sound like an adolescent."

"God forbid.. Maybe I should have said I find you to be an exceptional . . . "

"Too impersonal."

"Of course. Let's try this. 'You look sensational with wet hair'."

"Do I?"

"Without question. May I continue?"

"I am waiting."

"Right. Well . . .uh, . . .your long legs, your body, those eyes. All perfect." He watched for a reaction but there was none. "Was I too insensitive?"

"Did you mean it," she asked.

"Yes."

"Then I am not insulted."

"Thank God."

She ignored his attempt at humor. "In your country, how else do men show affection?"

This lady was driving him crazy. But if he dare utter that he'd be in big trouble. So he said, "Sometimes gestures are used when words aren't enough."

"Such as?"

"Well, I could take your hand." He held it gently. Rough patches covered the skin, every nail dirty and broken. Ragged cuts ran across the knuckles. He had never seen a lovelier hand.

"Yes?" she asked as if curiosity was her motive.

"And caress it like this." He brushed the palm with his lips and kissed it.

"And then?" Despite her dispassionate manner, he swore he could feel the heat of her body through her fingers. "I want to trace your lips with my thumb."

"Please do."

When he did, he felt her shiver. "Are you cold?"

"Not at all. This is most educational. Please continue. What is next?"

He cleared his throat. "Next is the simple kiss."

"And that is?"

"I place my lips on yours, thus creating a more intimate connection."

"A demonstration might be helpful."

"Happy to oblige." He positioned himself so that his lips were close to hers but not touching. No part of their bodies met. He lingered, grazing one cheek, then the other, then the chin. Yet, there was no firm contact.

He checked to see if her eyes were closed. They were, but only halfway. He studied her mouth and could not detect the slightest tremor. Was her breathing just a bit quicker? He thought so, but how could he hear it over his own? Then she bit her bottom lip and ran her tongue over it. How did such an innocent movement seem so damn sensual?

"Interesting," she murmured and stepped back. "And that is all?"

"Not quite." He leaned against the rock wall, held his hand out and almost pleaded. "Come here."

Would she chose to end it now? Just because he lost whatever common sense he once possessed didn't mean she had also.

For an instant she hesitated. Then with one step, she burrowed into his arms. His mouth was first to open, his tongue the first to taste sweetness. When she parted her lips, he understood she welcomed his embrace.

"Do you approve?" when they stopped to catch a breath.

She nodded. "There is more?"

"Definitely."

"Please show me."

"My pleasure." He wasn't kidding. His body responded to her more than he expected. Not ready to let go, he tightened his grasp on her waist. Her damp shirt against his chest did nothing to cool him off.

"Again, please," she whispered.

"Maybe this is enough for now."

"Why is that? Once more," she demanded and pressed the length of her torso against him.

"Well, if you insist."

At the end of a few minutes, she announced, "I believe I have mastered this."

"You sure have, lady."

"But just to be certain, perhaps one last time."

He did as requested, then forced himself to say, "The lesson is now concluded."

"If you wish," she commented. "Now, it is my turn."

"For what?"

"Cultural exchange. You see, in my country there are also ways to show affection." She took his hands and kissed each fingertip. "We do this also."

"Uh-huh."

"And this." She placed his hand against her cheek.

"Really," he managed to get out.

"And always this." Her mouth met his and she played with his tongue.

He wondered how much more he could take.

"But, we are not afraid to proceed further." She held his hand against her breast..

The move wasn't unexpected and he managed to summon enough strength to pull away.

"What is it?" she asked, her smile deepening to laughter. "This is not done in your country?"

"It's a universal practice, I'd say." Sure in hell was, he told himself.

"You do not find me desirable?"

He laughed along with her. "Are you kidding? I think you're desirable all right. Oh God, are you ever. But not now, not here."

"There may not be another chance. You are foolish, Riley." She stepped back, squared her shoulders and shook her head.

She was preparing for battle. He witnessed it several times since the start of their journey. Invariably, he lost. But this time he would have the last word.

"Now just listen for a minute." He pleaded rather than demanded. But he pushed on anyway.

"Right now. The only thing I want is to put my hands on you. All of you." He stopped to take a deep breath. "Hell, I'm busting to make love with you. But not here with the children and old folks so near."

"They can neither hear or see us," she argued.

But he went on. "And I won't take advantage of you either. Just because we've survived this long doesn't mean you have to repay me ....."

"Riley, shut up," she commanded and moved into his arms once again.

"Do we have to argue about this, too?" he asked even though he knew the answer.

"Apparently."

"You deserve better than a cold hard floor," he reasoned.

"We may not live long enough for better. And I know you want me. I can feel how you want me."

He threw his head back and laughed. "You drive me crazy, woman."

"Good. That is my intention."

"I know. But we are not making love here. Not tonight. Right?"

"I did not say that. You did."

He kissed the tip of her nose. "Don't you ever obey?"

"Not often," she answered with a smile. "I may listen to you. I may even fall in love with you. But I will not promise to obey." With a quick kiss, she loosened herself from his arms and left.

But he heard her last remark clearly.

"You are a hell of a kisser, Riley Taggart."

Shaking his head in amusement, he joined her by the fire. His shirt was dry and he handed it to her. "Here. Put this on. You have to dry your clothes."

They walked to the far end of the cave out of the firelight. He watched as she stripped off her wet clothes, with nothing underneath, and put on his warm shirt. Riley understood she wanted him to see her naked body and his eyes drank in every part of her.

"Will you put these near the fire," she asked, handing him the damp clothing.

"What? Oh yeah." He shook his head to clear it and did as she requested. She returned to the fire with the medical supplies.

"Will you remove your pants please."

"The last time you asked me to remove something, you stomped my sunglasses to pieces.

"I hate sunglasses. But I will not harm your pants. They can dry by the fire while I change your bandages."

"If you play nurse, may I play doctor?"

"Does that mean what I think it does?"

He laughed. "Forget it. Bad joke."

"You are afraid I may agree to play?"

"Yes."

"You are correct. Since you have withdrawn the offer, take the trousers off."

"Yes, ma'am."

He knew she watched as he stripped from the waist down. Quickly, he grabbed an old horse blanket, wrapped it around his butt and went to sit beside her.

As she worked on his injuries, she said, "We need a plan for tomorrow. Since you refuse to make love, we should talk of other things."

"Please don't joke about it," he begged. "You're not making this any easier."

"I have no intention of doing so."

"Of course not," he muttered.

"What of tomorrow?" she asked, still smirking.

He sighed. "Tomorrow, we wait until the storm passes. Then we try to make it down to the village."

"But, how can ... ."

"Hold your horses. Obviously, we can't move Francois or Antoinette. They stay here. Madeline will watch over them."

"What of the boys?"

"Yes, I know what you're about to say. We can't leave them here. They're liable to get into anything. So we take them with us. We'll go on foot to the village. If there is a village left. This storm is bad and the village is right on the beach."

"Riley, what do we do if we can not find Madeline's relatives?"

He reached out to touch hers. "We'll find them. Trust me."

"I do trust you. But I am not so sure that we will locate them. If we do not, then you will have to be a true miracle man. I can not leave them here."

"And you won't," he assured her. "I know you're worried. But you've got to believe that I'll do everything I can to save them."

He reached over and took her hand, their fingertips entwined. He made sure their bodies did not meet. He wasn't about to screw this up. Iniki was the woman he searched for all his life. She was what he needed. He loved her. And he would wait until it was right, damn it all. He would wait, he promised himself as he drifted off.

CHAPTER SEVEN

Day 3 ~ Daytime on the path to Nouvella
"Only females may exercise options."

She was not able to sleep. The rocky floor and chilling dampness did not help. But it was the ache she felt for the man, who twenty-four hours previously she barely trusted, that kept her awake. Now, she believed, he would lay down his life not only for her but for the twins; for Madeline and Francois; perhaps even for Antoinette, if she would let him.

Periodically, Riley stirred and reached over to find her hand or arm, to make contact. Then he would fall into a restless sleep, tossing and murmuring words she could not understand.

The storm died out in the dark hour before dawn. The wind was fierce enough to do much damage to a small seaside village like Nouvella. What would she do if there were no place to leave them? She would never abandon them, not even for Riley. Though in truth, she did not believe he would suggest it. They became a family in the last two days, a unit striving for a common goal. Perhaps Antoinette was not yet used to them. But Iniki believed she would come to love all of them. Maybe even Riley.

When Riley awoke at dawn, she pretended to be asleep. She felt him kiss her forehead but she did not open her eyes. She wanted to watch this man she was falling in love with.

He moved on bare feet, padding around like a cat. First, he checked on the twins. Michel woke as soon as Riley approached.

"Sir?" the tired child said.

"Hush. It's too early. Go back to sleep." The boy did as told, exhaustion overcoming his natural curiosity.

Iniki watched as Riley ran his hand over the head of each child, then put more wood on the dying fire. Carefully avoiding the space around Antoinette, he moved to Francois. The old man was awake but so weak he could barely raise his head. Riley bent down to feel the man's forehead.

Francois would not recover without medication and her heart broke as she watched Riley give the old man water and aspirin. How, she asked herself would they get what they need for Francois? Was Riley indeed capable of achieving the impossible? She prayed he was.

The horses were at the entrance to the cave. She watched Riley pour water into a hole in the rocks for them and feed them some hay. Then he walked outside. When he disappeared from sight, she smiled. She knew so little about him except that he had strength of body and soul, that he was intelligent and cunning. Yet he was capable of gentleness and sensitivity. Was it enough to observe a man for such a short time and be assured of his character? Was she a fool to give her lips and her body to him willingly and to want him as she did? She did not know. But the feelings he engendered in her were full of love and hope. She observed him with the boys and she was certain he cared for them almost as much as she.

She waited an adequate amount of time for him to do whatever he needed in privacy. Then, she got up and followed, wearing nothing but his shirt which fell almost to her knees.

Sunshine blinded her for an instant but when her eyes adjusted they were rewarded with a glorious view. The ocean in the distance sparkled like diamonds. White sandy beaches lined the coastline as far as she could see. She calculated the distance to Nouvella. It would take less than half a day to descend the mountain. After today, there were three days left to reach wherever it was he was taking her. With no exact idea of the rendezvous point, she could not estimate if they were close to their destination. Regardless, today was lost. Their sole objective was medicine for Francois.

She walked several yards to the point where the path took a sharp right turn. The tropical storm dropped enough water on the mountain to create a small waterfall between the rocks. Riley stood naked under the rushing water. He turned and let it run down his back and through his hair. Only when he stepped out of the direct flow and wiped his eyes did he notice her standing ten feet away.

He raised his hand in welcome, despite his nudity. This time he made no attempt to hide himself. Instead he motioned for her to join him. She felt no shame as she studied his body. A few scars were noticeable but they were not as obvious as his muscular frame.

Unbuttoning her shirt, she slipped out of it and walked toward his waiting arms. She stopped just out of his reach.

"I have decided that it is foolish to wait any longer. We are not teenagers, Riley." She wanted to win the silly battle once and for all.

But he shook his head no. "We wait until we reach our destination. Or until we're relatively safe. God, you're lovely."

"No I do not want to wait. I dreamed that death is near." This was a lie but she decided a little drama was called for. "I want you to love me before I die."

"Damn, lady. You wait until I'm naked as a jay bird to make that announcement?"

"A jay bird is not naked. No more than any other bird."

"It's just an expression. Must we argue about this again?"

"No. Not as long as you agree."

He folded his arms across his chest. She noticed that as much as he insisted they refrain, his body did not hear those words.

"May I join you?" she asked and moved toward him before he could formulate an answer. She made sure he noticed her study of his body.

"Well, do I pass inspection?" he asked.

"It is possible you will do nicely if you drop this foolish . . ."

She didn't finish her sentence. He grabbed hold of her, pulling her against him and under the flowing water. His mouth was on hers and when he prodded at her lips with his tongue, she opened them.

He swiveled, pushing her against the rock wall. Water poured down on both of them. He leaned his full body weight against her and continued to kiss her, moving his hands until they found what they were looking for. Her breasts felt swollen in his grasp.

His mouth moved slowly down her neck, then further still, until he was able to take the tip of her breast into his mouth., She heard him moan and did the same, aware that her passion was as strong as his.

"Do not stop," she told him.

He did not. His tongue caressed her belly button, her flat abdomen, the crease at the joint of the torso and thigh. He ran his teeth over that spot.

She pushed down on his shoulders to let him know what she wanted.

The message was clear. On his knees, he reached the place she directed him to. Her hands guided and he did not resist. He placed one of her legs over his shoulder and she braced herself. She knew what was coming and dug her nails into his skin. While he delved deep with his tongue, she whispered his name.

"Yes. Yes, please," she told him.

He continued, this time his fingers finding entrance. Again she moaned and felt no shame. This was part of love.

When he stood up, she asked, "Again?"

His response was a warm laugh. "What do you think I am? The man of steel? I do that again and all my good intentions go down the drain."

"Forget good intentions. They are silly. You must be the first man to make love to me."

He blinked once and said, "The first? But you and Marcel Valois . . . "

" . . were not lovers."

"Why did you let me assume . . .?"

"Because you already thought so. At that point in our relationship, you would not have believed me."

He took her face in both his hands. "My God, lady. You're a bundle of surprises. You know I want you. Not only now but always. So I must protect you."

"Protect me?" Somehow she knew he was not referring to government soldiers.

"Yes," he answered. "When we're safely off the island, we can be together all we want. But, I can't get you pregnant here in the middle of nowhere."

She saw he was in earnest but still could not believe what she was hearing. "Of all things to worry about, Riley. We may be dead tomorrow and you are worried about pregnancy?"

He frowned as he said, "Yes, I am."

"And the way to protect me is not to make love?"

He continued to frown as he said, "Exactly. Unless you can lead me to a store that sells condoms. So don't try to change my mind."

"I intend to do everything in my power to accomplish just that."

"Of course. How could I not know that? Now will you stop debating long enough for one more . . ."

When they heard the voice calling them, they froze. Then Riley shoved her behind him and peeked through the curtain of water.

"Good Lord," she said.

"Which one of those little twerps was that?"

"Michel, of course," she answered. "Who else can it be? Is it safe to go out there?"

"Well, we can't stay here all day. You wait right where you are. I'll go see where the hell he is." He ducked out before she commented on his vocabulary.

The boy was no where to be seen but Riley could hear Michel calling around the bend in the path. He motioned for Iniki to come out, threw her some rags to dry herself and her shirt. Then he pounced on his jeans, sticking both wet legs into them at the same time.

His pants were barely zipped when Michel appeared. In his hand was the ancient rifle. A quick glance at Iniki told Riley they were both presentable. Then he started to breath again.

"I have taken care to check the horses and also Madeline and Antoinette," the boy reported. "Our food supply is not good, sir. We must find more food. However, water is no longer a problem."

"Well done," Riley responded. "How is Francois?"

"Mathieu is feeding him the last of the broth. He heated it on the fire. You seem short of breath, sir. Have you been running?"

"No, no. I'm fine. Mademoiselle and I have been discussing important, er, plans."

"What are our plans, sir?"

Riley couldn't help but laugh. "Our plans are to go down to the village and find food, medicine and Madeline's family."

"All of us, sir?"

"No, the older ones stay in the cave where they will be safe. Mademoiselle and I will go."

"What of Mathieu and me, sir? We can help you. Protect you. You instructed me to keep an eye on you at all times."

Riley's eyebrows popped up. "You were not just watching . . .?" He looked at Iniki in embarrassment.

"Watching what, sir?" The boy exuded pure innocence.

"Nothing. Forget it. Go get your brother and the two of you come wash in that overflow there."

The boy ran off instantly.

Riley resolved not to touch Iniki again unless Michel were locked up somewhere. "You don't think he saw us, do you?"

Iniki shrugged. "If he did, it is your fault. You told him to watch you?"

"Well, sort of. I didn't mean when I was with you."

"Riley, you have much to learn about children. What you say is taken quite literally. But do not worry. I will help you." She turned and headed back to the cave.

He watched her go, smiling at her backside as she walked. Then, her words sank in. "Hey, what did you mean? You'll help me with what?"

She didn't answer.

An hour later, they left the cave, armed with water, some bread and a flashlight and minus Yankee Doodle, who preferred the pampered life by the fire. Riley led the small group, followed by Iniki and the boys. Michel controlled the rifle, a fact that Mathieu was unhappy about. The two argued for several minutes before Riley shut them up with a short lecture on sharing.

"Soldiers don't argue with each other," he began. "They're united against the enemy. They always agree."

"Pardon, Monsieur," Mathieu said , ashamed of his behavior.

Michel showed no such remorse. "But you and Mademoiselle argue. Yet, you are united, are you not?"

"Not until we find a condom," Iniki muttered under her breath.

"What did you say, Mademoiselle?"

"Nothing," Riley answered quickly. He threw a disapproving glance at Iniki and cleared his throat before he went on. "Mademoiselle and I do not argue. We disagree. Then we discuss our differences calmly."

Michel hesitated before he spoke. "Pardon, sir, but I do not find that statement to be entirely true."

"You don't?" Riley used a stern voice to cover his embarrassment. "What is it that is not accurate?"

Michel had no difficulty answering. "When you and Mademoiselle do not agree, sir, you often use a . . .loud voice."

"Yes. That is true." What else could he say? The kid was too damn smart for his own good.

"I notice, sir, that you do not argue so much anymore," the boy added. "Is it that you have now become friends?"

"Close friends," Iniki clarified.

Again, Riley scowled at her. To the boy he said, "And when you care . . . a lot about your friends, you try not to fight."

"I understand, sir."

The kid understands all right, Riley thought. God knows what else he will ask.

But Michel had only one more question. "And after you discuss with Mademoiselle, who wins?"

Damn, Riley thought. "Uh, the most reasonable plan."

Michel took a long look at Iniki. "I think I understand now."

"Good." Riley wasn't sure he himself did. "Now the two of you may take turns holding the bat and the rifle. Remembering, of course, that under no conditions do you fire that d . . .that thing without my order."

"Yes, sir," they said in unison.

Michel traded the weapon for the bat. His brother thanked him and the two ran down the path. Riley noticed they exchanged a few unfriendly swipes but there were no further complaints. Thank the Lord, Riley thought. He hoped to hell he handled the situation right. If not, he was certain she would straighten him out,.

"You did well," she commented.

He nodded, proud of himself. "Of course, I've been a mentor to the men under my command."

She laughed and he knew criticism was coming.

"The boys are children, not soldiers. They look to you for comfort and security because they have no way to attain those things by themselves. They trust you unconditionally."

"I know that," he answered indignantly. Nothing will happen to those kids on his watch. Didn't she realize that?

"Do not become angry, Riley. You did fine and I commend you. But you must acknowledge the emotional attachment they have with you."

He sure in hell did. Already the thought of leaving them on the island made him sick to his stomach.

The path became more difficult to follow because of the storm damage. Deep gullies were everywhere. The possibility of mud slides or falling boulders increased as the temperature climbed. Their progress was slower than Riley anticipated. His leg ached with each step and as they approached the base of the mountain, the danger of being spotted by the military increased.

The helicopters came just after the four reached the tree line. Under the protection of foliage, he observed the enemy make several trips down to the village and then back up over the mountain. He studied each craft with binoculars. Several carried medical personnel, judging from their uniforms. Another was equipped with stretchers. Though Riley didn't have a clear view of the village, he assumed it suffered from the storm's fury.

He recognized the man in black who rode shotgun in one copter. It made a pass directly over the summit of the mountain they just descended. The man also used binoculars, scouring the ground below. Riley said a silent prayer of thanks they reached tree cover in time. The helicopter did not land in the village. Instead, it made another sweep of the mountain before heading west. Riley checked every aircraft after that but did not see the man again. God or Lady Luck or maybe both watched over them.

"Are they still searching?" Iniki asked.

Riley noticed the dark shadows under her eyes and hesitated to tell her the truth. But what good would it do to keep her in the dark? She was an equal partner in this venture. She must know.

"Yeah. That jerk with the black outfit was in one copter."

He noticed her chin lift up and out just a bit. Then she said, "We outwitted him thus far. Now is not the time to let our spirits drop."

He caressed her cheek with his fingers. "You got that right. We've got two objectives. To find Madeline's family and to arrive at the rendezvous point on time. No matter what else happens, we keep working toward those goals."

"But the man will not give up the pursuit, will he?"

Riley shook his head. "We'll meet up with him again, I'm sure."

She shivered. "I am frightened. I know he is just a man but . . ."

"He's one man with a big army to back him up. And, yes, he's pursuing you. On the other hand, you've got me. This spirit of death guy won't get you as long as I'm alive."

She finally smiled. "No," she whispered. "I do not believe he will. So what is our next step?"

"My guess is the village is badly damaged. Those copters were evacuating the injured. Looks like we're stuck right here until it gets dark. If we go now, they'll see us for sure."

The two sat down in a bed of pine needles. The boys napped a few yards away.

"We are losing time, are we not?"

"Too much time," he remarked.

"Certainly you may tell me now about our destination. You trust me, I know."

"I never didn't trust you. Just thought it was better if you didn't know. In case we're captured."

"If we are captured, it will not matter."

"No," he agreed. "I guess not. The rendezvous is at Black Point."

"Yes. I know it well. When I was a child, my parents would hire a boat and travel around the island. Black Point was so beautiful. Maman always wanted to beach the craft there and have a picnic. But Papa would not allow it. He insisted it was too dangerous."

"It is," he said. "The undertow is crazy but the surf is usually calm because of the outcropping of volcanic rock that juts into the water on either side of the beach."

"It is secluded enough for a rendezvous, I believe."

"I've never seen it but my intelligence packet says just that. Military boats patrol regularly because of the American ships off the coast. But their coverage isn't tight. At least that's the information I have."

"I remember the water being flat like an ice sheet."

He nodded. "Normally the water is calm enough for that kind of operation as long as you don't have to swim any distance. That might not be the case now because the storm is out to sea. Regardless, the Seals will be there every night at midnight for four more nights."

"The Seals?"

"Navy Seals," he explained. "Trained to rescue people at sea.."

"Is that your job?" She whispered in a conspiratorial tone.

"No," he whispered back. Then in a normal voice, he said, "I do what you see me do."

"Rescue people?"

"Well, yeah." Then he shrugged. "Sometimes, other things."

"Like what?"

He wanted to explain, to show he kept nothing from her. But then, he thought, there'll be time for all that later. He answered her question with a kiss.

"The boys will see us," she warned.

"So what else is new? I've got the feeling they see a lot more than we know. Every time I turn around, one of them is behind me."

They remained quiet for moment before Riley summoned up the courage to make a request. He didn't know how she would react.

"Will you tell me about you and Marcel Valois?"

She hesitated before answering. "Why is that important?"

He was ready with an answer. And this time he had no misgiving about being truthful. "Because I love you. Because it's rare to meet a beautiful woman who has not had a sexual relationship. Because I believe you did love him at one time."

She smiled. "No one man has touched me where your lips and hands have been."

"Not even Valois?"

She shook her head and the brightness in her seemed to fade. "Marcel was a pragmatic man. He knew what he needed to run the rebel cell and accomplish his mission. Once he understood that I was willing to supply him with money, he had no reason to pursue me. There were plenty of women for that. I knew that. He made no attempt to hide it. A different one each night. I did fall in love with his zeal to fight for his country. I continue to respect that today. But I could not give myself to him."

"Then he did want you as a lover?"

"Yes. For one night. Perhaps two. Then there would be someone else. His true love was the role he played in the rebellion. No woman could compete with that."

"He hurt you?" He could see it in her eyes.

"Yes, I suppose. I vowed I would never allow a man to love me without some kind of commitment. Then you come along and I am doing exactly that."

"No, love. There's no way in hell I'm going to walk away from you, ever. That is, if you want me."

"Do you have any doubts about that?" she responded.

He shook his head and kissed her hard.

"Good," she confided. "Now, even if I die before we make love, I will be fulfilled."

"Dammit, stop saying that. No one is going to die. Do you hear me? I'm not going to let that happen."

She leaned closer to him.

"Please trust me, Iniki. Nothing will happen to any of us."

"I believe you. Now hold me tight."

As he complied with her wishes, he explained the rest of the plan.

"If we don't hitch up with the Seals by the sixth night, we'll be on our own. That was the largest window of opportunity they could give me. The political implications are not advantageous for the U.S. or NATO if this operation is made public.

"Will we make it, Riley?"

"Of course." He wanted to believe it was easy as it sounded. There was a damn good possibility he could get her to Black Point in time. But a number of vital tasks must be accomplished first. He must find medication for Francois and locate a safe place to leave the boys and elders. Only after that was achieved would he head for Black Point.

Attaining Iniki's freedom was his only official mission. But somehow each of the others, even Antoinette, wormed their way into his heart. He cared about them, his handful of followers. They were his responsibility. He willingly accepted that. No matter how difficult it would be to take them all to Black Point, he knew he would never leave them in danger.

Damn, he thought. How the hell am I going to pull this one off?

The general spent the entire afternoon in the helicopter covering most of the passes through the mountains in the central portion of the range. Military resources were occupied with transporting the dead and injured to the capital city. His available manpower to hunt for the fugitives was severely reduced.

The American's objective puzzled him. The general knew an American was leading the woman and child out of the country. There was only one logical area where they could be safely picked up by American ships offshore. Yet, they seemed not to be heading in that direction. Unless the helicopters missed them.

After many hours, the general ordered whatever spare aircraft he could find to go back to the eastern sector and search again. With limited air power, he could do no more at the moment.

"Where do you wish to be dropped off, sir?"

"Take me to the city. Sooner or later, they will reappear. I want every possible sighting reported to me immediately. No matter how insignificant."

They waited until dusk before inching the rest of the way down to Nouvella. The military garrison stood above the shore line a short distance outside the village. The storm battered the few buildings in the enclosure but sandbags prevented significant flooding.

The village was a different story. Clustered along the fringe of white beach, the homes were in ruins. Palm trees fell on flimsy beach shacks, crushing them to ruins. What the wind did not destroy, the ocean did. Erosion scarred the sand. Debris of every sort lay splattered about.

Iniki fought the urge to scream out at nature for finishing the carnage Simone started. Instead, she closed her eyes, blinking out the devastation. Then shoving grief aside, she pushed back her shoulders and faced the others. She would continue to give hope to the twins as long as she lived. Never would she abandon them. And, if Riley thought differently, he had a surprise coming.

"There are few people left," she said. "But the garrison is intact. We will find the pharmacy and get what we need. Right?" She addressed the question to Riley, aware the boys were listening.

"Absolutely," he answered. "If not, we use Plan B."

"Plan B? You have an option?"

"Will it make you feel better if I say yes?"

"Yes."

"Then I have a Plan B."

She beamed a smile to him, grateful for his attempt at humor.

When full darkness descended, they crept into what was left of the village. The place was deserted, save for an old man or woman here and there. Iniki explained they were in need of shelter and supplies and were looking for the Duvalier family. Madeline's people were known to the survivors but none could remember seeing them after the storm. Following directions, Riley found the place where the family lived. Nothing was left of it except for three wooden stakes sticking out of the sand.

"Dammit," Riley muttered just loud enough for Iniki to hear.

"*Mon Dieu*," Michel exclaimed, a look of disbelief on his face. The other boy said nothing but Iniki read fear in his expression.

She said a silent prayer. Because the hut sat on the edge of the beach, she knew the storm surge wiped away any trace of it. Both boys moved close to her and she grasped them tightly as if her arms alone would protect them from misfortune. Any hope of a new home for Madeline and Francois was washed out to sea. What happened to the family was too sad to speculate.

A very old man, pathetically thin, walked toward them. In French, Iniki inquired about the family. The man nodded his head and responded. Before he went on his way, Iniki took out a piece of bread from the store in her pocket and gave it to the man.

"He says the house washed away in the storm. He thinks the old folks were in it but he is not certain. The army evacuated the villagers to the city. He does not know if any of the family survived, but if they did they have been taken already."

"What about him?"Riley questioned. "He looks like he's not too well."

"Yes," she agreed. "The poor man lost his home and his wife. But he hides from the military. He will not go with them. He will die here on the beach if necessary."

"These people are starving. Instead of clearing out the population, why doesn't the government help to rebuild these miserable huts?"

She recognized the angry frustration in his words. It matched her own. "Simone's plan is to keep the people poor enough so that they can not rise up against him. This is just one more village he will not have to worry about."

She turned to the boys who heard the conversation. "We will tell Madeline that her family may have been evacuated to a hospital," Iniki suggested. "There is no proof they died in the storm. They may have been rescued."

"That's right," Riley confirmed. "We will not mention to Madeline what the old man said. Is that a plan?"

They nodded solemnly. "Does this mean we will not live here in the village?" Mathieu asked, his eyes focused on Riley.

"There's no village left to live in," he answered. "But we'll find a safe place. I promise you."

"I believe you, sir. It is as Piglet said, 'It is hard to be brave when you are a Very Small Animal.'"

"Piglet?"

"Yes," Mathieu clarified. "From *Winnie The Pooh* by A.A. Milne."

"Oh, I see. Well, you and your brother are extremely brave. In fact, braver than some of the men I have worked with. You make me very proud."

"Thank you, sir," the boy responded, smiling for the third time in their acquaintance. "It is you who gives me strength to be brave, sir."

Riley pulled the boy close and hugged him. "Don't worry, pal," he whispered. "We'll find a way."

The boy wrapped his arms around Riley's waist.

Iniki made no move to interrupt them. Did Riley understand that Mathieu was admitting he was afraid? The child seldom confided his feelings to anyone. In fact, she realized, the dialog between him and Riley was one of the few times Mathieu expressed emotion since his parents died.

Her eyes focused on Riley. As if he could feel her stare, he returned her steady gaze. Plan B better be ready, she thought.

The next order of business was medication and food. Those items they would find in the military garrison. Riley led them around the village outskirts and back to the mountain directly above the compound.

"Stay right here," he ordered. "I want to have a look around. Don't move." They nodded in unison. Riley prayed they would do as he asked. But his short association with Iniki told him he was foolish to expect it.

A quick surveillance of the area revealed little security, if any. After all, the villagers posed no threat. Some of the soldiers must have been evacuated since only a handful were in evidence. As far as he could determine, only one armed sentry stood at the front gate. The rear perimeter was unprotected.

He returned to his charges and was both relieved and suspicious that they sat exactly where he left them.

"My brother and I did not move, sir, as you ordered," Michel informed Riley, giving Iniki a sideways glance.

Riley knew there was a hidden message somewhere in those words. With Michel, there always was. "I believe you, of course. And you, Mademoiselle? Did you also follow my directions?"

"I did not," she confessed. "However, I investigated the back buildings to locate the pharmacy. I returned quickly."

"Yes. That is true, sir," Mathieu confirmed.

"I'm sure it is. Mademoiselle is a truthful person."

"I thought it would be easier if I gave you some help in the surveillance," she explained.

Michel chose that moment to say, "This is what you referred to when you said earlier that soldiers may disagree? They do not argue and the best plan wins?"

"Uh . . .yeah," Riley answered, trying to think of a good way to end the conversation without giving Iniki a reason to scold him. But he couldn't resist it. "However, some soldiers make a habit of disobeying."

Iniki interrupted with, "I was merely exercising an option."

"What is this option?" Michel asked.

"Choices," Riley explained, raising one eyebrow. "You don't have to worry about it, son. Only females may exercise options. Men don't have that opportunity."

"Is that fair, sir?"

"It all depends." Riley knew Michel would continue the discussion on and on if he could. Some of his questions were hell to answer.

"It depends on what, sir?" Another question.

"On how much you care about the female."

Michel thought for only a moment. "Yes. I understand. Females may decide to exercise an option regardless of orders."

"This discussion is over," Iniki insisted.

"You hit the nail on the head, Michel."

"I assume that indicates I am correct, sir?"

"Undeniably, my boy."

"That is enough," Iniki exclaimed. "Riley, do you wish to know where the pharmacy is located?"

"Of course." He enjoyed how Michel's questions annoyed her.

"It is directly in front of us."

Riley included all of them in the making of the plan. As reluctant as he was to expose the boys to danger, he knew leaving them to their own devises would be worse. Besides he needed every hand available. When they found what they needed, he intended to take as much as he could carry. The backpack that was normally Yankee Doodle's home would come in real handy.

He demonstrated how to rub dirt on their skin to eliminate reflection of light. Michel thought the idea was splendid and was covered in no time. He helped his brother to finish up and offered to assist Iniki. She politely refused and instructed him to quiet down. The boy obeyed. But Riley noticed that Michel couldn't stand still for very long. He bounced on the balls of his feet and swung his arms back and forth, waiting for the adventure to begin.

Riley studied both boys. Michel burst with energy and enthusiasm. Mathieu sat motionless on the ground, his arms wrapped around his bent legs. These kids deserve so much, Riley decided. If he ever had children, he wanted them to be just like these two.

When they were ready, Riley led them down to the building Iniki identified as the pharmacy. No guards stood on duty. The place was small, a one room cement structure with two barred windows on either side. It was tucked behind other buildings, hiding it well from the central courtyard.

They made their way around to one side where Riley signaled to crouch down and wait. He alone approached the door, secured with a padlock. Taking a small tool from his pocket, he fiddled with the lock until it opened. He hoped every obstacle they met would as easy.

The others joined him and together they entered through the dark doorway. Once inside, Riley held the small flashlight so that it did not shine through the windows. As they searched, he pointed to whatever he thought they needed while Iniki and the boys packed it up. He intended to be in and out in five minutes. None of them uttered a single word.

Penicillin and antibiotics were found in a locked glass cabinet. Riley had no choice but to break the glass with his elbow. The falling glass made noise but it was worth it. He pointed to the medication and some morphine and Iniki grabbed them. Then he found aspirin, bandages and ointments. He did not bypass a supply of condoms and stuffed one box in his pocket without the others noticing, he hoped. There was no food in the place and Riley didn't want to stay any longer.

Flipping off the flashlight, he led the group back to the exit. It was then that a soldier appeared in the open doorway. Most of his body was hidden by the glare of his flashlight. Riley and Iniki were behind the open door. But the boys were directly in the path of the flashlight beam. Both froze as if they had turned into ice.

The soldier appeared to be confused. He did not expect to encounter two frightened boys. He sighed in relief, then reached for the switch on the wall. A dusty ceiling fixture blanketed the room in a dull orange glow. Then, it flicked off. Riley took advantage of the distraction and smashed the open door into the soldier, who fell to the floor in a clatter of noise.

"That'll bring someone. Come on, let's move," Riley instructed. Grabbing the knapsack he reached out to pull Mathieu along. "Stick close to the building and follow me," he shouted. "Iniki, take Michel."

He knew he had to chance it now or they would be lost. The sound of voices and thumping of boots became louder. Running as fast as he could, he no longer cared if they made noise. As the first shots rang out, they rounded the back corner of the building. Riley didn't stop, urging Mathieu on, never letting go of his hand. Whistles began blowing in the compound below him as he reached the trees.

Still he continued on. He led the boy up through the trees and beyond. He had to put distance between them and the garrison. Based on their quick response, there were more soldiers than he anticipated. Added to that, he had no idea of their fighting capability. The last thing he wanted was to be caught in the beacon of a helicopter.

He pushed ahead until he noticed Iniki dropping behind. They were well above the compound. He didn't know if they were being followed. Regardless, he ordered a five minute rest to catch their breath.

"Good," Iniki blurted out between gasps. "I do not know who was pulling whom back there."

"Pardon, sir," Michel interrupted.

"Just a minute, Michel."

"But, sir!"

Riley wished his breathing would settle down as well. He was getting too old for this. Only the boys appeared able to climb higher up the mountain.

"Monsieur," Michel said and poked Riley in the side with his rifle.

"For God's sake, what is it?" Riley spouted.

"They are coming, sir. You see the lights through the trees?"

He was right, of course. They were coming much to close for comfort. They would search farther and farther up the mountain . He did not want to lead them to the cave. The trail had to go dead in this area.

"We need to find somewhere to hide," he explained. "I want them to lose the scent right here."

"There." Mathieu pointed to a natural outcrop of rocks which formed a hollow roundish area.

Where it would normally be dry, the storm deposited plentiful water. The natural pool was about ten feet wide and several feet deep.

"Good eyes, son. You may have just solved the problem."

"I hope so," the boy responded.

Riley hid the guns and medications high up in a tree. Then, he climbed over the rocks and into the water. He invited the rest to do the same, instructing them to squat down so that only their heads were above the surface.

"There may be snakes in here, sir. They hide in the rocks."

"Thank you, Michel," Riley groaned. "We needed to be reminded of that."

"You are welcome, sir."

Iniki added, "It is better to die of a snake's venom than to be taken by Simone."

"Wow! You guys are a barrel of fun to be with on a mission," Riley said, trying to be upbeat.

"That is an odd expression, sir," Michel commented. "Please explain what it means."

"Not right now, Michel. The flashlights are coming damn close."

"Damn close," Michel agreed.

"Dear God," Iniki muttered.

CHAPTER EIGHT

Day 3 ~ Nouvella
"Didn't your mother teach you not to hit girls?"

Then soldiers trekked a quarter of a mile up the mountain and they were tired. Their enthusiasm for finding a couple of kids hooked on drugs was drained by long hours they put in during the hurricane and cleanup. They searched the woods halfheartedly, talking among themselves in French.

"What are they saying?" Riley whispered. "Do they know who they're looking for?"

Iniki shook her head. "I do not believe so. Not them. They complain they are overworked and underpaid."

"What do you mean 'not them'?"

"The commandant, whoever he is, insists they find us. He mentioned my name to these soldiers."

"Dammit! Your name?"

She ignored the curse. They were literally up to their ears in trouble. This was not the time. Besides, it wouldn't stop him. He was who he was and she rather liked him that way.

She continued the translation. "The helicopters that followed us across the flats have reported in. They know we are in the vicinity. The commandant concluded we broke into the pharmacy because of what we took. Drug dealers do not sell penicillin and bandages.,"

"True enough," Riley muttered. "I should have foreseen that."

"How could you know?"

"I'm paid to know. Go on. What else?"

She went on, "His second in command tells him that the soldier you disabled in the pharmacy reported he saw only two boys. They know about the twins."

"How does that connect to you?"

"It does not, at least not yet. Except this commandant is not a foolish man like some of the soldiers. He wants to find me because he know it will further his career."

"He said that?"

"Yes. The other officer keeps mentioning that the men are weary. He thinks the boys could have stolen the medications to sell to the villagers."

"Who's winning the argument?"

"The commandant. But he can not afford to leave the garrison unprotected. After this area is searched, they will go back."

"Terrific," he whispered. "Be ready for anything. If they come near here, I handle the heroics, understand? You take care of the boys."

"Yes, sir," she quipped as if they were on a Sunday outing. In her heart, she knew they were in grave peril. Except for the knife and the gun, Riley had no defense against so many. She prayed the soldiers would leave soon.

The men spread out in a fan pattern searching behind and under every bush. They followed orders but when the officers' backs were turned, they took it easy, not straining themselves. Their disinterest proved lucky for Riley's gang as the search moved closer to the rock pool.

"Be prepared to duck beneath the surface."

"For how long, sir?" Michel quietly asked the obvious question.

"Until you can't any more. Whatever you do, do it silently. No noise. Got it?"

The three nodded. The boys huddled close to Iniki and she took them into her arms. Together they waited as the soldiers came near.

When one of them walked up to the opposite end of the pool, put his hands on the rock wall and looked into the water, Riley used his arm to push the other three down. They all disappeared beneath the surface without a sound.

Iniki suspected Riley was trained to hold his breath for longer periods of time but he wouldn't stay down long. She was right. She felt him rise slowly until he was submerged to just below eye level. She did the same. She was in time to see the soldier scooping water into his hands to drink. In order to do that, he put down the flashlight. Her breath caught in her throat when she realized they might be caught in the beam of light. Instead the torch slipped into a crevice, the light shining up to the sky. The soldier was on the other side of the pool and the night was moonless. He failed to see the four refugees. The boys came up for air without a ripple. They waited in place while their enemy took another drink.

If he invites his comrades to share the wealth, they were lost, Iniki told herself. The steely look in Riley's eyes meant he had the same worry.

Again he applied gentle pressure and again they slid beneath the surface. She knew they could not hold their breath much longer. When the twins rose for air, she followed. No one stood at the pool.

"I think they were ordered to retreat." Riley whispered.

Iniki let out a sigh of relief. She rubbed the backs of the shivering boys. When the commanding officer spoke, she again translated. "They will leave one man here. The officer believes we are still in the area."

Four pairs of eyes watched in silence as the lone soldier saluted and stood at attention just long enough for the platoon to retreat. Then he put down his rifle and sat down against a tree, pulling his hat over his eyes.

Riley signaled them to remain where they were as he climbed out of the pool. He moved slowly and carefully and Iniki realized he did this work may times. Once more, the thought occurred that he moved like a wild cat He circled around the guard. Holding a large rock, Riley crept up on his victim. Standing beside him, Riley tapped the man's shoulder, scaring the guard half to death. The man strained to waken, but too late. Riley used the rock to put him back to sleep.

The boys leapt from the pool at Riley's wave and Iniki followed their lead. Their watery hangout left them cold and uncomfortable. But it served them well, thought Iniki. They were still alive.

"Is he dead, sir?" Michel was interested in the details as he examined the rock used on the soldier's head.

"Just knocked out. There was no need to kill him. He'll be out for a while but we've given away our location. When they find him, they'll know we're headed up the mountain."

"We still have two hours of walking to reach the cave," Iniki said. "Will they search that far?"

Riley shrugged. "I don't know but I can't take that chance. We'll have to find somewhere else to hide."

Iniki disagreed. "We can not move Francois yet. Not until he has more medicine. And he needs time for it to work."

"Then we start for the cave now and medicate him. The boys need to rest. You and I will come back down tonight for food. It's a big risk but one we have to take. Tomorrow morning we leave the cave. If we stay longer, we'll be caught for sure." He looked at his watch. "It's not yet midnight. We have time to return. Then when Francois has a couple of doses of penicillin, we clear out."

"To go where?" She was not convinced.

"I wish I knew," he stated.

They made the cave in less than two hours. Riley felt guilty for pushing so hard but time was running out; time to avoid the military and time to make the rendezvous. Once back in the warmth of the cave, Iniki saw to the boys, getting them into dry clothing and then to sleep.

Riley lectured the twins the entire way up the mountain on how they will be responsible for the elderly while Riley and Iniki go back down for food. After he expounded for some time on their responsibility, Michel summed it up with one sentence.

"In other words, sir, you do not wish that we do anything that we have been told not to do."

"Correct. I do not wish you to leave the cave unless you feel you are in danger. I do not wish for you to leave the cave, period. And, if there is something you think of, that I have not mentioned, don't do that either. Until you check with me first."

"It seems we are to do nothing," the boy summed up.

"Now you've got it." Riley wondered what he forgot to say. With this kid, what he didn't say was just as important as what he did.

"Did I leave anything out?" he asked Iniki.

"It is of no consequence. If Michel gets an idea in his head, he acts on it. Mathieu goes along only to protect his brother."

"Good God. We're doomed, you know," Riley whispered.

He guessed on the dose of penicillin for Francois, hoping his doctoring didn't kill the poor man. Then, refilling the water jug, they left. Iniki wiped a tear from her cheeks as they made their way down the mountain one more time.

"What is it, Iniki? Are you ill?"

She sighed, hating herself for showing weakness. "No. I fear we may never see them again. Is this a fool's errand that can only lead to trouble?"

He pulled her to a stop, cupped his hands around her face and laughed. "This is funny, you know."

Sorrow turned to irritation. "What is funny?"

"You. You're funny. You're the one who refused to move from your home unless I agreed to take along your whole tribe. And you were right. I admit it. They would die and I would be responsible. You're the one who insisted on the side trip to Nouvella. And if we hadn't done exactly that, we wouldn't have found Antoinette's hut and the wagon. We would be caught unprotected in the storm. You convinced me to drag Antoinette along. Again, a smart idea since she led us to the cave. Above all, it's your fault that I care for you and the boys more than I thought possible. You're the cause of this situation and I'm not sorry a bit. Yet, you're crying and doubting we'll make it. Do you really think I will let anything happen to any of you?"

"I will not leave them in Nouvella, Riley. I will not leave them on this island." She was angry now at herself and Riley. Better to let him know now, she decided, before they went any farther.

"I won't leave them either," he said calmly.

"What?"

"Wherever we end up, they come along. All of them. And God help us."

He surprised her once again. "You are a good man, Riley. Thank you."

"I try to please, lady. If dragging that bunch to Black Point will make you smile again, then that's what I'll do. Besides, I won't trust those kids to anyone else to bring up and I've gotten attached to Madeline and Francois. Antoinette is another story but we seemed to have reached a truce, so who knows?"

"Will we make it?" She knew he had no answer.

"We can only try our best, lady," he answered. "And there's no place I'd rather be than with you, wherever we end up."

She was a lucky woman, she told herself. Despite their predicament, she was thankful she met this man.

"So no more crying," he ordered.

She grabbed the front of his shirt. "Do not tell me not to cry. I shall cry whenever I want."

He laughed. "Sorry, I lost my head."

"Kiss me." She wrapped her arms around his neck.

"Yes, Ma'am. Always happy to comply with your request." But when one kiss led to another and another, he pulled away. "Come on. We have too much to do, dammit."

She let the curse word pass. How could she reprimand him for saying aloud what she herself thought.

They spoke little on the journey to the village, avoiding the area of the rock pool. Riley gave the garrison a wide berth, entering the village from the opposite end.

"Okay. We're here. Where do we get food?" Riley asked. "You know these villages, don't you?"

"Somewhat. Antoinette mentioned a place in the village center where the farmers would come from around the area and sell their produce. That will not happen tonight, I am sure."

"Where else can we look, then?"

She chewed on her bottom lip in nervousness. "In the garrison, perhaps. Their stores are usually well supplied. We can not take from the few villagers that are left."

"I do not intend to. I was hoping for some sort of market to break into."

"Riley, I think the only place is the garrison. Even the people here have to get some supplies there."

"Okay. But we'll approach from the beach side. Less chance of meeting soldiers there."

They skirted the edge of the deserted village and walked along the sand, dashing from one broken-down hut to the next. Near the last of the ruined structures Riley motioned for them to rest.

They sprawled out on the sand. Riley enjoyed wanting this woman. The wanting was just as exhilarating as the having will be, he thought. More than he ever imagined, he reveled in this new found love. They rested on the sand looking up at the cloudy sky.

"Would it not be wonderful if we were carefree like lovers should be?" she whispered. "Make love without fear of certain death?"

"We will. Not long now."

"I want to play in the ocean with you," she went on. "Naked as jay birds."

"Jay birds aren't naked," he corrected.

147

"I will swim away from you and make you capture me. I will squirm out of your grasp like a slippery eel and you will have to catch me once more."

"Stop. Please stop. You're making me crazy."

"That was the intended response."

"It worked."

"Riley, . . . " She rolled on her side facing him and put her hand on his chest.

"Oh hell," he murmured as he pulled her on top of him. He ran his hands down her back. "You are bad, lady."

"Good. Another intended response." She pushed her hips into his and felt how much he wanted her. He grabbed her long hair in one hand and forced her to kiss him, while he placed his other hand on her buttocks and thigh. He almost abandoned all reason when he heard it.

"Shush," he whispered, releasing his grip. "Did you hear that?"

"No. I hear nothing. What was it?"

"No idea. Came from that direction." He pointed to the remains of a nearby hut on the beach.

It was badly damaged. Riley reckoned the water swept over it causing it to collapse onto itself.

He sprung to his feet and pulled her up beside him. "Let's see what it is."

"What do we do when we find it? We can not call attention to ourselves."

"No. But it may be an injured animal in need of help. We can try."

They approached the hut, listening carefully. There were no further sounds since the initial faint cry he heard. Riley pulled away some fronds of a coconut tree that covered the wall. The quiet murmuring came again.

"Whatever it is, it's alive," he commented. "Help me dig out this wall."

They worked for a few minutes pulling away debris as quietly as they could. No more sounds came from within. When a small opening was cleared, he squeezed through and squatted under the remaining refuse. Only then did he use his flashlight. What the beam revealed, he couldn't believe.

"*Mon Dieu*," was his only comment.

"What is it?" Iniki whispered from outside. "You sound like Michel."

He laughed. "I thought I would say it for him."

"Why? What is it you see?"

"Hold on. I'll show you." He crawled on his stomach to reach his objective. Iniki heard a gurgle come from the hole. Suddenly, Riley held up an object about two feet long, wrapped in a wet blanket.

She grabbed hold and knew immediately what they found. It smelled awful and was soaking wet, but seemed uninjured.

"*Mon Dieu*," she repeated.

A baby smiled up at her, thumb in mouth.

"Riley, it is a girl. About nine months, I would guess."

"Is she okay?" he asked, realizing the child's condition was important to him.

"She is wet and dirty but appears to be fine."

Thank God, he said silently. He rummaged around in the ruins, gathering certain objects he thought they could use. When he retrieved all that was worthwhile, he climbed out.

"*Petit ange*," Iniki cooed.

"In English, please." He was amazed the tiny creature survived. She was a hardy little thing, he concluded. All arms and legs.

"Little angel," Iniki translated.

"Angel, yes," he confirmed. When he touched one tiny hand with his finger, the child grasped onto it and tried to bring it to her mouth. "Hey, look at this. She's got my finger. Won't let go. How do you like that?" In that moment he knew his heart was captured one more time. "Another to add to the collection."

"What collection?"

"Well,"he began, almost indignant at her inability to understand. "The baby's parents are both in there. Drowned. She was in a cradle set up high. Somehow she survived. Can we leave her here to die?"

"Oh, the poor little one."

"Hey," he said. "We found her. That was good luck. Obviously no one is looking for her."

"We will take her with us?"

"Of course," Riley stated. "Do you think I want to leave her here? We can't turn her over to the authorities. Of course, I won't leave her. She'll starve to death if typhoid doesn't get her first."

"Then, we need milk," she told him. "And food."

"How about coconut milk? There's plenty on the beach and I found some stuff in there. Some clothes and a bottle. Pretty dirty but it'll do after it's washed in the ocean. She's wet though. And these clothes are wet too. We need to wrap her in something dry."

He took off his shirt and handed it to Iniki. "Here. This will do for now. Until we break into the garrison."

"With her?"

"We can't leave her here, can we?"

"No . . . ."

"Ah. Agreement at last. Lucky for us she's too young to remember her first excursion with her new parents was breaking and entering."

Iniki seemed surprised. "Her new parents?"

"Of course. She lost the ones she had. We will take care of her." Why in the world did Iniki look so dumbfounded?

He tore off a square of his shirt. Twisting the material in the middle, he made a funnel of sorts. Then he grabbed a coconut, opened it with his knife and filled the makeshift bottle with milk. The baby accepted it with no problem.

"You amaze me, Riley."

"Care of Babies in the Field 101," he quipped. "Required course for every young operative."

"You are joking."

"Not really. This trick was taught to me if I needed to feed a wounded comrade. Works for babies as well."

"She must be hungry, Riley. We need to find food."

"Here. Put some coconuts in the knapsack. When we are away from here, I'll mash together some coconut meat and milk. That should hold her for a while. Hand her to me."

He took the baby and cradled her in his arms, rocking back and forth. Iniki packed up the baby things and they were ready to head for the garrison.

Army Stores was not difficult to locate. An armed guard stood in front. Unlike his comrade on the mountain, this one was wide awake. Riley did recon while Iniki stayed out of sight.

His investigation uncovered a way to bypass the guard. To try to attack him would be foolhardy. Riley intended to complete the burglary undetected. The two-storied building sported open windows on the second floor. With the assistance of a sturdy drainpipe, gaining entry was a snap.

He found what he needed. Bread, fruit, nuts and biscuits were abundant. He packed salted fish and dry sausages into the knapsack and a pillowcase he found. On the first floor, he dared a search, even with the sentry outside. An adequate supply of army shirts and a blanket were things he didn't expect to find. He grabbed them..

He was about to make his exit when he heard noises outside. Changing of the guard, he hoped.

He made his way up to the second floor and climbed out the window, holding on to the drainpipe with one hand and the pillowcase with the other. He told himself he would make an excellent second story man.

Suddenly he smelled smoke. The source of the odor nearly caused him to drop the pillowcase. A soldier, probably the one who was on duty before, relaxed on the side of the building puffing on a cigarette. The voices Riley heard had been one man relieving another.

Not a hell of a lot of options, he told himself. Either he tried to jump the guy, which meant a drop of about twenty-five feet or he remained where he was, like a cat up a tree, until the soldier went away. Riley decided on the second course of action, not because he was reluctant to fall the whole way down. His concern was that he not be discovered.

The commandant of the garrison was alerted about Iniki already. If one of his men were found injured, the missing food would be noticed. That would bring out the entire platoon up the mountain. The commandant was no dummy. Common sense would tell him there was no where else to hide but on the mountain. The cave would be found twice as fast.

So he waited, as the soldier enjoyed every last puff. Riley's concern was that other men would come around the corner of the building. From that angle, they would not miss Riley dangling there.

A few minutes later, the soldier crushed out the butt and moved along, crossing the compound and not turning back.

"About damn time," Riley told himself as the man disappeared from view.

Iniki was asleep with the baby cradled against her chest when he returned. Gently Riley shook her awake, trying not to disturb the infant.

"Oh," she whispered. "I must have dozed off."

"Come on. We need to get out of here. The longer we stay the more danger we put ourselves in."

"Did you find food?"

Riley was proud of himself. "Sure did. And clean clothes and a blanket for the baby."

"Good. She will need so many things."

They left the way they came, along the beach, running from one spot to another to avoid being spotted. They were about to head up the path when Iniki saw laundry thrown over some rocks to dry.

"Wait," she said and stood her ground. "Those sheets and towels will be perfect for diapers."

Riley shook his head. "No. We've been lucky so far. I'm not taking any more chances."

"It is only a short distance to those rocks," she whispered. "Stay here with the baby. I will go."

"No." He reached out to stop her with his one free arm but she took off too fast. He didn't dare to raise his voice as she ran down the path, turning off to reach the laundry. Riley watched from the trees as she gathered up a few towels and a sheet. The white material shown clearly in the dark night.

Riley knew this was a dumb move. He started toward her intending to drag her away if need be. But the dark figure creeping up on her stopped Riley dead in his tracks. Before he could warn her, a flashlight illuminated her face. She turned toward the light, saying nothing. Riley watched as she squared her shoulders and straightened her posture. She plans to talk her way out of this, Riley thought.

But the soldier wasn't stupid. He blew his whistle and spoke to her in French. Riley couldn't hear the conversation but when she dropped the laundry and put up her arms, he understood the gist of it. The soldier spun her around while taking hold of one arm. The appendage was twisted behind her but she made no sound.

Soldiers came running. Riley knew he had no chance against so many especially with a baby in one arm. He watched as the military encircled her, the first soldier binding both her hands behind her back while another fondled her dark hair. She held herself straight and answered their questions. Riley was sure she was telling them some farfetched story but he knew it was futile. The men were briefed and ready for her. No more questions were asked. With one soldier on each side, she was pulled roughly toward the garrison entrance. Her eyes stared straight ahead. Not once did she look in Riley's direction.

"You're something else, lady," he said to himself. Then he looked down at the sleeping baby. "Hope you were sent to us for luck, Angel. Because your second field trip with me will be a more serious felony than the first."

Slipping through the woods, he traced the progress of the soldiers as they led her into a building at the center of the compound. Riley assumed it was the commandant's office. The same man who mentioned her name earlier near the rock pool. He would have no trouble figuring out her identity.

Riley's training came in handy. The little person he carried did tend to complicate matters. When he returned to the states, he planned to recommend that all operatives pass a course on how to accomplish a mission while holding a baby in one hand and coconuts in the other.

He recognized the man crossing the compound as the commandant. The man adjusted his uniform before entering the building where Iniki was imprisoned.

Time to act, Riley determined. In a concealed spot above the garrison, he transferred the coconuts to the bottom of the pillowcase and put everything else on top. The baby would travel in the knapsack on his back. When the baby fussed, he found a biscuit in the pillowcase and handed it to her. Her tiny fingers reached for it and stuffed it into her mouth. For the moment at least, she was content.

With his gun in one hand, pillowcase in the other and baby on his back, he was ready to get the job done.

"Okay, Angel," he said softly. "Let's do it."

He took off down the slope and into the compound, flitting from one building to another. He managed to come up behind the commandant's office. The back door was locked but unguarded. It presented no particular problem.

"You see, Angel," Riley instructed in a low whisper. "This is how you get into a locked building in two seconds flat. When you're a little older, I'll teach you," he whispered. "Better if you don't tell your mom, though."

Iniki refused to cry out in pain. Her helplessness made her hate the man towering above her that much more. The commandant made sure he took advantage of a female who could not fight back. She was tied into a chair with rope that cut into her wrists when she struggled. Her feet were tied, one to each chair leg; after she gave one soldier a hard kick to the groin when he tried to touch her.

Luckily the second in command was present and stopped the men from entertaining ideas of having some fun. He immediately called for the commandant who was smarter and crueler than any of the men.

He slapped her hard across the face before he addressed her. The attack took her by surprise but she did not make a sound. The commandant was not pleased with her fortitude. He whacked her again but she did not whimper.

"Your name?" he requested.

She did not answer and prepared herself for another blow.

It did not come. Instead the man laughed. "You do not have to speak, Miss Beaumont. Iniki Beaumont. I know who you are. And let me assure you that your value to me is limited. Once I notify the general, you need not be kept alive longer than necessary. Perhaps for an hour or two in my quarters. We shall see how good you are to me."

She stared up at him in hatred.

"You will be begging for mercy in a short while, my dear." He raised his hand and followed through but stopped short of touching her face. She winced in anticipation and gasped when the pain did not come.

The commandant finally received the reaction he was looking for. He laughed in her face, a disgusting high-pitched giggle that made Iniki wish he would hit her instead.

The lesser officer observed the situation disapprovingly but his superior was running the show. "Commandant," the officer interrupted. "We have strict orders about this woman. Perhaps we should concentrate on finding the American."

"You are dismissed," his superior barked out. "I will handle this."

When the aide left, the officer circled her chair. From behind, he massaged her shoulders and stroked her hair. She stared straight ahead, her chin jutting out, eyes wide open. No reaction showed when he began to rub his hand up and down her arms.

"Good girl," Riley said softly, as he watched through a crack in the door.

The one-sided conversation turned to French but Riley needed no translation. The commandant intended to enjoy his prisoner before execution. Riley felt an anger so intense, it was almost a living entity. He would kill the man. But he would be patient. So far, she was not badly harmed. But he knew he had little time to get her out of there.

The decision to act was made by the commandant himself. As he came round to face Iniki again, he rubbed his hand across her face, then hit her hard. That was more than enough motivation for Riley. He kicked the door open and pointed the gun at the man.

"Is that the only way you can get a woman's attention?" he said in a raspy voice. "You should read up on that, you know. Intensive therapy may help. Now untie the lady."

Riley moved into the room, took the man's gun and tucked it into his waistband.

"Who are you?" The commandant looked confused at the unshaven half naked man with a baby nestled on his back.

"I'm the one with the gun. You're the one with no gun. Now untie her before I get nervous."

When Iniki was free, he ordered the man to sit in the chair himself. "Tie him up tightly." Then taking the man's tie, he gagged him.

After he checked the ropes and decided they were secure, he leaned so close to the officer's face that Riley could smell the man's foul breath.

"Didn't your mother teach you never to hit a lady?"

The man was unable to speak with the gag. He stared at Riley with cold eyes.

Riley just snickered. "Just so you know. If I ever see your face again, I will kill you. That is a promise." With that, he landed a right jab that knocked the man out cold.

"Bastard," Riley said.

"You should have killed him now," Iniki spat out, rubbing her wrists.

"I thought you were the non-violent one?"

"I am," she explained. "But he is an animal."

"Agreed," Riley commented. "I just have a hard time doing that with a baby watching. Don't want to damage her psyche at such a early age."

Her smile returned. "You are a maker of miracles, Riley."

"I don't know about that. A miracle is needed to get out of here without being caught." He took hold of Iniki and handed her the pillowcase. "Can you manage this and I'll lead the way? No more side trips. Understand?"

She nodded and made a silly face at him.

They met a potential problem as they exited the encampment when the baby started fussing. Riley found another biscuit and she quieted down. Except for the sparsely located sentries, no one was about. The three reached the mountain path in no time.

When they traveled far enough to feel safe, they stopped. Iniki was too quiet since the ordeal. Her unusual reticence unnerved him. In an attempt to lighten the mood, he sniffed the air. An unpleasant smell came from the sleeping infant.

"Guess the biscuits worked their magic, huh?"

But she didn't smile. Instead she asked, "How are we going to survive?"

"Okay." He recognized the after effects of trauma when he saw them. Motioning for her to sit on a small boulder, he stood before her. "Think we better talk about this now. I saw what he did to you. Tell me what he said."

In the darkness, her face looked tight and drawn. But he recognized anger in her eyes and sighed in relief. She'll be all right, he told himself.

She began to explain. "He knew who I was. He planned to have some fun first and then call in the general."

"Who's the general?"

"I do not know his name but I suspect it is the man in black. He gave orders to kill me immediately as I was no use to anyone alive. But first, I was to tell him about the man who was helping me. The American, he called you. He said you were the prize the general wanted. Once he caught you and handed you to the general, the commandant would receive a promotion. He wanted to leave the garrison and return to the city."

"Anything else? Did he mention my name?"

"Not your name, but a description. The general will be so pleased," that wretched man repeated, "if the commandant delivered you. They will make laughing stocks of the Americans," he said.

Riley nodded. "Not wrong there. We'll have to be sure we don't get caught, I guess."

She continued on. "That is not all. They are convinced that the twins who were seen in the pharmacy are working with you. If they find them, they will be shot on sight."

He put his hands on her shoulders. "Listen, lady. I told you they won't get us. Forget that man and what he tried to do. Concentrate on the task before us. And remember what we, you and I, feel for each other."

"Yes. But what is it we share together?"

"You need me to explain? I thought it was evident. Between us there is a powerful need. One that won't go away. Plus, at last count, we have a baby, whose name is Angel, by the way. I took it upon myself to name her. We have two precocious twins who have stolen my heart. Then we have Madeline and Francois who will be with us until they die. And then the cranky eighty year old who thinks I'm after her body."

She waited a moment and then added, "Do not forget Yankee Doodle."

"Right. And a *chat*."

CHAPTER NINE

Day 4 ~ Morning at the cave
"You let them escape, you imbecile!"

Shortly before dawn, they reached the cave.

"Do not disturb them yet," Iniki suggested. "It is still dark. Let them sleep."

"Sounds fine to me. I'll go in and give Francois his second dose of medicine. Then he'll have a few hours rest to allow it to work. You stay here with the little lady."

The baby fussed for the last half hour of the journey. Angel was hungry and needed changing.

"Poor darling," Iniki cooed. "Let me make you more comfortable." She put her down on a clean towel.

"Whew," Riley remarked. "She sure has a good digestive system."

"Babies are known for that."

He kneeled down beside her. "Another thing I have to learn, huh?"

"If you want to be a good father."

"No doubt about that."

"None at all?" she dared to ask.

He shook his head and ran his finger across her cheek where a bruise formed from the commandant's treatment. "Maybe I should have killed the bastard. Your face is turning purple."

She touched his hand. "Now I am happy you did not. I want our relationship to be built on love. No room for hate."

"Then you have nothing to worry about." He stood up and let her proceed with the baby. "Hope I can get in and out of the cave without waking Batman and Robin."

"Who?"

"Michel and Mathieu."

"I wish you luck. They hear and see everything you do."

"My buddies." The thought was pure joy. "Be right back."

He bent to kiss the top of her head. The baby gurgled happily, her legs straight up in the air and arms moving a mile a minute. "God, she's so pretty. We'll make a baby that beautiful, my love."

"I agree. Then, we will not need the bloody condoms."

"Watch your vocabulary, lady. We're in the presence of a minor."

"Go, Riley."

"Right."

She rummaged through the pillowcase and found material for a diaper. With the biscuits and milk, she mashed a gruel. Tending to the baby gave her time to relive the terrifying minutes she endured tied in that chair. The episode left her with a new understanding of fear. She would not forget the emotion, never lose the realization that humans are capable of enormous cruelty. She was consoled by the fact she did not cower. She fought against the horror she felt as a captive. She did not grovel at the evil man's feet. Somehow, that made her stronger, confident she could face danger and not allow it to conquer her.

By the time Riley returned, the baby was washed, changed and fed. The fussing stopped. Angel's almond shaped eyes were closed.

"I hoped I could play with her before she fell asleep. She's something else, isn't she?"

"Yes," Iniki replied. "Do not dare disturb her."

"Yes, Mother," he teased.

"How is Francois?"

Riley nodded. "His brow was cool to the touch. Temperature went down, at least. I gave him a smaller dose and told him to sleep." He looked at his watch. "I want to be cleared out of the cave by noon. Maybe you and I should rest, too. We may not get another chance for some time."

She looked his way and cocked her head. "Is that what you wish to do?"

"I'm open to suggestions."

"Where are the twins?"

"They were sleeping or doing a pretty good imitation. I think we've got some time before Michel shows up with some cock-and-bull story about searching for us."

"How much time?"

"Enough. Of course, if you continue playing twenty questions, we'll waste half of it."

She laughed. How she enjoyed everything about him! "What did you have in mind?"

"Come here and I'll show you."

She put her hands on her hips. "There is nothing I want more. But you will not . . . complete."

"Complete the job?"

"Exactly."

He reached into his pocket and pulled out a soggy box. Silvery packets fell from it as the cardboard disintegrated in his hand.

"And those are . . .?"

"Just what the doctor ordered. Condoms straight from the garrison."

"Show me."

He opened a packet and demonstrated with his fingers.

She was amused. "That little thing will protect me, as you are so fond of saying?"

"I guarantee it. Now stop fooling around and come here. I want you."

She took the two steps necessary to reach his arms. This time he was not passive, not holding back, covering her mouth with his and pressing his body into hers. "I love you," he whispered.

She blinked away the tears she felt coming. "Riley . ."

"Hush. Kneel down with me."

She did as he asked and they faced each other. He kissed her hard and she wanted his tongue. She wanted all of him but felt like a foolish schoolgirl on her first date. When he opened her shirt and slid it off her shoulders, she gasped. Her nipples felt like they were on fire. Her whole body burned at his touch and the delicious ache between her legs consumed her.

Gently at first, he took her nipple into his mouth. Then he increased the intensity of the caress. He unzipped her jeans and ran his hands down inside the back, feeling her buttocks. She could do no more than moan. When he slid his hand down the front, she held her breath and leaned her head against his forehead.

"Lie down for me. Please," he begged, his voice cracking.

She did as he wished. With shaking hands, he pulled off her jeans. His hands took hold of her knees and separated them. He studied the uncovered spot.

Was it possible to experience shame and desire at the same time, she wondered? The combination was explosive. But his fingers stopped further rational thought. She moaned and caught her breath.

"What is it, love?" he asked, as he slid his finger into her.

"I am so wet, Riley."

"Never be ashamed of that. It's a compliment to me. That shows you want me."

He stretched his body down on top of hers and kissed her deeply. Then he kneeled up again and unzipped his pants. "Iniki, look at me. This shows how much I want you."

"Yes, I know." She reached for him and he didn't stop her. She felt the hardness with both her hands.

He slipped on the condom quickly. "I may make you uncomfortable for a moment. Just the first time . . .I . . please just trust me."

"Riley, stop talking and proceed."

He entered her then, thrusting hard to break the membrane. Then he pulled out.

"Do not stop," she begged. "Please . . ."

He laughed. "Not a chance. Are you all right? Did I hurt you?

"A sweet, wonderful ache. Please do not stop now."

Then he kneeled up and positioned her hips against his so that he could reach deeper into her. So deep she thought she would bust.

"Don't wake the baby," he said and pushed into her over and over.

"I can not wait, Riley. I do not think . . ." She shuddered with exquisite passion. She felt him do the same.

They lay together for some time. "Not yet," she begged when he tried to move.

"You are incredible, lady. The first time can be painful."

"And magical."

"Ah. That's a better word.,"

"Riley. I think I may love you."

"Good. That fits right into my plan."

"What plan?"

"I will explain it all. But not now. I hear noises from the cave. If I don't miss my guess, Michel will be out here any minute now."

"Oh my God," she cried and tried to get up.

He laughed out loud. "Hold on there. We're still attached. You will do damage to both of us."

He rolled off and helped her rise. Collecting her clothes, she ran behind a tree to get dressed. She slid into her jeans and slipped the shirt over her. While she buttoned it, she watched the man she knew she adored.

Riley zipped himself up and checked on the baby. "Hope you didn't hear any of that, Angel," he murmured. "Going to be damn hard getting in some nookie with all you kids around."

As if on cue, Michel appeared as predicted, his rifle at the ready. He marched toward Riley unaware that Iniki could see him.

"Sir. I thought I heard your voice."

"And I thought you were not to leave the cave."

"Quite correct, sir. As I recall, you said not to leave the cave unless there was great danger."

"So? Where's the danger?"

Michel cleared his throat. "When I awoke you were not back. I did not know you were outside here. So I decided to investigate."

"You did, huh?"

Michel ignored the question and countered with one of his own. "Where is Mademoiselle?"

"She's washing in the rocks. We have another Mademoiselle with us now."

Michel looked at Riley in amazement as he pointed to the small package sleeping on a blanket a few feet away.

The boy took a closer look. "Hot damn!" he shouted.

"Michel, what did you just say?"

"Oh, pardon, sir. I heard you say it earlier. Is it not a good saying?"

"Well, it's not so bad. But I wouldn't recommend you use it in front of Mademoiselle."

Michel smiled. "I understand."

"Good," Riley confirmed. "Now, will you pick up Angel and show her to the rest of the gang?"

"Angel? That is her name?"

"Sure is. She was sent to us for a reason. She's our guardian angel."

"Very good, sir. I will welcome a sister."

Riley smiled as he watched the boy carry the baby cautiously into the cave. Iniki came out from the trees.

"Do you see what I mean about cursing? He is already picking up your bad habits."

He raised his eyebrows at her and held her nipple between two fingers. "I'm not the only one with bad habits."

She flushed. "No. Well . . .Michel is thrilled with her, I see."

"She's going to charm the pants off everyone."

"I beg your pardon."

Riley chuckled. "An inappropriate expression. Actually, she won't be doing that for a great many years. She's not allowed to date until she's thirty. And then we'll see."

"Mmm. Well, isn't that what you just did to me?"

He bent down to kiss her lips, still puffy from their earlier exercise. "How do you feel?"

"A strange feeling. I am so wet and I hurt but that only makes me want you more. Is it possible to feel sated and still go on wanting at the same time."

"It is, love. Nothing unusual about anything you're feeling. Stay that way. Wet and wanting." He grabbed her and held her close. "Dammit. I want you again."

"Not unless you enjoy an audience. Here comes Mathieu."

Angel made a hit with Madeline and Antoinette. Francois smiled at the curly haired child with enormous brown eyes. But her greatest fans were the boys who adopted her as their own.

Angel's needs were not a problem. The women set about ripping their petticoats for diapers and washing the clothes Riley found. The twins took turns holding her and she surprised them by crawling around on the cave floor.

"Isn't she too young to do that?" Riley was confused, a condition Iniki enjoyed seeing in him.

"We don't know how old she is. Many babies crawl before they walk."

"Walk?"

"Of course. Do you intend to carry her around forever?"

Riley laughed. "If she will let them, the twins will do just that."

"They have learned to love her already," Iniki commented. "She is a miracle."

"You know I am realizing the boys have no toys, no special possessions they carry with them. Just the rifle, the bat and Yankee Doodle."

Iniki agreed. "The gun and bat are weapons and not toys to them. Only the cat is special. And now they have the baby. They have not had the luxury of a childhood."

"They damn well will as soon as we get them to the states."

"Riley, please do not swear. Now there are three children to hear you."

He sighed and hugged her tight. "Angel can't tell one word from another yet. And the boys . . They know right from wrong. You know, if I didn't adore you as I do, I'd get tired of your frequent lectures."

She smiled coyly. "Too late to change your mind. You behaved wickedly and ruined my innocence."

"Bullsh . . . I wasn't the only one behaving badly back there. You kept up with me every step of the way. No shyness from you, lady. I seem to recall you begging me not to stop."

She felt her face redden. "I have a masterful teacher." She deliberately stared at the bulge under his pants.

"Then, lesson number . . whatever. Don't talk to me like this when you expect me to be logical."

"I shall talk like this any time I wish. But only to you, that is."

He smiled again. "You got that right."

Their conversation was interrupted by Mathieu who mentioned that Angel had no last name.

"We do not know her parents' name." Iniki hugged the boy to her.

"When we get to the states, she will become Angel Taggart," Riley said with certainty.

Mathieu stared at him with wide eyes. "You are taking Angel with you?" His face assumed a hurt expression.

"I'm taking everyone with me," Riley assured him.

"Everyone but . . ." The boy had no chance to question further.

Riley stood up and addressed the entire group. "Listen, guys. Gather round. We must leave the cave today. The military are on to us. We need a plan to get to Black Point as fast as possible. I'm ready to listen to any ideas."

"You let them escape, you imbecile!" The general ranted at the commandant who buried any hope of a promotion in the deepest recess of his mind.

"The American, sir. He was formidable."

"Aha. He caught you unawares, huh? What were your orders about the woman?"

"I did not touch the woman, sir. She was tied here in my office but I made no move to . . ."

"Then how were you overcome by him?" the general interrupted.

"He had a gun, sir."

"And you did not?"

"Yes, but it was holstered as she was tied to a chair."

The general shook his fist at the stupid man. "You are an idiot, one of many in this army. Did it occur to you to assign an armed guard to her? You knew she wasn't traveling alone."

The commandant put his head down. He kissed his promotion goodbye. He would be lucky not to be sent to a worse hell hole than Nouvella.

"Describe the American."

"What?"

"The American. Describe him."

"Yes, sir. He was tall, more than six feet. Definitely spoke with an American accent. Light brown hair."

"What distinguishing marks?"

The commandant shook his head. "None, sir. He had no shirt."

The general frowned. "What kind of gun did he have?"

"I am not sure. It was small."

"Imbecile. You do not remember the gun pointed at you?"

"No, sir," the man answered. "Perhaps I was distracted by the baby he carried on his back."

"Baby? Explain."

When the commandant finished his story, the general removed his cowboy hat and scratched his hairless head. The commandant was stunned when he saw that the man was bald. He never saw the general without his hat. The baldness and the ink-black glasses made the man more frightening than usual.

"That confirms they are in the area," the general concluded. "Obviously Nouvella was their objective for some reason. Since they are traveling with a baby and at least one small child, perhaps they planned to leave the children here. Once the storm hit, their plan was ruined."

"But where are they now?" the shamed officer asked.

The general smiled. "Up on that mountain, hiding out. Get horses and a platoon ready. I will fish them out myself."

"Do you need helicopters, general."

"No. They managed to avoid them so far. I will have an easier job tracking them down with horses. I have extra equipment which enables me to continue the chase in darkness when they are traveling. For now, I will take some men and begin by the only passable route. I am convinced they are headed for the Black Point area to rendezvous with the American ships. If they are not captured soon, I will get them there."

"I am sure you will," the commandant said, hoping to gain some forgiveness.

His effort was useless. "If you reported the first incident of the medical supply theft, I would have been here when you captured the woman. She would not be rescued by anyone."

"Yes, sir." He waited for the axe to fall.

It did. "You better hope that these people are found. Otherwise, your head will roll for this. I will do the job personally."

Iniki reminded him they had two problems. The first was to move Francois, who was not able to walk on his own. Antoinette was the second problem. The swelling around her ankle was not as severe but she would never make her way on the rough terrain.

Riley did not seem to worry about it. "We have the horses. Antoinette will ride one. I don't want to make Francois ride. He's much too weak. However I have a solution that the boys can help me with. Our largest problem is how to get to Black Point two nights from now."

"If we go down to the shore again, we may be able to find a boat." Mathieu was thinking hard. "Would it not be faster to sail to Black Point than to walk?"

"Definitely faster but not safer," Riley said, patting the boy on the head. "Remember, we can't go near Nouvella. The soldiers are searching for us and before the end of today, they'll find this cave. So we need another route."

Iniki turned to Antoinette, who was holding Angel. In French, Iniki asked if there was another way to Black Point. The woman nodded and smiled at the baby. Then, in rapid French, she came up with a solution.

"She says we backtrack for a half mile or so. There is a trail that traverses the mountain range. She knows the turnoff to Black Point but she claims the path goes by another village with a military outpost."

Riley frowned. "We'll decide what to do about that when the time comes." He turned to Antoinette with a smile. "Thank you," he offered. The woman scowled at him, then smiled at the baby.

"At least she didn't scream at me," he whispered to Iniki. "We may be making progress."

The rest of the morning was spent packing horses with everything they needed. Food and water were not immediate problems. Dark rain clouds threatened and the twins were in charge of water collection on the journey. They were entranced with what Riley built out of heavy branches and some horse blankets.

"This is called a travois, a sort of sled that the American Indians used to transport supplies long ago. They also used buffalo hides. Since there are no buffalo readily available, we'll make do with horse blankets."

"I do not know buffalo," Mathieu said.

"Yes, you do," Iniki interrupted. "I showed you pictures of the western part of the United States in our school. They are large animals with . . ."

"Yes. Now I remember. Large with big fur around their heads. The Indians hunted them and used every bit of them for a purpose. No waste."

"Right," Michel continued. "They were plentiful until the white man ..."

Riley ended the history lesson right there. "We can talk about that later. We need to get ready to leave."

Iniki smiled at her lover. "Go on then. I will help the women."

Riley watched her go off. "I love her," he said under his breath. "Who would have guessed it?"

"Guessed what, sir?" Michel had very good hearing. Riley must not forget that.

"Nothing. Hey, let's get back to work here."

"Who will pull this?" the boy asked.

"The horse, hopefully. I'll attach it to the saddle and Francois will be strapped in. When the path becomes difficult, we men may have to carry it ourselves."

"Yes," Mathieu commented. "We will do that, sir."

"And who will carry Angel?" Michel asked.

"I am most willing," Mathieu interjected.

"As am I." Michel threw his brother a jealous look.

"Neither of you," Riley ordered, foreseeing another disagreement in the making. "I need both of you to help with the horses. Mademoiselle will carry her in the knapsack. Angel likes that."

Neither boy was pleased but discussion ended. The twins helped Riley finish the long sled and attach it to the second horse. Francois was secured and the horse seemed able to pull the travois with the frail man on it.

"One problem solved," Iniki said.

"What other ones do we have?" Riley saw the concern on her face.

"Nothing we can not handle except for one. The military are coming up the mountain path."

"How many?"

"At least ten men."

"Dammit!"

"Riley!"

"Yeah, yeah I know. Okay, are we ready to push off?"

"Yes. I suggest we go now."

"Good idea. You walk with Madeline behind the second horse. Keep the binoculars with you. If they continue to track us, let me know."

He led the first horse with the supplies and Antoinette atop while the twins took the reins of the second horse pulling Francois. In the daylight, the path was not as scary as when they first came. But it was extremely narrow. Riley wondered how they were able to travel it without falling to a nasty death.

Less than an hour later, Antoinette called out and Riley stopped. He shouted to Iniki to come forward to talk to the woman. Again, in rapid French, the old lady chattered, waving her arm in an easterly direction. Iniki nodded, asked a few questions and then turned to Riley.

"She says to follow that pass there around the mountain top. After many hours of travel, we will come to the place where there is an army garrison. From there, the path dips down to the coastline and we must follow that for many more hours before reaching Black Point."

He shook his head. "That's cutting it real close. But there's no other choice. Ask her if she knows a place we can stay if we need to."

Iniki did as asked. "She remembers many deserted huts that are used by travelers. However, she does not know exact locations."

"Okay. We'll continue on until we can't anymore. Something will turn up. Always does."

"I wonder who else we will meet and add to our traveling party?" Iniki laughed as she made her way back to the rear of the caravan.

"Don't even joke about it," he called out to her. "Wait until my boss sees this bunch. He's going to have my head."

"As long as I may have the rest of you," she answered.

The general was only a little more than an hour behind when he discovered the cave. There was no need to spend much time investigating what had been left behind. The embers in the fire were still hot. There were remnants of food and evidence of horses.

"This was their hideout during the storm."

His adjutant agreed. "It is obvious quite a few people stayed here. I would estimate five or six. Is it possible we have the wrong group of travelers? Does it not seem strange that the American sent to rescue one woman would travel with so many others?"

The general nodded. "I agree. Not standard procedure. Yet, this is where they were. I'm sure of it."

"What are your orders, sir?"

"We track them from here. I am convinced they are headed for Black Point. We know they didn't head down the mountain to Nouvella so they must have gone in the opposite direction. The trail will not be difficult to pick up. Look at the map and determine the quickest route to Black Point.

The aide did not have to work hard for an answer. "There is one possible route if they decided not to go by water."

"No. He would know that is too dangerous with our patrols."

"Then the only other way they are headed is through this indistinct path which cuts across the mountains and then ends near Black Point." He traced the route with his finger.

"That is where they have gone. I will bet on it."

The adjutant was puzzled. "Even if it takes them directly past the military garrison at St. Lucille?"

"Yes. The American will think of an alternate plan before he reaches there. In the meantime, we follow that same direction. We won't be far behind. Traveling with so many people will slow him down."

Riley compared the new path to a roller coaster. It was nothing more than a series of ups and downs. Each decline gave everyone a break. But the inclines were bone-tiring. Twice he disconnected the travois from the horse. The twins helped him carry Francois. After a long while, Riley tied the travois around his chest and shoulders and pulled by himself. The boys were too tired. Just before nightfall, he decided to get a fix on their position and find out if they were still being followed.

He remembered the contempt on the commandant's face the night before. By now he reported what he had seen in his office to the guy in the black hat. The man followed them every step of the way like the posse that pursued Butch and Sundance in the movie. Riley was certain the man would not pass up any chance to capture an American operative and do away with Iniki at the same time. Whoever the guy was, he was in this for personal gain. Delivering an American into the president's hands would be a coup. Even that idiot commandant would profit if they were caught. Riley knew what would happen to the rest of his group. Everyone but himself would be murdered on the spot.

Not if he could help it, Riley vowed. He met these kind of men before. The only difference between then and now was that all his people were helpless. The very thought enraged him.

As the sun set, he stopped the caravan. They were at a high point on the path. From that location, he could see for miles on both sides of the mountains. Riley thought he could make out the lights of the American carrier that sat just beyond ten miles of the island.

Iniki came to him then. "We must stop soon, Riley. They are all exhausted."

"I know. May I use the binoculars?"

He scanned they area they covered in the last hours.

"What do you see?"

He heard the fear in her voice. "Lights," he said. "Flashlights. They're moving, following along the same path we're on."

"Dear God."

"They have a long way to go before they catch us but the garrison Antoinette mentioned concerns me. They may be informed of our presence. I don't want to meet a platoon coming toward us on this path and be trapped between the two."

Iniki took a deep breath. "What do we do?"

"If I were alone, just you and I, we would go over this mountain, then leave the path, cut through the wooded area on the other side of the mountain and head down to the coast. From there, we travel just inside the vegetation along the shore."

"They would not expect us to do that?"

"No. It is foolhardy to try it with the old folks. Especially Francois. And the horses will be difficult to control going straight down."

"Is there another option?"

"Nope."

"Then?"

He shrugged. "What the hell! We go for it. Do they trust me enough to follow?"

"They do. Even Antoinette."

"I find that hard to believe. Okay, we rest for ten minutes. Then we go on where the path winds closest to the mountain top. We descend from there."

"And we pray."

"That, too," he said. "It's been a long time since I asked God for anything. Think he'll listen if I tell him how much I care about you? How much I need all of us to come out of this alive?"

"He sent us Angel, did he not? He knows we need special attention."

Riley ran his hand over the baby's soft curls. "Hey Angel. Are we doing the right thing?"

The baby gurgled and smiled at him. Then she reached out for his finger and popped it into her mouth.

"Ouch. There's something sharp in there."

"She has teeth, Riley."

"Is that normal for her age?"

"Of course. You know we make a good pair. You know nothing about babies but a great deal about making them."

"And you?"

"I enjoy your lessons very much. I will help you to be the best father."

He looked at her in surprise. "Yeah. That is what I want to do for the rest of my days."

His band, as he referred to them, followed him as he led them away from the path. Not one raised an objection or complaint. They traveled slowly for two hours. Then he stopped and gave instructions to make camp. He knew they could go no further without rest. Trying to navigate down the path in the dark with an ill man and two horses was nearly impossible.

"We rest here until dawn. Then we continue on. No fire though. I know it's cold and about to rain. Protect yourself as best as you can. But no fire."

They formed a circle and huddled together. With the ingenuity of engineers, the twins forged a tent-like structure out of large branches and with horse blankets spread on top. Francois seemed better with each dose of medicine that Riley fed to him. Food was shared and soon most settled down to sleep.

When all was quiet, Riley led Iniki away from the others. "I'm going back up to where we left the path," he told her.

"Why? Please do not, Riley."

"I need to cover any tracks we left when we turned off. And I want to see who's following us and if we fooled them. Please stay with the others here. Be sure there is no noise."

"Riley, you will put yourself in terrible danger."

"True. But it's better to know where we stand. If I go, I can pinpoint their location and judge how safe we are. I need your understanding on this."

"You know I will do what I must."

He pulled her against him and kissed her hard. "I'll be back by daybreak. If I don't show up by ten, you'll have to find a way to get them to Black Point without me." He held her tightly once more. "They are our family. You must save them if I can't."

"I will. I promise, Riley. I know you will come back to me."

"Keep that thought in your head. Don't think about anything else. Think only about this morning and how many more times we'll do that again."

CHAPTER TEN

Day 5 ~ Morning on the path to Black Point
"Shoot the damn gun, Michel."

Riley was back on the path quickly. With no one but himself to look after, he moved faster and more efficiently. Yet, he didn't enjoy the solitude, the freedom of movement. He preferred Iniki and the others with him. The thought amazed him. Throughout his career, he worked alone and was successful. Four days with his ragtag band of refugees erased that satisfaction. He decided he didn't want to work alone. In fact, he was done with the job entirely.

He climbed to the top of a cluster of rocks and held the binoculars to his eyes. The approaching flashlights weren't hard to make out. They were close. Riley estimated the platoon would reach his location within the quarter hour. Each man was on horseback. Leading the line was the same man in black, the general, the spirit of death. Whatever the hell his name was, Riley knew he was one dangerous whack-job.

On the other hand, he admired the man's perseverance. The chase began at the Beaumont Plantation and so many miles later, he still pursued. If Riley outsmarted him this time, it was not the last time the two would locked horns. The guy would pursue the quest to the end. The thought of Iniki and the children in the grasp of the general chilled Riley to the bone.

He jumped down from his perch and with dry brush wiped away whatever marks the horses made when they turned off the path. The ground was rocky and the soil somewhat dry despite the storm and frequent rain showers. It would not yield clues easily.

Yet, this enemy was not an ordinary soldier. Riley knew he could not erase every trace of their route. Sooner or later, the general would backtrack until he found where his prey went. Since it was dark, their tracks would not be noticed until much later. Regardless, Riley learned never to underestimate the enemy. He would not do so now.

He found a good hiding place directly above the trail. The wait was not long. Within minutes, the caravan of soldiers approached. Riley strained to get a look at the enemy. The general wore a black hat, in the style of the American cowboy, pulled down low on his forehead. U.S. Army-issue infra-red glasses encircled his neck. The others were similarly equipped. Once they discovered the spot where Riley and the refugees veered off the path, the soldiers would have little trouble tracking them. The glasses picked out moving objects utilizing not light but the amount of heat the object generated. Riley's gang must stay well out of range to escape the long reach of the glasses.

"Crap," Riley said in a whisper. The general had a whole bag of tricks up his sleeve. No wonder he managed to project the frightening image he enjoyed. With those glasses on, he and his men resembled something out of sci-fi movie. How many more weapons did he carry courtesy of the U.S. mail order catalogs?

Riley studied the man, taking note of the proud and determined way he sat on a horse. Riley read much about a man from his seat on a horse. This guy was no one to trifle with. He wanted Iniki and Riley like a big game hunter stalks his prey. And if he got them, he would display his prizes in much the same manner.

Riley heard little conversation. At one point, the column stopped and the leader turned to the second in line. "How far are we from the garrison?"

"Five to seven kilometers, sir. Most of it is downhill."

"Excellent. We need more men to help flush them out."

The line resumed its forward march. Riley studied the contingent. Ten men. Not a large force considering the trouble Riley and the gang caused so far. The general was sure of reinforcements. That meant he alerted the outpost at St. Lucille. Riley knew he made the right call when he led his band off the path before it was too late. The troops from the garrison at St. Lucille could not be far off.

He watched until they disappeared on the downward path. Then, he followed them for a half mile more, keeping the binoculars on the soldiers. When he came to a high rock formation, he climbed up and could see far into the distance. The mountains were lower here and easier to cross. Up ahead, so far away that he wasn't able to judge the distance accurately, he observed the glow of lights. They were stationary, indicating a permanent place.

"St. Lucille," he said aloud.

He delayed no longer. He needed to move the gang immediately. Even with the soldiers deliberate slow pace, it would not be too long before they reached the garrison. Once there, they would determine their target left the path. Riley needed to move his people off the mountain and into the heavy vegetation on the coast before sun up, well ahead of their pursuers. If they remained on the mountain side at night, the infra-reds might pinpoint them. Once down on the beach, they would travel through the vegetation to avoid the helicopters that were sure to come.

Iniki was awake when he returned. He embraced her and quickly explained his plan.

"Do they have the strength to do this?" she asked.

"We have no choice. I wondered why the Army didn't use helicopters to trace us today. Now I know. He knows exactly the way we are headed. He doesn't need confirmation."

"Who are you speaking of?"

"The guy dressed like a cowboy with bad taste."

Her hand went to her throat. "The general."

He took hold of her shoulders. "Yes. The general. With plenty of the latest technology to trail us. He has a purpose, just like us. His purpose is to find you. And me, most likely. But we have a purpose just as strong. We want to get off this island in one piece. Just because he's still on our tail doesn't give him supernatural powers. He's a soldier with the resources of Simone's army to back him up. But a bullet will stop him just like it will me and you. Do you understand?"

She nodded. "Yes, of course. He is not a spirit or a specter."

"Exactly. He eats, sleeps and urinates just like the rest of us."

She laughed softly. "You and your words, Riley. What will I do with you?"

"I have several excellent suggestions. Unfortunately, they have to wait. Ask me that question when we get on the ship."

"Will we make it, Riley?"

"I saw it. I saw the ship out there at sea. It's waiting for us and we will make it. Because I have so many people I love and I want to keep them safe." He kissed her hard then let her go. "Mustn't do that too much. It distracts me. Forget everything but you."

"I am happy and not a bit ashamed about my behavior."

He shook his head in wonder and brushed his hand across her breasts as he walked away. "Let's get them up. We have a long distance to go before we can rest."

Again the refugees woke, packed up and set out without a word of complaint. Riley marveled as he encouraged them on. He was born an American and, as such, knew freedom his entire life. He took it for granted. The two old women and one sickly man were never totally free. The twins were the same. And Angel's chances of survival were less than zero before they found her. They wanted their freedom and were willing to do whatever was asked of them. Whatever else happened, Riley knew these people must be saved. If it was the last act he performed as an employee of the U.S. government, they would have their wish.

Iniki thought also of these folks but in a different way. She was so proud of them. Even Antoinette, who was not the most pleasant of women, did what she was asked without hesitation. Madeline and Francois never uttered a word of doubt about this crazy journey they were on. They followed her wherever she went. And the boys proved they were made of greater strength than even she suspected. They adopted Riley as their hero. What a role model, she thought. But in the next breath, she chided herself. Except for his vocabulary choices, he was every bit the man she would wish the boys to emulate.

What would happen if they did reach America? Would Riley keep them? He acknowledged that Angel would become his daughter. What of the boys? What of her, for that matter? She loved Riley more than she ever imagined possible. But her people were her responsibility. If Riley wanted her, he must accept that she came with baggage. Was that expecting too much of a man who had been a bachelor his entire life? It would cause her much pain if he wanted only her and Angel. But she would have no choice. She never would abandon the rest of them.

Francois managed to walk the last mile downhill, a feat for which he was congratulated. He was on his second full day of medication and it made a dramatic change in his condition. Even his gunshot wound was healing and infection free.

Madeline and Antoinette took turns relieving Iniki of carrying Angel in the knapsack. The twins begged for a chance to do the same but Iniki insisted they stay with Riley at the head of the line in case he needed help with Francois.

"You are the only ones with weapons. He needs you."

Once they reached the beach, Riley gave them time to rest. He pushed them hard to get down the mountain not knowing where the enemy was. He led them to a rock outcropping with heavy green growth overhead and asked that they stay put.

Then, once more he backtracked up the mountain. He did not travel far when he heard the soldiers and horses making their way down.

The general and his soldiers wore the infra-reds but were on foot leading their horses. The terrain slowed them right down. Otherwise they would have caught up to Riley long before.

Riley squatted behind a large rock and watched, barely moving. He would be picked up in a second if he were in the open. The men talked in French and the general listened intently. Riley understood very little but the word helicopter and St. Lucille were mentioned more than once. With dawn approaching, the men turned the horses and headed back up the mountain. Riley froze and waited to see what came next. Not following his men, the general scanned the area once more with the glasses. Riley felt the man's strong will and was sure he didn't want to suspend the search. Somehow, Riley knew the general was aware of his presence.

"You are an interesting adversary, American. But I will get you. Only an American can sniff out another." The words were shouted out and meant for Riley's ears.

Ten minutes passed before the general took off the glasses and turned to follow his men.

Riley didn't move for a long time. He understood the general was a formidable opponent. The odds were even.

Only after the last of the men disappeared from sight and the area was silent did he consider moving. But he waited until the birds began to sing again.

The general did not want to leave. He could feel the nearness of the American. He was close by. Probably watching me, he thought, from behind some rock. Not moving to avoid the penetration of the infra–reds.

Three times the general stopped his trek up the mountain and turned, surveying the area. Three times he picked up nothing with the glasses. The sky brightened with impending dawn. The heat sensors were not so accurate in daylight.

Still he was certain the American was there. The hunt would not end pleasantly for him.

At the same time, the general acknowledged a growing respect for his prey. The American operated just as he himself would do if the tables were reversed.

"Well done," he shouted as he turned a final time and joined his men. He would meet the American again.

They trudged on in an easterly direction for the remainder of the day, eluding the helicopters that flew low every hour or so. Heavy vegetation caused the refugees to travel at a slow pace. Progress stalled when they encountered large rock masses. Riley took no chance being spotted on the beach. His only option was to retreat inland around the giant jetties, losing still more time.

Less than thirty-six hours to reach Black Point, he calculated. The water supply was adequate. The boys devised several ingenious methods to collect what fell from the occasional showers. But the food situation was not good. The adults could manage without much food for the time being. But the boys and Angel could not. Several smoked sausages remained along with some canned fish. Biscuits and bread were saved for the children. Scraps went to Yankee Doodle who grew skinnier by the day but seemed satisfied sharing Angel's milk and biscuit gruel.

As nightfall approached, Riley found a spot on the edge of the beach behind a cluster of rocks that formed a three-sided protection. The high rocks blocked the wind off the ocean and the sand was warm. He was convinced the general was not far behind them. For that reason, he did not dare to build a fire. After dark he accompanied Madeline down to the water to search for shellfish. She seemed to know where clams and mussels lay in abundance. Her catch made a fine dinner feast for the older ones who had little else to eat.

"What is your plan?" Iniki asked as they settled Angel down for the night.

"We'll stay here until just before dawn. Then into the brush again for the last leg of the journey."

"How do you know the distance?"

"I don't."

"Then?"

"I know we're in the general vicinity. While I watched the platoon coming, I saw the lights of St. Lucille. If it's on the path to Black Point, as Antoinette claims, then we aren't far away. When we reach it, I'll recognize it, even if Antoinette doesn't"

"She may. I have seen it only from offshore and that was many years ago. I am not certain I could say for sure."

"That's the least of our problems," he advised. "We'll continue along as we have before. Can't risk being in the open in daylight. Not with those copters. Lucky for us, there is so much beach for them to cover."

She sighed and admitted, "I have come to hate helicopters."

He laughed. "Can't say I'm fond of them myself."

"Will they send more?"

"Sure. If you were the guy who followed us from your plantation, would you give up now?"

"That is what frightens me."

He smiled wryly. "No time to be frightened. Fear dulls the wits. True, we are as vulnerable as we can ever be. So we have to keep sharp and on our toes. They know the direction we're headed in and they'll use every means to find us."

"That does not make me feel better, Riley."

He noticed the slump of her shoulders. She was drained from the stress and anxiety. Yet her voice betrayed nothing. It was strong and determined.

"Try to channel fear into positive action."

"Is that what they teach you in spy school?"

At least her sense of humor was intact. "Here's what you do. Make a mental list of what we need for one more day. Everything else, chuck into the trees. No sense carrying extra baggage."

"You are confident we will meet with the Seals?"

"Sure." And if they didn't he would die trying. "Now go around and make sure everyone is comfortable. Tell them to lighten their load. I'll keep watch for helicopters but I doubt they'll be around. They know we won't camp out in the open."

"Where are the boys?" She looked around nervously.

"Over there in the brush. I'll go see what they're up to."

They should be exhausted, Riley thought. Instead, Michel bounced around playing soldier with the rifle. His brother squatted down investigating something in the sand. Only one more day, Riley told himself, and they would no longer be on the run. He stopped a few yards away, aware they didn't notice him.

"Will he take us with him?" Mathieu asked his brother without looking up from the object he studied.

"Monsieur? But yes. He will not leave us."

"I mean to his home in . . ."

"Virginia," Michel interjected.

"I know it is Virginia. But will he take us as he says he will take Angel?"

The all-knowing Michel seemed to have no answer. "I do not believe he will take Angel from us. Mademoiselle will not allow that."

Mathieu shook his head sadly. "Mademoiselle is in love with him. They kiss and kiss."

Michel stopped dead in his tracks and plopped down beside his brother. "They do? I have not seen that."

"Because you are always pretending you are a brave soldier with that stupid rifle. But I watch," he went on. "They sneak away and I have seen them kiss several times. Mademoiselle may forget about us now that she has him."

Michel was outraged. "You should not spy on them. He has been good to us. Mademoiselle will be upset. And you are not allowed to use the word 'stupid'."

"I did not watch when they started to make love."

"Make love?" Michel's eyes seemed to pop out of his head. "What do you mean?"

"Sex, my brother. I know you have heard of it."

"Yes. But Mademoiselle?"

"I told you I did not watch. This is not what is important. I am afraid that they will marry. And go away from us."

Riley heard the entire conversation and was baffled. Should he interrupt and put an end to this talk about love and sex? What would the two of them think if they knew he was snooping on them? He decided to do what Iniki would do if she were in his position. Then he realized he wasn't so sure of that either. So he remained where he was and continued to listen.

Michel appeared disgusted with his brother. "You should be ashamed. How can you doubt Mademoiselle's love for us. She has protected us since Mama . . ."

"You do not have to preach," Mathieu responded in a voice full of shame and fear. "But I am still afraid."

"Then you are foolish. If you continue to watch them when they are alone, I will tell them myself."

"You will not," Mathieu cried. He tightened his fist and swung at his brother, connecting on the upper jaw bone.

Michel gave as good as he got. They exchanged a few blows before Riley reached them and broke up the fracas.

"What the hell was that about?" Riley asked knowing the answer full well. Better to play dumb. See if they confide in him. Out of breath, he sank down on the sand beside them.

"We are in disagreement," Michel answered.

"You are the master of the understatement, my boy."

"What does that mean, sir?"

"Never mind. What did you disagree about?"

"About . . . the rifle . . again."

Riley understood he was lying and was about to lecture on telling the truth. He opened his mouth, then closed it again. The kid lied to protect his brother, Riley realized. Michel's behavior was normal. He did what any kid would do in the same circumstances. Hell, Riley wondered, how do I handle this?

Mathieu resolved the dilemma. "Pardon, sir. I will tell you. It was not about the rifle. Since I now have Yankee Doodle, we do not argue about the rifle. I allow him to carry it. It makes him feel like a big man."

"It does not. That is a lie." Michel was incensed.

"Hold it, both of you. This isn't about the rifle or the cat. Now which one of you is going to tell me the truth?"

They put their heads down. Neither dared to glance at Riley.

"I will." Mathieu was first to speak.

"No, I will," Michel insisted.

Riley played referee, quieting both boys. "Mathieu, you spoke up first. Let's have it."

"Let's have what, sir?"

"The truth," Michel said with contempt. "If you are going to live in the United States, you must learn what the Americans mean when they speak."

"I know what they mean!" Mathieu threatened with a sandy fist.

"You did not just then!"

Riley interrupted before the war escalated. He raised one hand and the boys froze. "Now, Mathieu, you were about to tell me?"

But Mathieu could say nothing. His cheeks were beet red, a color Riley saw even though the night was dark.

Again, Michel sighed in disgust. "My brother is ashamed. As he should be. He thinks you will not take us to your home as you said you will do with Angel. He thinks we will go to a *orphelinat*.

"What is that?"

"A place for boys with no parents."

"And what do you think, Michel?"

With complete assurance he answered. "I do not believe you will leave us anywhere. You will keep us with you and Angel and Mademoiselle. She will never leave us."

"That's why you were beating on each other?"

"Yes, sir." Michel did not mention the part about the sex.

"Mathieu," Riley addressed the boy. "You believe I would put you in a home for boys? Do you know how much I love you guys?"

Tears streamed down the kid's face. "Yes. But you love Mademoiselle more. You will want to marry her and have baby Angel as your child. My brother and I are not as young nor as easy to handle."

"*Mon Dieu*," Michel groaned.

Riley said the same to himself. Here he was sermonizing about honesty. He better damn well be truthful himself.

"Yes." He paused to clear his throat. "It's true. I do love Mademoiselle. And I love Angel and I love you two. I love the entire gang of you. And all of us will live in my home together."

"We will?" they said in unison, faces beaming.

"Hell, how could I get along without my two sidekicks?" Riley tousled the dark hair on both heads. "Now no more fighting. That causes weakness in our ranks which is what the enemy wants. Do you understand?"

"Yes, sir,' they parroted.

"By the way, how did you know that I love Mademoiselle?"

"Because you kiss and make . . ."

"*Mon Dieu*," Michel said again.

"And how do you know that?"Riley asked, suppressing a grin.

Michel attempted to save the day. "We always watch you and follow your orders. Remember when you said not to do anything unless you tell me?"

"Right," Riley agreed.

"Well, we always keep our eyes on you so that we do not miss an order."

"Yes. Very good. And what do you see?"

"Nothing, sir. I see nothing," Michel said in truth.

"Nothing," Mathieu answered. After a slight hesitation, he continued, perhaps determined not to lie. "I leave when you start to undress."

"Bloody hell," Michel muttered under his breath.

"I see," Riley said, straining not to react. "Well, let me explain something to you."

"We do know about sex, sir," Mathieu assured him. "Mademoiselle told us about in school."

"Good. But maybe you don't understand about making love. It's different in a special way that someday you'll understand. Someday, when you're older. Much older. Very much older. In the meantime, I need you to promise me two things. Then we can forget this discussion." Please God, Riley thought.

The twins nodded, their brows frowning in exactly the same shape.

Riley cleared his throat once more. "First, never tell Mademoiselle about this."

"Yes, sir."

"And second, do not follow Mademoiselle and me when we go off. Not unless I tell you. Got that?"

Michel, of course, answered for both. "We got it, sir. We are to do nothing...nothing," he emphasized. "Unless you tell us or we ask you first."

"Right," Riley acknowledged. "I think we understand each other, boys." He knew in his heart that wasn't true but what the hell?

The general was irritated. His helicopters spotted no trace of the refugees. What was worse, he received calls from the idiot president every hour on the hour. During the last call, Simone insisted the general return to the capital city to report in full. As if an adequate accounting could not be given over the phone.

He agreed to the demand only because there was nothing more he could do at St. Lucille. Continuing the search at night was pointless unless he had a specific idea where to look. Instead, he decided to center his efforts on the spot he believed was the final destination. And there was no doubt that was around Black Point. His prey did not reach that area yet. Not traveling on foot. But by the next morning, they would be close.

Beginning at dawn, he ordered boat patrols along a ten mile stretch of coastline and instructed the helicopters to fly in patterns from Black Point east.

With those strategies in place, he grudgingly climbed into a helicopter for the flight to the capital.

Riley sat up most of the night. Their position, though camouflaged, was still in the open. He felt it necessary to watch. They were too close to their objective to screw up now.

He didn't suggest going into the darkness with Iniki. Though she slept at his feet, he didn't touch her. From now on, he vowed love making would occur behind locked doors only.

Somewhere in the early morning hours, he dozed. But he woke and roused his people before sun up. They must be off the sand before daylight. Helicopters would hunt them today, he was sure, considering their trail went cold in the past twelve hours.

Again they all followed his lead. The camp sight was cleared, leaving no trace of their presence. Even the opened clam shells were buried. Everything was done with speed and silence. Too silent, Riley thought and looked around.

"Where are the twins?" He turned to Iniki and felt the color drain from his face. She looked around frantically. Everyone did. The two were nowhere to be seen. No one remembered seeing them since the night before.

"I made sure they fell asleep. And I checked on them before I settled down. They may have gone into the trees to relieve themselves," Iniki suggested. She started to move in that direction.

"No. Stay here," Riley said. "Get everyone ready to go so that we can take off as soon as I find them."

Madeline came to Iniki and whispered in her ear. Riley recognized the panic on their faces.

"What is it?"

"Madeline says Yankee Doodle is gone also."

'The cat? The damn thing is so lazy he wants to be carried everywhere. How can he be gone?"

She shook her head. "I do not understand. I believe the cat has something to do with their disappearance."

"God damn it," Riley swore, pointing a finger at her. "And don't lecture me. This is no time for them to take off like this."

"They would never do that. You know they would not. If they are gone, they have a good reason."

Riley scratched his head in frustration. "Let me look in the bushes. I'll be right back."

He searched for twenty minutes, calling out their names as quietly as he could. There was no response. The fear in the pit of his stomach ate away at him. Iniki was correct, he told himself. They wouldn't leave on their own. Especially after their discussion the night before. He assured them they would live as a family. So why would they suddenly vanish? And why didn't they wake him?

The cat. It had to do with the cat. That ball of fur hardly took a step on his own without Mathieu scooping it up and carrying it. Had they gone for food? For fish? He scanned the ocean but there was no sign of them.

However, something more dangerous was coming toward them. In his worry for the twins, he didn't notice the Army jeep with the machine gun mounted on top. It headed straight for the rocks where the group waited.

"Dammit, Taggart," he said aloud. "Pay attention."

He had only fifty feet to cover to get to his people. Before he got very far, he noticed Mathieu come out of the bushes holding Yankee Doodle. Detouring, he ran to the boy, picked him up, and yelled to the others to run into the trees. But it was too late. One of the soldiers in the jeep began firing into the sand at Riley's feet.

Riley stopped immediately. The soldier then turned his attention to the others, aiming over their heads and forcing them to cower on the ground. Iniki, with the baby in her arms, stood her ground.

The jeep pulled up and stopped about twenty feet from them. The driver got out and motioned for Riley to join the other refugees. Riley put Mathieu down and took his hand, leading him to the others. The second soldier remained in the jeep, seated behind the machine gun.

The first soldier began to ask questions in French and Iniki did the talking. Riley didn't understand much of the conversation and made a mental note to enroll in a French class as soon as he got back home.

Iniki introduced her people using false names for each. Madeline was Jeanne D'arc. Antoinette became Brigitte Bardot. Francois was Vincent Van Gogh and Riley became Claude Monet. Riley waited for the expected reaction but the guy didn't even flinch. He wrote each of the names in his book. Then, he took out a picture and studied it, glancing to Iniki several times. That's it, Riley told himself. Even he could understand when the soldier called her Iniki Beaumont. He motioned for her to approach. She stood still, defying his orders until the soldier spoke again. This time she acknowledged his order and began to walk slowly toward the man. Her actions were out of character for the woman who didn't take orders easily.

"What did he say?" Riley whispered to Mathieu, who stood beside him holding Yankee Doodle and the bat.

"He knows who we are, sir. He told Mademoiselle to come to him or he would put a bullet through the baby's head."

Every muscle in Riley's body tensed. He had no chance against the machine gun even if he managed overtake the one on the ground. Before he could approach the jeep, the rest of them would be dead.

Iniki walked up to the soldier with her head high. He grabbed the baby from her and slapped Iniki across the face, forcing her to the ground. Angel started to cry. When Iniki tried to move, the soldier shouted at her.

"It's okay, Mathieu. Tell me what he said and focus on me and what I do."

"Yes, sir. He told her to lie still. When they take care of the rest, she is their prize."

Riley had to act. The situation wasn't going to improve by itself. He took a moment trying to decide how to change the odds. No matter what plan he devised, someone was going to get hurt. Dead, more likely. He decided the best thing was to protect the children and Iniki. If need be, he would die for them. Iniki would get them to Black Point if he couldn't.

"Where is Michel," he whispered under his breath.

"He is there," the boy responded and slightly raised his hand.

"Don't point. Tell me in words. Where is he?"

"Behind the jeep, sir. We were . . ."

"Not now. Later." If we live long enough, he thought.

Michel was indeed behind the jeep. He carried the rifle in his hand as always. And something else. He watched as the boy put down the mysterious object on the sand. A rock? What was he doing with a rock? He had the gun, didn't he?

They watched while Michel took time to load the gun. Then he stood, the gun resting on the top of his shoulder, looking through the eyepiece. But he didn't fire.

The soldier on the ground held the screaming baby with one arm around her middle. Angel cooperated by making enough noise to cover the conversation between Riley and Mathieu. When the soldier asked a question of Madeline, she could not hear him over Angel's strong lungs so he moved closer to them. He began to question each one. What they said was a mystery since Riley couldn't hear them or understand. He was waiting for Michel to do something with the gun. Anything.

"What the hell is he doing?" Riley muttered in frustration. "Why doesn't he shoot the damn thing?"

"Because you have not given the order, sir," Mathieu explained. "You said we may not fire until you give the order."

"*Mon Dieu*," was Riley's reply.

The soldier approached Riley next, pushing his weapon into Riley's stomach. Riley didn't understand the man's question, of course. While he tried to formulate some sort of answer, Antoinette solved his problem. She grabbed Riley's arm and pressed her eighty-something old body against his. "*Il est mon mari.*"

Mathieu translated. "You are her husband, sir."

"*Oui*," Riley agreed with a smile. He bent over and kissed the snow white hair atop Antoinette's head. She, in turn, reached with her right hand and grabbed his head. Then she forced his lips smack into hers. He tried his best to pretend a kiss though who he was fooling was anyone's guess.

The soldier obviously never heard of May-December marriages. He slammed a fist into Riley's stomach, doubling him over in pain.

Riley fell to the ground and was yanked up by the hair. The gun again was shoved into Riley's gut.

Now or never, he decided. If the guy didn't speak English, they had a shot. Looking directly into the soldier's face, he yelled as loudly as he could. "Shoot the damn gun, Michel!"

A brief look of surprise danced on the boy's face as the long-awaited order was given. Michel fired, though it was difficult to determine what he aimed at. But whatever it was, he couldn't have hit a better target. The bullet from his weapon, which boomed like a cannon, hit the machine gun, splintering it to pieces. The man standing at it was hit with shattered metal and collapsed.

Riley took advantage of the confusion and grabbed Angel from the other soldier's grip.

"Mathieu," he shouted. "Catch." Not waiting to see if the boy understood, he literally threw the baby in Mathieu's direction and turned to face the soldier. A swift jab to the jaw put him out of commission.

Mathieu did just what Riley said. Yankee Doodle was rudely displaced as the boy dropped both cat and bat. He caught Angel with the skill of a major leaguer.

"Excellent," Riley said and patted the boy on the back. He took Angel and handed her to Antoinette. "Thank you," he said to her. She actually smiled back.

The force of firing the rifle knocked Michel over backward. He was still sprawled on the ground when Riley reached him. "Did I do it, sir?" he asked eagerly.

"Well, you got the gun which was a smart move on your part."

"I was aiming at the gun, sir."

"You were?"

"Yes, sir. You said 'Shoot the damn gun' and that is what I did. Did I not follow the order correctly?"

"No. Yes. I mean you did that perfectly," Riley confirmed. They were all safe. At least for the moment.

"What's this?" Riley reached down and took hold of the white object. He brought up a white bunny.

"It is a rabbit, sir. And it is not to eat. Mathieu has his cat and I have my rabbit."

"Okay. But where did it come from?"

"It is my fault," Mathieu admitted. "In the night, Yankee Doodle ran to the trees. You were sleeping and I did not wish to wake you. I did not realize it would take me so long to find him. When I did, he was chasing after the rabbit."

"And I followed, of course," Michel added. "I need to protect my brother since I have the only rifle."

"Of course." Riley shook his head to clear it. How the hell was he going to channel the energy that these two boys generated. The thought made his jaw hurt more.

"What do we do now?" Iniki finally spoke up, thoroughly drained but ready to go on. She hugged each twin and kissed the tops of their heads.

"We clean up this mess, tie those two so they are out for a while. Then we create a diversion."

"A diversion?"

"Yes. A fire will do nicely. I don't think it will last long. The ground is still wet under those trees. But it will be enough to take some of the military off the hunt for us."

CHAPTER ELEVEN

Day 5 ~ Midnight Black Point
"I won't kiss you goodbye."

"I have named my rabbit, sir."

Riley looked up from what he was doing. He discovered it was necessary to pay attention to every word Michel said. A vital piece of information could slip by and be missed.

"And what is your rabbit's name?"

"Madonna."

"Madonna? That's a strange choice. But I like it."

"Thank you, sir. Madonna is a word that means mother. Mademoiselle taught us that in school. It is English. I thought it proper to choose an English name since we will live in America."

Riley hesitated a second, frowning at the boy. He knew there was another question he should ask. But he had no idea what it was.

Iniki watched the man she adored and the child they both loved. She laughed to herself as she overheard the conversation. She knew Michel and his habit of sharing information in subtle ways. Where Mathieu was straightforward, direct and painfully honest, Michel delivered a message in a round-about way. She wondered if Riley would pick up on it.

"How do you know Madonna is a female, Michel?"

Riley stopped what he was doing and listened.

"Female? She's a female?" he repeated. "How can you be sure?"

"Even a small child could tell, sir." Michel appeared stunned at the question.

Riley glanced at the rabbit, then at Iniki. "Something tells me I'm not going to appreciate what I'm about to hear. So tell me quick."

Michel complied. "She expects babies, sir."

"Babies?" he echoed. "When?"

Iniki laughed. "I am sure Madonna would tell us if she could."

"She will let us know when she is ready," Michel assured him.

Riley could only shake his head and laugh.

"What is the problem, sir?" The boy was confused at Riley's reaction.

"Not a thing, my boy. Congratulations on becoming a father. And so quickly. I've only one request. Tell her to wait until after tonight. That's all I ask."

"I shall relay your message, sir. But I cannot guarantee she will wait. Just in case, I have designed a sort of sack to carry her in. She can give birth in there if necessary."

"Excellent thinking. I'm sure you can handle the situation."

"Yes, sir. Madonna's babies will not hamper our progress. I must tell the others the good news."

"Swell," Riley muttered as the boy ran off.

Iniki enjoyed teasing her lover. "That will make you a grandfather. You are making progress faster than I thought. After all, we have been together only once."

"Once is not enough," he said slyly, deliberately running his eyes over her body. "Your face is still red where that bastard hit you. That is the second time a man has slapped you. The third time, he dies. Are you all right?"

"I am now."

"Good. And while we are on the topic of procreation," he said to change the subject. "I think we'd better table our lovemaking until we're off the island."

She raised her eyebrows but waited for him to explain.

"Seems the boys, Mathieu in particular, have a habit of watching me. At all times."

"Oh no!" Horror washed over her face.

"Be calm. He assured me that he left when we started to undress."

"Good God," she said, sinking down on the sand, her face scarlet red. "I worry that they see so much violence in this world and I am the one showing them . . ."

"Showing them love," Riley said. "And even if they sat and watched the entire proceeding, which they did not, they would conclude one truth. That love between a man and a woman is beautiful and sacred and nothing to be ashamed of."

"I am not ashamed," she answered sharply. But she was embarrassed, no matter how Riley tried to rationalize the problem. "I should have realized what they were capable off. They are with me for so long now."

"Okay. But the deed is done, he reasoned. "From now on, we wait until we can lock a door behind us."

He was right, she told herself. There was nothing she could do to change it. "I am embarrassed, I suppose."

"I don't know why. Mathieu wasn't embarrassed in the least. Besides we've got bigger problems. And the last thing we need are baby rabbits. How the hell am I going to deliver the whole menagerie to one small rubber raft?"

"Perhaps we should have built an ark?"

"Not funny. Still the boys now have a pet to love. They don't have much else."

"Their parents death traumatized them and for a long time they were afraid to love anything or anyone for fear of losing that also. Now with Angel and Yankee Doodle and Madonna, they are feeling again. I do hope Madonna's babies are born tomorrow."

"Why?"

"It is my birthday. Madonna's babies will share my feast day."

"Birthday, huh? Well, we'll celebrate on the ship."

She liked that idea. For a brief moment, she allowed herself to daydream. "Do they have birthday cake?"

"Sure."

"And ice cream?"

"No question."

"And doors that lock out nosy children?"

"Damn right. But, first things first. I'm going to have a hard time explaining this crew to the captain of that ship out there. And, I know we won't all fit on the raft together. We'll have to make several trips. Somehow, we need to pull this off."

"We will. I can feel it. With a little luck," she added.

He smiled and proceeded to douse the jeep with the remaining gas he found in the vehicle. He positioned the vehicle on the edge of the undergrowth so that it stood half on the sand and half under the trees.

The two soldiers were bound with their own clothes and left naked at the edge of the of the water, away from the fire but not close enough to be caught in the rising tide. Riley thought seriously about letting them drown after their treatment of Iniki and the baby.

She was repulsed by the idea. "How can you do that in front of the boys? They will learn that murder is acceptable."

"What do you think they were going to do with you?"

"I am fully aware believe me. But cold-blooded murder is never to be condoned. Unless we teach out children, we cannot rid the world of violence."

"I love you, my beautiful lady, but you may be a bit altruistic and idealistic. Naive may be the best word."

"Riley, sweet words will not change my mind."

"Of course not. But it was worth a try."

As she knew he would, Riley honored her wishes. The captured men were left in no danger of drowning.

When preparations were finished, Riley asked her, "Are we ready to roll?"

She answered with, "They are. Will you light it now?" She did not approve of his plan to burn the jeep.

"Yes. We've lost too much time. I don't know if we'll make Black Point before midnight."

"Then, why leave a calling card like a burning jeep?"

"It's no secret we're in the area. This a message to your spirit man that his men are not so smart. Besides, they'll need helicopters to put out the fire. That means less of them looking for us."

She did not like the plan. Even one tree destroyed was against everything she believed in. A small fire could escalate, wiping out both vegetation and small animals. She argued with Riley but he was adamant.

He waited until the group was far enough away before he lit up the jeep. The wind blew in the opposite direction so smoke was not a problem. He pushed them along at a rapid pace. Almost immediately, they heard helicopters.

"They can see the coastline from St. Lucille," Riley commented. "That was a fast response."

"I hope they extinguish the fire before it reaches the trees." She sent him a critical look.

"Okay. Okay. Some day we'll come back to that spot and I'll replace every damn burned tree with a new one. Will that make you happy?"

"It will do."

"Good."

"For now."

"Of course."

But the plan almost backfired. The diversion brought so many helicopters, the refugees were forced to go further inland under denser tree cover. The walk was difficult and he had to cut through vinery to continue. They stopped once to eat their final rations. From now on, the adults ate only coconuts and water. Angel and the boys shared the rest of biscuits and fish.

To further lengthen the final leg of their journey, Riley was not sure of the exact distance to Black Rock. Every hour he ordered a brief rest while he scouted out the coastline ahead. Each time, he recognized nothing familiar. He took Antoinette with him once after he discovered a small fishing village that was wiped out by the storm. Antoinette knew of the place but she had no recollection of its closeness to Black Point.

The news was disappointing to the others, particularly the older couple. They were on their last reserves of strength and fortitude and while they rested more often than before, they looked to Iniki with questioning eyes.

At one such stop, she sat with Riley for a moment. "What does the map look like for this area?"

"Here," he said as he handed the map to her. "See how the coastline juts in and out? If Nouvella is there and we crossed two mountains, then we camped last night right about here." He pointed to a spot where he put a big X.

"How far have we traveled today?"

"Due east, about two miles, maybe less."

"Riley, we are not moving fast enough. We need to be closer to the water."

He thought for a moment. Then he touched her hair and pulled her close, looking around for prying eyes. When he saw none, he kissed her. "I love doing that."

"I love you doing that also. But we must focus on our journey. How will we move faster. Maybe a boat?"

"And teach the boys that stealing is okay?"

"Only when a maniac is trying to kill you."

"No." He shook his head emphatically. "The boat idea is no good. They must have patrols out there. A boat is impossible to defend. They'll blow us out of the water."

"Yes. I believe you are right."

"Will wonders never cease? I'm right?"

She enjoyed the jibe and countered with one of her own. "Oh, you have been right a few times."

"You are a wicked woman," he whispered.

"Do not forget it." She pulled him to her by the shirt collar and returned his kiss. They scanned the bushes for voyeurs. If they were there, they were well hidden.

"We better get going, dammit."

She nodded and went to prepare the others to leave. "You will be relieved to know that we will follow the beach from now on," she announced, hopping the news might boost their sagging spirits. "Riley believes we are very close now."

The elders smiled gratefully and the twins saluted each other. She watched as they gathered the provisions and followed the man who brought them on this quest. She felt a surge of hope and realized how thankful she was to have lived through the past few days.

"Bring me the men who were found on the beach." The general was not amused. The adjutant knew enough not to ask questions when his boss was angry. The two men were delivered, fully dressed, to the general's room in St. Lucille outpost. They shook with fear as they entered.

"So," the general began, 'You were captured by a bunch of old people and children?"

One of them answered. "There was a young woman there, sir, who was the fugitive we are looking for."

"Yes. Iniki Beaumont."

"Yes, sir. I recognized her from photo that was circulated. I arrested them but there was a loud explosion behind me and the tall man overtook me."

"Tell me about the man."

"He was tall and lean, sir. He did not speak when we came upon them. Only the woman spoke. And an old wretch who claimed the man was her husband."

"What did you do when you heard that?"

"I did not believe it, of course. Still, he did not speak. Only after we were captured did I hear his voice. He spoke like an American, sir. Like you."

"And how did you both become captured?"

The second soldier spoke up. "There was a young boy behind the jeep, sir. He fired at the machine gun and somehow shattered it. I was injured by flying debris and the corporal here was overcome in the confusion."

"Brilliant piece of work," the general roared.

The soldiers stood at attention, trying to control their embarrassment.

"So my initial statement about being taken by children and the elderly has some truth in it?"

"Yes, sir."

"In your report, you mention three children?"

"Yes, sir. A baby girl and two boys who appeared to be twins." The soldier who struck Iniki was not so macho.

"That matches the report by the man attacked in the medical stores at Nouvella. The others were three older people and the American and the Beaumont woman?"

"Yes, general."

"Did you hear any conversation which might indicate where they were headed?"

"They burned the jeep as a diversion. I could hear the American and the woman argue."

"Why were they arguing?"

The soldier shrugged. "I heard her say their time was short. She did not want to waste time moving the jeep and setting it afire."

"What else?"

"I heard nothing else, sir. My partner was still unconscious so he heard nothing. But I did see them head east into the trees."

"Were they armed?"

"I did not see other weapons other than the rifle the boy used."

"Anything else?"

The man hesitated, then decided to say it. He was in enough trouble as is. What did a little more matter? "I received the impression that the young woman and the American were romantically involved."

The general smiled. "Why do you say that?"

"The American frequently caressed the woman, sir. She did not seem to mind."

"Good observation. There may be hope for you yet."

He dismissed the men and sat back digesting what he learned. Actually the idiot soldier revealed quite a bit. He knew how many fugitives there were and who they were in terms of age and sex. It was beneficial to know your enemies. He now knew their potential weapons power, though he must assume that the American was armed. Most importantly, he knew of the relationship between the woman and the American. An Achilles heel for the man. What kind of second-rate operative did they send in there? A true subversive never gets attracted to his target. Love relationships like that only happen in the movies. In real life, involvement was suicide. Yet this man expressed affection for the woman? He was a fool.

And why, the general wondered, did the man agree to drag along the rest of the party? Old women and children? In the general's view, those people were expendable. The operative was an amateur.

The general smiled. All the easier to catch them. In the end, the American would regret his foolishness and his desire for the woman.

The adjutant appeared when called.

"Increase security in the area east of where the incident took place. That's where they are headed. Their time is growing short."

And the game was getting tedious.

It was past sundown when Riley ordered another rest. The traveling became easier when they move along the tree line on the beach. But that brought new problems. Riley had to be on constant watch for military jeeps. Helicopters covered the area in low patterns and patrol boats came in close to shore when they could. Riley pushed his people further into vegetation to hide when they appeared. Added to that were huge masses of lava rock that they met often. In the daylight, they could not climb over them, though it was most direct route. The elders would be in a vulnerable position if the helicopters passed while they were on top of the rocks. Not able to move quickly, they would be picked off easily.

"This is the final push," Riley told Iniki. "I know we're close. We have to be."

"They are becoming disheartened, Riley. I am afraid they are losing the will to fight."

He disagreed. "No. They're exhausted and nearly spent. But they're not willing to give up. They've been asked to do more than most undercover agents I've trained. I give them so much credit."

"I told you they would serve you well. They believe in you. As I do."

"They believe in you, lady. And because of that, they trust me."

"Then you must save them."

"I'm trying damn hard."

"Riley . . . "

"I don't want to talk about swearing right now."

"I am not going to. Plenty of time for that later.. I do suggest that we leave them here now that it is dark. We will travel faster without them. Over that rock mass and beyond. We will locate Black Point and return to take them."

He nodded. "Good idea. They'll be safe here as long as they stay put."

"How much time do we have until midnight?"

"About two and a half hours."

"Then we must go."

Iniki strained to keep up with him. He moved fast climbing over rocks and pulling her up behind him.

"How far have we gone?" She was slightly out of breath.

"About a quarter mile. Stay here and rest. I'm going over that next jetty and see what's on the other side."

"I want to come also."

"No. Listen for the sound of a motor. If you hear it, lay flat face down on top of the rocks. Understand?"

He was off before she could answer. She knew they had little time left. How could they all get to Black Point on time? For the first time, she felt despair. She felt like a traitor when Riley was striving so hard to save them.

Her growing doubt almost blocked out the sound of an approaching boat from the west. A spotlight mounted on top of the craft washed the beach with blinding light.

Fear almost consumed her. Where was Riley? Did he hear the boat or was he on the sand on the other side of the jetty? She lay flat down as the spotlight neared, but the beam was focused on the beach itself. The top of the jetty where she hid remained in darkness.

A second later, a pair of hands surrounded her waist and a body lay atop hers.

"It's just me," he whispered in her ear and rolled to the side.

She relaxed, attempting to control the hysteria inside her. "Thank God. I was afraid. . ."

"The boat? That's not our immediate problem."

"What do you mean?"

"Black Point is on the other side of the next jetty."

She felt a flood of relief. "We have made it?"

"Not yet, love." His lips were in her hair. "We've got to go back for the others. That will take us far beyond midnight."

"How much time left?"

"Less than an hour."

"Then I will go back," she said. "You go on to the rendezvous point. When the Seals come, you tell them to wait."

He shook his head. "No way. First, you can't move them as fast as I can and second, I can't risk bringing the Seals onto the beach until we are ready to put people in the raft. But your idea is a good one. You can get to Black Point and wait. The raft will be about fifty feet offshore. They'll flash a light once. I'm to return the beam and they'll come in."

"But if I see it, I do not flash back?"

"No."

She found it hard to take deep breath. "What about the patrol boat?"

"I'm timing it. They're covering a certain area and go by here at approximate intervals. The last one was eight minutes ago. 11:17. Here, you take my watch and time the next pass. Get to Black Point and time the next pass. Remember, even if you see a signal from the Seals, don't respond. They'll be sitting ducks.

"Riley, will they wait?"

"I hope so."

She would not tell him she was terrified she would never see him again or the twins or Angel or any of them. She would conquer her fear and do what he asked. "I understand what to do."

He rubbed her back for a brief moment. "It's all right. Just wait for us to get back here. Don't bring them in until we've got someone to put on the raft."

She nodded. "I will see you shortly."

"Yes, you will, love. I promise."

"Riley . . ."

"No," he said as if he read her mind. "I won't kiss you goodbye. This is not goodbye." In the next instant, he was gone.

She picked herself up and scaled down the rocks until her feet touched sand. Running like she was chased by demons, she crossed the narrow strip of beach and came to the next jetty.

Again she scrambled up the rocks and reached the top just as the patrol returned. She looked at the watch. 11:28.

"About eleven minutes," she said out loud. Then she lay flat and waited for the boat to pass. She waited for her boys and Angel and the others. Especially for Riley. Could he get them all here and produce a miracle?

The next thirty minutes were the hardest. Patrols came by like clockwork., scanning the sand with their spotlights. But they did not stop, continuing on down the shore line. Helicopters resumed the search but covered ground further inland. They hovered over the beach for a second only, then moved on.

She stopped worrying about them. Her heart ached only when she thought of her people. Would Riley be able to get the old ones here? God would not allow them to fail when they worked so hard throughout the journey.

The sea was black and angry from the storm a few days before. Waves of five to six feet broke close to shore. Madeline and Antoinette would not last long in the surf, to say nothing of Francois. In order to board, the raft must be beached, she decided.

She wondered how many would fit in the raft? How far was it to the American ship? How long would it take for the raft to make a return trip? She was so absorbed in thought, she almost forgot to duck as the patrol made another pass. It was 12:04

As soon as the craft went along, she scanned the dark ocean. There was no moon but her eyes became accustomed to the blackness. Pacing up and down along side the jetty, she searched for a place that would hide her from the search lights. A perfect place presented itself, close to the water's edge. A deep gash cut into the rock wall resembled a small cave. It afforded enough room for everyone to hide until the Seals came. If they came, she thought. What good would any place be if they didn't come? She searched the dark sea until her eyes ached. There was nothing out there. No one to rescue them.

Two more hours passed and still no signal. Still no Riley and the others. She was on the verge of panic. "As if that is helpful," she said aloud in an angry voice.

"Talking to yourself, love. I think you've been alone for far too long."

She jumped in surprise but Riley grabbed her, hugging her hard. "My poor brave love."

'The others? Where are the others?"

"Right here behind me. I couldn't risk taking the horses any closer. So Antoinette rode on my back. And now we have five new additions to the family."

"Madonna?"

"Mother and babies are doing fine. Michel is a nervous wreck."

Iniki said a silent prayer thanking God for the hopeful promise of new life in the form of baby bunnies. Then she showed them the hiding spot she found.

"Good location," he commented. "Are you interested in a career in undercover work?"

"No thank you!"

"Have you met many patrols?"

"Yes. At intervals as you thought. Before I saw one helicopter but no more since."

"Yes. I heard it too. It never came back. But it will."

"Do you think so?"

"Hell, yes. I don't like this. Something is weird. Too easy."

"Easy?" she gasped. "What do you mean? The boats never cease and there is no light from the raft. There is nothing out there."

"Yes, there is. They have to find the right window of opportunity to come in. They'll have to beach it. Meanwhile we wait."

"Should we signal?"

"No. We wait."

"Why?"

"Because they know what they're doing."

She sincerely hoped he was correct. "What if it is too late for them to come?"

"Lady, are you losing trust in me?"

She sighed. "Of course not. But I will admit I am frightened."

The group settled into the protection of the tiny cave. The boys and Francois fell asleep on the sand. Just outside the opening, Riley and Iniki scanned the darkness for more than an hour.

When it came, the signal was so brief she thought she was dreaming. With the blink of an eye, it could be missed.

"Riley?" she whispered.

"I see it. Give me the flashlight."

She handed it to him and checked the watch. "Only seven minutes before the next patrol returns."

"Wake the boys . Hurry. I'll get Francois. The rest of us wait until the next trip."

"Angel and the animals?" She knew the boys would not leave without them.

Riley understood immediately. "Grab them too. Hurry."

The twins were groggy but cooperative. Michel had his hands tied with the harness full of bunnies. Yankee Doodle was tucked safely into Mathieu's knapsack so Iniki handed him the sleeping baby and her bottle.

"You must carry her and protect her, Mathieu," she instructed. "Do not allow her to cry. Use the bottle."

"Yes, Mademoiselle. I am no longer afraid. I will see you on the ship."

"I promise you that."

The raft appeared out of nowhere. It made no sound at all. One of the two men on board took a look at them and frowned. 'We cannot fit everyone."

"Take them in shifts," Riley said. "Are you timing the patrols?"

"Affirmative, sir."

"On the next trip, there are two older women."

"Yes, sir. How many trips are needed?"

"Three. Go now."

"Aye, sir. Our ETA at the ship is twenty minutes. So plan accordingly."

"Roger that. And thanks."

The entire encounter took less than a minute. Iniki stood with Riley as the craft slipped away. She could see Michel waving as if he were on a great adventure.

"Please God," she said. "Keep them safe."

"He's been pretty good to us so far, love."

"I am terrified, Riley."

"So am I. Not for the kids. They are safe now. But I won't feel safe until we're gone from the island."

The general boarded the helicopter as the clock passed midnight. He did so for a specific reason. The moonless night was ink black. Perfect for a rendezvous. He felt the nearness of his prey in his bones. His premonition was bolstered when he himself found two horses lingering at the edge of the beach just west of Black Point. He ordered the pilot to land.

The animals bolted when the noise and wind from the aircraft spooked them. It took some time for the general and the pilot to corral the horses. On one, he found a bag containing pieces of coconut and dried sausage. There were a few bandages and other items. No doubt, these were the pack horses used by the fugitives. If they abandoned the horses, it meant one thing. Rescue was close upon them. Less than a quarter mile to the east was Black Point. That beach and the two after it going east were ideal for amphibian craft.

"Head for Black Point," he instructed.

"Yes, sir. But the president wishes to speak with you. We are ordered to return to St. Lucille.

"Negative. We go to Black Point. I'll call the president when I'm damn well ready."

When the second signal came, Riley moved the two old women down to the water's edge. They shook with fright but uttered not a sound. Iniki talked to them in soothing tones, reminding them that Francois and the children were waiting, safe and sound. Soon, they would be, too. She asked them to take charge of the children and animals until she arrived.

Giving them a job encouraged them and as soon as the raft beached, Riley picked up each of the women and handed them to the Seals.

"Okay, lady. You're next," he told Iniki quietly.

"What?"

He picked her up and moved toward the raft. "You can fit in there. You're small."

"No," she shouted. "No. I will wait with you." She struggled to get free of his arms.

"Like hell," he said and standing in waist deep water, he threw her not gently into the raft. "Take off."

"Damn you, Riley," she cried.

She warned him she did not take orders easily, especially from men. As the raft slid back into the blackness, she stood up and jumped into the surf. A wave caught her and she went under.

The Seals tried to help but she refused to cooperate and tried to make it to shore. The powerful undertow, however, dragged her further out. Her one and only thought was that Riley was probably right this time.

Riley dove into the water immediately. He grabbed her hand, the only part of her he could see. The Seals could do nothing to help. The leader determined it was a waste of valuable time and backed the craft away. Madeline and Antoinette, witnesses to the drama, cried out. They were told to be still. The raft disappeared as silently as it came.

The next patrol boat approached from the east, its motor humming loudly.

Riley yanked on her arm while trying to keep his footing. Iniki came up, choking and gasping for air. She clung to his arm with every bit of strength left in her. Slowly, he stepped back, pulling her along, until he was almost out of the water. "Damn it, woman. You are the most obstinate . . "

He attempted to lift her but the receding water acted as weight pulling her away. She slipped from his grasp and he lunged forward to grab her again. In the same moment, the patrol's spotlight caught him in the beam. Iniki lay on the sand, her energy drained. She tried to rise but her body felt so heavy.

The first burst of gunfire ran along side her. She screamed and rolled away from it. Riley tried to hold on but a huge roller came in and separated the pair. Iniki pushed herself up on her elbows and witnessed Riley get hit with two or three bullets. He doubled over and fell to his knees in front of her.

She wanted to scream but didn't. That was a waste of time. She must get up and pull him to safety. Suddenly, her body was light as a feather. Her legs carried her to his side in a second.

"Get into the water along the end of the jetty," he shouted. "Hold on to the rocks." Blood streamed from his upper torso, only to be washed clear by the next wave.

"Do what I say, Iniki," he pleaded. Then, without warning, he stood up and ran back away from the surf. The spotlight attempted to follow but he took them by surprise. They scanned the beach over and over in circles. Bullets pelted the sand everywhere.

Riley's diversion gave Iniki the chance to position herself against the rocks at the point where the jetty and the water met. She knew exactly where Riley was. The fissure she found where they all hid. She must get to him, she told herself. That was her only thought as she climbed the rocks. Once on top, she sidled from rock to rock.

Taking a quick look at the boat, she noticed it was inching closer to shore. But the surf was too heavy. They would not risk being slammed against the boulders on either side of the beach.

If she could only reach Riley, she thought, then corrected herself. She would find him. She had to.

He was tucked into the tiny cave when she saw him. She thought he was unconscious. Pushing panic aside, Iniki slapped his face in an effort to wake him. Her hand came away covered in blood.

"Damn you, Riley. Wake up," she shouted. She was furious with him and did not know why.

"No swearing," he answered in a whisper.

"Oh, thank God." She was so grateful he was alive. "Are you able to stand? We must go to the end of this jetty. They do not shine the light there. But you have to help me."

"No, love. Go yourself. Wait for the raft. It'll come back for you."

"Shut up, Riley. I am going nowhere without you. And you know it."

He cried out in pain when she helped him to stand. But she did not stop. If he was hurting, he was alive. Dead men do not complain, she assured herself.

"The spotlight is on the other side of the beach," she said as she urged him on. "We need to move now."

She knew she had only seconds to cover the space down to the water. She pulled with all her strength and somehow, he stayed on his feet. They reached the water and then he collapsed. But she had the buoyancy of the ocean to help her. She clung to the rocks like a black mussel as the waves came rushing in. Once or twice she almost lost hold but she held him by the belt in a grip that would not loosen. They will have to pry her finger off, she vowed.

Both were up to their knees in water, with every wave washing over them. She wedged herself into a deep crevice so the waves pushed rather than pulled. She held on, struggling to hold him up, waiting for whatever came next.

"They have been spotted, sir. On Black Point beach," the pilot shouted over the noise of the rotor blades. "Just as you predicted."

"Our ETA?"

"We are coming up on it now, sir."

"Good. Radio the patrol boat that we'll handle it from here. I want the American alive."

"Yes, sir. Should they stay on station?"

"Affirmative. But no shooting."

CHAPTER TWELVE

Day 6 ~ Early morning on the ship
"It's not like I haven't seen you naked before."

S he dared not move, fighting to maintain her position as the waves broke over her. Through it, she clung to Riley's belt like it was her life line. He showed no signs of life, no reaction to the pounding surf. When she whispered his name, there was no answer, no curt reply, no smart jibe. Only silence.

Without him, she inherited the job of finishing the mission. She needed to act as he taught her, not in lessons but by example. He never allowed fear to conquer him though there were times when she suspected he was as alarmed as she. He focused solely on the obstacle in front of him, not on those down the road. One problem at a time, he cautioned. Well, she told herself, she was not a stupid woman. She was able to do that.

The patrol boat flooded the beach with light. Would they request land troops to search the area? They had not yet, she reminded herself. The patrol boat could not come in any closer to shore and no helicopters arrived overhead. But that situation would not last forever. Troops from St. Lucille might arrive any minute. How long was she able to hide with Riley before she was found? Until dawn? If the raft did not return by then, they were both lost.

"Stop it," she said aloud. Why bother worrying about what might happen? Was there a way to change it? Her prime concern was to stay alive and hidden. And that she would do.

But what if she was holding a dead man? She tried to pull him close enough to feel his breathing. Each time she attempted, the surf fought her. Finally she gave up. Of course, he is alive. Until she knew differently, she would proceed on that assumption. Only God determined life and death.

The fingers on her left hand bled as she clung to the rocks. Her right arm was numb from the steel grip she had on Riley's belt. Nothing to do about that either. She closed her eyes and remembered happy times. She relived their love making under a mountain waterfall and outside the cave gazing up at the night sky. She smiled at his insistence on using a condom. In order to protect her, he revealed his soft and vulnerable underbelly. That was what made him so lovable. That was why she trusted him. His love for her blotted out all the evil moments. And she would be forever grateful for the experience.

She was so involved in her thoughts, she did not notice the patrol boat move out to the east. The beach again was black as pitch. At first, she was elated. Had they given up? Something told her it was too good to be true.

She soon found out how right she was. From out of nowhere came the helicopters, two of them, casting their white light down on the sand. They crisscrossed beams several times starting at the shoreline and progressing inland. Iniki was forced to duck under once more, dragging Riley down with her. The beam passed over them so fast and the darkness was back. When she surfaced, she heard Riley gasp. It was indeed the sweetest sound.

"Land on the beach. Instruct the other pilot to remain aloft and wait for my signal. No firing."

"Yes, sir." The pilot followed orders and brought the aircraft down without a bump.

The general smiled. "Perseverance pays off," he said to the pilot as he unbuttoned his harness and jumped onto the sand.

The bright lights illuminated the whole area. Iniki watched the tall man. She saw him remove his cowboy hat and toss it back into the craft.

"Bastard," she said quietly as she regarded the bald head glistening in the lights. The black glasses were in place as they were the last time he confronted her. He hunted her like she was a wild animal. He followed her to this place. And he did so because he wanted something. Not from her, but the half-dead man she held onto.

The general strutted in front of the copter's spotlights. There he appeared as a dark shadow with light radiating from his body. If the devil possessed a physical form, it would be like this, she thought.

She held her breath but made herself stare straight at him. He was "only flesh and blood", as Riley said. He was right. The general was just a man, one who possessed many fearsome toys.

He pulled a set of long glasses to his eyes and raised his right hand in the air. Both aircraft shut down the lights, cloaking the beach in blackness once more. She needed to blink several times before her eyes adjusted to the change. She knew about the strange looking glasses that traced the body heat even on the darkest night.

She watched transfixed as he stepped down to the water's edge, twenty feet away, and looked right and left. Riley was pushed under once more. She was sure the man saw her and remained frozen in place. Every hair on her head tingled. Finally, when the turned his gaze away, she pulled Riley to the surface. Only his nose and the top of his head were above water. This time no sound came from him.

The man covered the length of the beach, strutting up and down atop the jetties on both sides. He steered clear from the water line. Perhaps he disliked the ocean, she thought, and that prevented him from studying the very end of the rocks. His only effort was to come to within several feet from the end. This he did on either side of the beach, at one point standing only a few yards above Iniki's head. She heard his boots clicking on the rocks above.

Her heart did not stop pounding until she saw him climb down to the sand and head for the helicopter. As he crossed in front of the craft, the searchlights came on and the man stopped abruptly. He removed the alien glasses. Iniki remembered the blood that was on her hands as she helped Riley to move. They must have left of trail of blood from his hiding spot down to the water. If the general found it? If he followed it?

He knew the American was there. He could smell him, smell the closeness of the enemy. And if he were there, then the woman was also. Three hours until dawn. The general couldn't stand on that beach until the sun rose. He had to move on, even though he was convinced the wounded man could not travel very far.

The American was here, on this strip of beach, watching from a dark hiding place. At daybreak, he would flood the area with troops. The man and woman would not have blackness to shield them. And then the chase would be finished. But, he admitted to himself only, the victory would be bittersweet. The game became a challenge and the American did himself proud. Perhaps, the general concluded, he felt a kind of twisted kinship with his unnamed prey. He was the general's equal when it came to skill and cunning. The American would be caught. The general then would leave this hell-hole of an island and never come back.

She watched with a thankful heart as the man boarded the copter. The two aircraft took off to the east, and she was sure they would search the adjoining coastlines. For the present, she succeeded in foiling the general's plan. Her next obstacle was harder to accomplish. She must wait for the Navy to come back.

"If you are out there, now would be an excellent time," she said aloud.

As if they heard her, the raft emerged onto the dark beach. At first, she believed it was an apparition. She continued to think it even as she struggled to pull Riley behind. It was an impossible chore. If she let go of the rocks, the receding waves could pull her under. In the last instant, when she knew she could not fight the surf, she yelled out. Immediately one Seal ran to help her. He secured a rope to both of them

"Hang on, Ma'am," he instructed. "The commander needs to go first."

She nodded, still clinging to the rock and watched as Riley was pulled unconscious from her hand. Letting go of him was the hardest part. The Seal carried Riley to the raft and pushed him over the side with the help of the second man. Then he returned for Iniki.

"Grab onto me, Ma'am." She was reluctant let go of the rocks, but obeyed the order. He wrapped a life preserver around her neck and they were pulled to the raft by the other Seal. The two men easily got her into the craft where she was pushed face down onto the black bottom next to Riley.

He was on his stomach as well. Blood covered his face and his upper body. Clinging to any hope whatsoever, she told herself he was alive. If he were dead, he would no longer bleed.

"Damn you, Riley. Do not dare to die on me,"she whispered to him. But there was no response. She fought the urge to shake him awake. Anything to assure her that he was alive. She noticed then that the quiet engine hum stopped. The two Seals assumed a prone position with one paddling with his arm over the side. The patrol boat returned. She heard its engine coming closer.

They drifted for what seemed to be a long time. No words were spoken. She waited for the light and the bullets. But blackness remained and the only noise came from the patrol's crew. Each of the Seals sidled down beside her and Riley. Both were armed with unusual short weapons, pointed up. A quick look in that direction revealed the hull of the patrol boat. The raft silently bobbed in the water on the ocean side of the larger craft.

How long they remained there, she could not tell. Riley uttered not a sound. She tried to reach his wrist but the Seal stopped the movement with a shake of his head.

After the warning, she remained silent. Riley was alive, dammit, she thought. She determined not to shed one tear until someone in authority told her different. Her job now was to lay still. She could do that. She allowed a cold numbness to drift over her, dulling every sense and emotion.

Finally, the raft motor started. The Seals sat up, their weapons still at the ready. Whatever foe was out there, she did not see. She let the Seals do their job because that was what Riley would do.

They made no attempt to examine the unconscious man, not even to take his pulse. They did not look at him or her. She shivered in the cold and searched for a sign that Riley was reacting to the damp cold. She saw nothing. She edged as close as she could to him and took his hand in hers. But she felt nothing with the shriveled tips of her fingers.

The carrier loomed out of nowhere. The tall grey structure rose high above the tiny raft. So high that she was reminded of skyscrapers she saw in pictures of New York. Suddenly, like magic the small craft was hoisted out of the water and she was lifted by a sailor and taken out of the raft. "Are you hurt, Ma'am?" he asked kindly.

"No. But you must help him."

"Yes, Ma'am. We will take care of him." Gingerly he put her down on the deck and wrapped her in a blanket. "Are you able to stand?" he asked.

"Yes. It is Riley who is injured." She made a move toward the raft where Riley still lie unmoving surrounded by dark clothed men.

"You better get to your quarters, Ma'am. They'll do everything they can for the Commander."

"Commander?"

"Yes, Ma'am. Let me show you to your quarters."

"No, "she insisted. "I will not leave him. He saved all of us. Do you not understand? He needs me." She was furious and yet she understood that poor man was following orders. Still she clung to the rail, refusing to move. Riley would never abandon her. She must do the same for him.

"I know you are distressed, Ma'am. Please let me explain. Those officers working on the commander are medical staff. He will receive the best care possible. I promise you that."

"Fine. Then I will stand here and watch."

The ensign shook his head. "I'm sorry, Ma'am. That is not allowed. If you don't come with me, a higher ranking officer will take my place. I will do everything I can to get information to you as soon as I know."

She sighed in frustration but conceded. "Yes. Yes. I will come." She took one last look at the raft where Riley lay. But she could see nothing of him. The medical personnel blocked him from view.

"I must see my people first. The two boys and the baby. Are they safe?"

"They are, Ma'am. Snug as a bug in a rug. The cat and bunnies are fed and resting comfortably.

"The elders?"

"The women are in their cabins. I believe they may be sleeping also. The old gentleman is in sick bay."

"Sick Bay? Then I must go to him."

"Ma'am, why not wait for morning? You need to rest."

But she would not be appeased. She insisted on checking each of the children. The ensign was right. They were given showers and clean clothes and fell asleep. A nurse sat beside Angel in Sick Bay where she slept peacefully.

Assured they were fine, she asked to see Francois. The old man slept, his face tired and drawn, but showing a healthier color than before.

Before leaving Sick Bay, she asked again for Riley. The ensign went to talk to a nurse in charge. When he returned, he shook his head. "I'm afraid you can't see him now. I'm sorry."

"Please tell me if he is alive." She willed the tears to go away. She would not cry. Not yet.

"I'm so sorry, Ma'am. I wish I could give you some information but they are not talking yet."

She must make plans, she told herself. Her responsibility to her people did not change even if she was alone to face it. For a short time, Riley shared the burden with her. He promised to save them and he did. And if he were gone, the twins and Angel would need her twice as much.

The nurse offered something to help her sleep but she declined, accepting a clean change of clothes and a few toiletries. She needed to think. What would she do if Riley were no longer in her life?

Sometime during the night or what was left of it, she fell across the narrow cot in her quarters and finally slept. She did not eat or wash or change her damp clothes. Her dreams were filled with dark shapes that swallowed everything up. She cried out for Riley but he was not there. Despite searching through her dreams, she could not find him. She woke close to two in the afternoon. It took a moment to realize where she was. The pain of losing him smothered her once again.

Without showering and still in her battered clothes, she insisted on leaving her cabin. The sailor on duty outside her door informed her that he was her escort.

"Fine," she said boldly. "Escort me to Commander Taggart."

"That is not possible, Ma'am."

"Of course not," was her angry reply. "Then I demand to see the children."

"Yes, Ma'am," he said and saluted. She was taken to a large room where Mathieu and Michel held court over Yankee Doodle and Madonna and her brood. A Navy nurse played with the bunnies. Iniki made much of the new arrivals. "They are beautiful just like their mother," she noted.

"What of Monsieur," Michel asked. "Is he injured?"

"I believe so. I will find out more and tell you. But you must remember that you will be with me always."

Mathieu came to her and hugged her waist. "I am sure Monsieur is fine. He loves you too much to leave you alone."

She willed away the tears and changed the subject. "What are the names of the baby bunnies?"

"I plan to ask Monsieur first. I think they should be American names, don't you?"

"Of course," she answered, blinking away the wetness from her eyes.

In another room, Angel was the center of attention. Iniki was told Angel would move in with the boys for the duration of their stay.

Madeline and Antoinette sat beside Francois' bedside in Sick Bay. He was making excellent progress and would soon be on his feet, the nurse told her. When Iniki asked about Riley, she received the standard answer. Only the doctor could give out that information.

"Then bring me to the doctor."

"He is not available right now," the nurse answered. "However, I will give him your message."

Frustrated and heartbroken, she returned to her quarters. A little more than twelve hours before, she let go of Riley on the rocks. Since then, no information on his condition was available. If he were dead, they would tell her. She couldn't believe they would not. Yet, they were unaware of their personal relationship. Did they not think she cared if he survived or not?

Everything depended on Riley. The children must have a home and schooling, she thought. She was able to provide that. Perhaps Paris? No, she decided. Riley wanted them to go to Virginia. If he recovered. He will recover, she corrected herself. But the long hours without him started to take their toll. Doubt and fear flooded through her body and she could not control it any more.

Heading to the door, she yanked it open, ready to confront anyone who tried to stop her. The ensign who was so kind to her when she came on board stood guard. The fury she felt dissipated when she saw the man. "Please tell your superiors that I want... need an answer about the commander's condition. I understand you must follow orders. But I must know what has happened to him. Tell them I am surprised they are withholding this information from me. Do they realize how vital he is to the children and me? Does the captain of this vessel know we are worried sick? Ask him what the hell he thinks he is doing?" She felt her voice rising. "I am so sorry to speak to you this way. I do understand your position. But I need help. Please do whatever you can."

The ensign nodded. "Ma'am, I will go to Sick Bay right now. Please remain in quarters with the door locked until I return." He left in a flash.

She locked the door and leaned back on it. She fought to control the emotions racing through her. But the fury was spent, the rage subsiding. Anxiety took their place followed by a deep despair.

Stripping off her dirty clothes, she entered the bathroom and turned on the shower. She remembered the last time she bathed. That beautiful morning when she and Riley discovered and explored each other for the first time. She could still feel the touch of his hands on her skin.

With almost all hope gone, she allowed herself to cry. Bitter wrenching sobs racked her body. Sorrow poured out of her yet the supply within her soul did not diminish. Warm water ran over her, mixing with relentless tears.

Only when numbness took over did she use the shampoo and soap. Ridding her skin and hair of dirt and salt made her feel no better. No pleasure would be the same again.

He was gone from her, she finally admitted. Never again would he hold her or kiss her or touch her. Never again would she look into his eyes and recognize the longing there. Never would she see that special expression on his face. Together they had magic. Part of her would always belong to him.

"He's dead, Mr. President. I gave direct orders not to fire but the patrol boats did anyway. His body washed out to sea. Unfortunately, I can do nothing to change the incompetency of your army."

The adjutant showed no expression as he listened to the general's explanation of how their prime opportunity slipped through his fingers.

"The woman? I'm afraid she is lost also," the general went on. "There is no indication that she survived. No indication any of her party survived, which was our objective. I'm quite certain they perished in an attempt to reach the American ship. We discovered a trail of blood leading directly into the ocean."

The adjutant walked to the window so as to hide his grin from his superior.

"I will be leaving tomorrow, Mr. President," the general continued. "My work here is done. If you'll kindly have a check ready for me. I'll be in the city tonight to collect it."

When he ended the call, the general grabbed his hat and placed it on his head. Then, without a word to his second in command, he left the building and boarded a waiting helicopter. The pilot greeted the man in black cordially but no return gesture was made. The black glasses completely blocked whatever expression was in the man's eyes.

She shut off the water and reached for a towel. Standing inside the stall, she dried her hair. Despite the warm water, she was cold. No more tears came. Her heart and soul were drained. Perhaps, she thought, her tear ducts were as empty as the rest of her. Then she heard it.

"How the hell long are you going to stay in there, lady?"

She knew the voice on the other side of the bathroom door.

"Open the damn door," it continued. "It's not like I haven't seen you naked before. Besides this candle . . ."

She rushed to comply with the man's wishes. Riley, swathed in bandages, leaned weak-kneed against the wall. He held a birthday cake with one lit candle on top.

"Happy Birthday to my lovely lady," he said with a smile. "Blow out this bloody candle before it goes down to nothing."

She took the cake and did as he asked. Say something, you fool, she demanded of herself. But words would not come.

"If I get these bandages wet, the Doc will have my head," he went on in the same wise-cracking voice she was used to. "So before I touch you, love of my life, please dry yourself off. If I had use of two hands. I'd gladly do it myself."

"Riley," she finally managed to say. "I thought you were dead." Her mouth did not want to do anything but smile and her breathing was far too difficult.

He cocked his head to one side. "Who told you that? I'll have them put in irons."

She managed to laugh but could not stop a tear from falling. "No one told me. They would not tell me anything." Another tear dripped down.

"Don't just stand there, love. Dry off so I can touch you. And why the hell are you crying?"

Instead of trying to formulate an answer, she made fast work of any remaining dampness.

He took in her naked body with eyes. Every inch of her. "That ensign outside sent me a message after you had your little snit. He felt sorry for you and told me you were distressed. He was under orders not to open his mouth about me. The Navy gets its kicks out of keeping secrets. But when I found out how worried you were, I decided to come see you myself. Your ensign helped me here and is stationed outside for the duration. No one is getting past that locked door."

Bandages covered his chest and half his scalp. His right arm was in a sling and a soft cast wrapped his wrist and hand.

She frowned, "You are hurt badly. Why did they let you out of bed?"

He shrugged and then winced in pain. "My injuries aren't that serious. I look worse than I feel. They didn't appreciate my plan to leave Sick Bay. But with the ensign's help, I succeeded. Besides, my friend the chef delivered the cake so I needed to bring it to the party."

She smiled. "For once, I will not argue. I will nurse you back to health in this tiny room. They will not take you away from me again."

"Of course not," he agreed. "I outrank the bunch of them, anyway. Try the cake. It is your birthday."

"You remembered?"

"Of course, I remembered. I told myself I had to be with you on your birthday. The gift will have to wait until we get ashore."

"I need no present. I have you."

She ran her finger along the frosting on the cake. Then after tasting it, she put her finger to his mouth. He sucked it until the frosting was gone.

"Almost as good as you taste," he said. "Which reminds me of why I locked the door."

"No, Riley. We can wait. Now that I know you are safe."

"Listen, lady. I'm a little damaged in certain places so I need to lie flat. But the parts needed to function for this particular operation are in excellent working order. So, don't tell me 'no'."

He caressed her face with his one good hand and kissed her. Within the next ten seconds he decided he was well enough for anything. At least, where Iniki was concerned. He wanted to formally propose but elected to postpone it for an hour or two. Neither of them were going anywhere.

He pulled her against him after getting rid of the towel she held. Then, holding on to her, he managed to make it to the bed. Grimacing in pain, he laid flat on his back.

She was already protesting, he noticed.

"This is not such a good idea.

"Are you kidding? This is the best idea I have ever had. Now quiet down. My injuries are confined to the upper portion of my body. Nothing wrong with the rest of me. Except I wish I had both hands. So, you're going to do more of the heavy work." He put his good hand out to her. "Please come here."

She approached the bed, a concerned expression on her face. Before she could object, he let her know that what he wanted was the best medicine he could have. Reaching down, he untied the string on his pajama bottoms. "I need you, love. I won't recover unless I have you right now."

"Riley, you are so hurt."

"Stop saying that. Okay," he conceded. "I was going to wait until I could get down on my knees. But, what the hell. This question requires a yes or no answer. This is not the time for discussion."

She sat on the side of the bed and leaned toward him. "What is it?"

"Will you marry me?"

Her eyes opened wide. "The children . . "

Riley wanted to scream. "No debate. Not right now, if you don't mind. I'm in a rather vulnerable position, here. So, yes or no? Everyone is included. Baby, boys, and the older ones. The cat, too. And the damn rabbits. Who did I leave out?"

She didn't answer and he wondered what he said that was wrong. There was always something.

"Iniki, you know I love you. And I love all the rest, too. Even Antoinette. I adore her. Well, maybe not adore. But we're friends now. And I give you my word I will never swear again. Well, I'll try as hard as I can. But it may happen, once in a great while. After all, I am human. Not that I'll use that as an excuse. But, it is a possibility at . . ."

"Riley," she said as she climbed on top of him, her thighs straddling his hips.

"What?"

"Stop talking."

EPILOGUE

Three years later at Beaumont Children's Hospital
"Like hell you will."

She stood, hands on hips, bare feet planted solidly in the soil, surveying the fields that were planted every kind of vegetable that grew on the island. She breathed in the sweet smell of earth. Fertile, productive earth that gave life to the plants held in its tight grasp.

Beaumont Plantation was doing well, each of its fields brimming with unharvested food. The men and women who tilled and planted would realize a good profit at market. Their windfall would enable them to purchase seed for the next growing season as well as provide produce for the Beaumont Children's Hospital.

Iniki Beaumont Taggart turned to look back at the building that resembled the house she once lived in. The estate was rebuilt as a hospital, giving prenatal and obstetric care as well as pediatric services. With the help of the U. N. and the United States government, and a generous trust set up by her family, the hospital would continue with substantial funds.

She smiled and dug her toes deeper into the soil. This is so right, she affirmed.

The stone veranda at the back survived the fire and it was there that government officials from different countries gathered for the ribbon cutting. She waved at the man standing at the back of the crowd. Riley waved back. He stood right about where he did the first time she saw him.

Three years ago she stood in the same spot in despair. Now her life was full and happy and her beloved land was used to assist the people of the island. They now received decent care at a price they could afford. The tyrannical government was gone, replaced with one that answered, for now, to the United Nations.

In the intervening years, her private world became more and more crowded. Riley needed a few weeks of rehab at the Navy hospital near Norfolk. Out-patient, of course. By the time they were married, in a beautiful ceremony on his Virginia estate, she was two months pregnant. She often teased him that he did not know the proper use of the condom. He countered with a retort that Simone's military did not know about expiration dates. Regardless, the use of condoms was futile that first time. Iniki gave birth to twin girls exactly seven and one-half months later to the day.

Mira and Marissa Taggart enjoyed the constant love and attention of their older sister, Angel and their brothers, Mathieu and Michel. She and Riley adopted the three of them as soon as they married. Yankee Doodle became a husband and father a few times over. Madonna never stopped producing. While Riley constantly complained about the farm becoming overrun with animals, he was first on the welcoming committee when the kids brought home another orphaned stray.

For their first trip to St. Phillipe since their near fatal escape, they left the little ones at home in the care of Madeline, Antoinette and Francois. Michel and Mathieu did come along. The boys shot up several inches and were almost as tall as their dad. Riley attributed their rapid growth to the fact they ran barefoot through the horse manure on the farm.

The boys adjusted well to life in Virginia. Mathieu became a top student and his proud parents were constantly attending some ceremony where he was honored. Michel, on the other hand, was better in only two subjects; sports and girls. Riley found himself at school just as often for Michel, attending conferences with teachers about the boy's rather exuberant outlook on life. If Iniki and Riley argued about anything, it was that Riley considered the kid's antics not so serious, while Iniki was embarrassed by her son's misconduct.

On this particular day, both boys were on their best behavior. They stood in front of their father, dressed in sport jackets and ties. Riley had one hand on each of their shoulders. His pride in them never diminished.

Carrying her shoes, she slipped back into the crowd. Riley wrapped his arm about her waist. "Hey, lady," he greeted her. "Your feet are dirty. The way they were when I first saw you. With your feet planted in the soil like an unmovable oak."

She leaned against him. "I would have died here if not for you."

"No, my love. It was written in the stars. You and me and the girl twins and the boy twins and Angel and Francois and Madeline and Antoinette - she's very fond of me now - and Yankee Doodle and Madonna and how ever many those two have managed to produce. We were meant to be together."

"You forgot the others."

He looked at her in confusion. "Who?"

She looked down at her stomach. "Another set of twins. Six months from now, according to the doctor."

"That's wonderful," he said softly. "How do you like that? Have you told the boys yet?"

"No. And we will not right now because we do not want to interrupt the ceremony."

He nodded, a smile beaming across his face. "Hot damn," he said loudly, drawing the attention of the boys, who could not stifle a laugh.

"Riley .. .."

"Oops. Sorry. I know. No swearing. I'll be good."

"Like hell you will."

ABOUT THE AUTHOR

Nancy James has worn different hats in her professional career. An elementary and middle school teacher, she has an intrinsic knowledge of children. After retirement, she worked as a editorial assistant at a local newspaper. Her love of writing started there. She is a past president of the Rhode Island Romance Writers and is presently a member of Mystery Writers of America. She resides in Wakefield, Rhode Island with her husband, Michael.

www.ingramcontent.com/pod-product-compliance
Lightning Source LLC
Chambersburg PA
CBHW070556130626
46556CB00001B/182